M or F?

M or F?

a novel by

Lisa Papademetriou
and Chris Tebbetts

M or F?

a novel by

Lisa Papademetriou
and Chris Tebbetts

razOr
bill

M or F?

RAZORBILL

Published by the Penguin Group
Penguin Young Readers Group
345 Hudson Street, New York, New York 10014, U.S.A.
Penguin Group (USA) Inc., 375 Hudson Street, New York,
New York 10014, U.S.A.
Penguin Group (Canada), 90 Eglinton Avenue, Suite 700, Toronto,
Ontario, Canada M4P 2Y3 (a division of Pearson Penguin Canada Inc.)
Penguin Books Ltd, 80 Strand, London WC2R 0RL, England
Penguin Ireland, 25 St Stephen's Green, Dublin 2, Ireland
(a division of Penguin Books Ltd)
Penguin Group (Australia), 250 Camberwell Road, Camberwell,
Victoria 3124, Australia (a division of Pearson Australia Group Pty Ltd)
Penguin Books India Pvt Ltd, 11 Community Centre, Panchsheel Park,
New Delhi - 110 017, India
Penguin Group (NZ), Cnr Airborne and Rosedale Roads, Albany,
Auckland 1310, New Zealand (a division of Pearson New Zealand Ltd)
Penguin Books (South Africa) (Pty) Ltd, 24 Sturdee Avenue,
Rosebank, Johannesburg 2196, South Africa

Penguin Books Ltd, Registered Offices: 80 Strand,
London WC2R 0RL, England

10 9 8 7 6 5 4 3 2 1

Copyright 2005 © Razorbill
All rights reserved

Interior design by Christopher Grassi

Library of Congress Cataloging-in-Publication Data

Papademetriou, Lisa.
  M or F? : a novel / by Lisa Papademetriou and Chris Tebbetts.
    p. cm.
  Summary: Gay teen Marcus helps his friend Frannie chat up her crush
online, but then becomes convinced that the crush is falling for him instead.
  ISBN 1-59514-034-4
  [1. Gays—Fiction. 2. High schools—Fiction. 3. Schools—Fiction.
4. Friendship—Fiction.] I. Tebbetts, Christopher. II. Title.
PZ7.P1954Maor 2005
[Fic]—dc22
                                        2005008149

Printed in the United States of America

M or F?

🧍 One

I'm thinking this whole thing will make a good movie someday. It will be the first feature from Tributary Productions, which will be my company. Tributary, as in, out of the mainstream but always going somewhere. Productions, as in, life is one big. . . . Frannie says I'm a drama queen. I prefer to think of myself as someone who knows a good story when he sees one.

So. Opening credits roll. Camera tracks down the hallway of a typical high school. Make that painfully typical. Everyone you see looks like someone else you already know. Geeks and gods and everyone in between are either hanging out or jostling along, all of them wearing clothes that look like they came from the same mall, which they probably did. The camera passes by a big banner on the wall; it used to say GO BUCKS, but now the word YOURSELF is scrawled after it, with the S in BUCKS crossed out. A grumpy looking thick-necked teacher with a bad tie is taking the banner down as the camera passes him by and pushes into a crowded cafeteria.

Move in on a small table at the far corner, where someone is sitting with his back to the camera. He's sixteen, has straight dark hair that shags over his ears, and wears a bright green T-shirt with BOOLIO on the back in black writing. The way the camera is positioned, you think he's eating alone, but then a girl's face comes into view as she leans a little to the side to look at something over his shoulder. She's the same age but more put together than he is, with lots of curly dark hair pulled back from her face and a wavy fade-stripe top that almost looks out of focus and definitely didn't come from everyone else's mall.

That's me and Frannie, or at least the movie versions of ourselves, who of course will be better looking. (Hey, it's my movie; I can do what I want.) The camera moves in closer. Frannie's eyes register something across the room and she says:

"Hm."

And that's really how this all began. Not even a syllable. I didn't think much about it at the time, but I did look up from my bowl of Fruity Pebbles.

"What?" I asked her.

"Nothing," she said, as in, something, but I was going to have to ask twice to find out.

"*What?*" I asked again.

"That girl, Astrid." Frannie was still staring over my shoulder. "She's just hanging all over him."

"Who?"

"Astrid. That girl from Germany. The exchange student with the big lips and the stupid shoes."

"No," I said, knowing better than to turn around conspicuously. "Who's she hanging on?"

But now Frannie was back on her sandwich like it was the most interesting thing she'd ever eaten. She might as well have had the word *oops!* in a little cloud-shaped bubble hanging over her head. I knew right away she had said more than she wanted to, which was strange for us. We always told each other everything, so of course I was more interested than ever. Now I gave myself permission to turn around and look. I did it subtly, without letting my eyes stop in any one place, then turned back to face Frannie again.

"Jeffrey Osborne," I said. That's who Astrid was hanging on. "Good choice."

Jeffrey Osborne was all the right things and wasn't any of the wrong things, either. He was hot—blue eyes, long eyelashes, sexy little smile, nice arms—but he wasn't stuck-up about it. (I don't think he knew how good looking he was, which always makes a person better looking.) He was also nice but didn't seem sugary sweet. He was quasi–high profile at school, but he wasn't mainstream, either. As far as I knew, he didn't really slot in with a particular group or clique, but he always had a swarm of people hanging around him.

And hanging was exactly what Astrid was doing. She had one hand clamped on Jeffrey's shoulder like she couldn't stand on her own. They were working a table in the cafeteria, getting volunteers signed up for something to do with Green Up Day. At least, Jeffrey was working the table. Astrid was just working Jeffrey.

Frannie, meanwhile, was plowing through her pastrami on rye like it was Astrid's head.

"I can't believe this is the first I'm hearing about this," I told her. "How long have you been window shopping him?"

"I don't know," she lied. That meant a long time.

I leaned in close. "Do Jenn and Belina know about this?" Jenn and Belina were Frannie's girls on the side. I had best friend status, but sometimes they could get things out of her that even I couldn't.

Frannie shook her head. "There's nothing to know."

"That's so not true," I said. This was about the hundredth deep dark secret Frannie had ever told me, but as far as I knew, it was the first one she had ever held back before telling. That meant something. I tried wearing her down with a heavy stare for a few seconds but then realized something else.

"Wait a minute. This isn't just an eye candy thing. You're *big* smitten, aren't you?" That's why she wasn't talking. If silence speaks louder than words, right then Frannie's silence was saying *crush, crush, crush,* which is different than *hot for, hot for, hot for.* Hot was all she'd ever been for anyone until now.

I walked my fingers across the table and up her arm. "So what are we going to do about this?" When I reached her ear, she squirmed off to the side.

"*We,*" she told me, "are not going to do anything."

"Yeah," I said. "That's exactly the kind of line people give right before they do the thing they just said they weren't going to do."

"This is real life, sweetie," she said. "Not a movie. Remember?"

"It's the same thing," I argued.

"Actually, it's not."

"Well, it ought to be."

We both took bites of food at the same time and chewed in silence. End of round one.

I started round two almost right away. "Just go see what this Green Up Day thing is about," I told her. "You don't even have to do anything. Just get on his radar."

"And say what?"

I patted Frannie's hand. "You're so cute when you're stalling. Let's see, how about . . . 'Hi. What's this Green Up Day thing all about?'"

"It's bad timing," she said. "Astrid's right there. She's practically stapled to him."

"That means it's perfect timing," I told her. "Time to send in the staple remover."

"Ooh, office supplies. Very sexy," she said.

"Ooh, changing the subject. Nice try."

Frannie rolled her eyes. Translation: she knew I was right but didn't have a comeback.

"Seriously," I went on. "You're thinking about it too much. If you want, you can pretend in your mind that you're not interested in him, but then don't act like you're not interested in him when you're over there. It'll help you balance out."

"Okay, one." She started counting out her responses on her fingers. "I'm not even sure what you just said. Two: saying that something is easy doesn't make it easy. And three: remember the guy at the Thai place? I didn't see you going for it and getting all bold. Let's see, what happened? Hmmm. Marcus got lost in his pad ki mao and never said a word."

"That was some stranger in a restaurant," I said. "This is someone we know at school."

6

"*Barely* know," she interrupted.

"Whatever. It's totally different."

The other difference was that this was her we were talking about—not me. It's always easier to know what someone else should do. Not to mention the fact that Frannie's odds were so much better than mine. Roaring Brook High School wasn't exactly crawling with out and eligible gay boys. I couldn't even find someone to have a realistic crush on, much less think about finding a boyfriend. This Jeffrey thing, on the other hand, had some potential.

"Just go," I told her, but I could see she wasn't ready. She looked over in Jeffrey's direction again with this expression on her face like a kid in a toy store with no money.

"Maybe later," she tried.

"Maybe later he'll be with Astrid," I said, and then right away, "I'm just kidding," because she was a little fragile right now, although we both knew I wasn't completely kidding.

I snuck another look, taking Jeffrey in with fresh eyes. I'd noticed him before, just because he was nice to look at, but I'd never really *considered* him. "He *is* cute," I said to Frannie. "Not necessarily my type, but I can see where you're coming from. And he definitely makes more sense than Ronald McDonald." That was my nickname for

Frannie's last and strangest crush ever: Ron McHauser. The guy played everything-ball, had one gigantic eyebrow, and was only an animal pelt away from looking like a natural history museum display: early Cro-Magnon Jock. Frannie had started the school year with this thing for him that I had never been able to understand. And in fact, she had gone out with him exactly once. They'd gone to Taco Bell (strike one) on their way to seeing some Vin Diesel movie (strike two), where Ron had skipped the popcorn and gone straight for Frannie's crotch. The end.

"I'm going to buy Ron McHauser off of you," she said. "How much to never mention him again?"

"I'd say one conversation with Jeffrey Osborne would about cover it."

She rolled her eyes again, in that if-I-didn't-love-you-I'd-hate-you kind of way. At the end of the eye roll, though, she was looking over my shoulder in Astrid and Jeffrey's direction.

"Hm."

Just one vowel away from "him."

Sixth period after lunch Frannie had Latin and I had geometry. Standing at our lockers just before the bell, I gave her an assignment.

"Okay," I said. "Remember how you made that list—"

"What, the pros and cons of getting gold highlights?"

she said, reading my mind. "Not exactly the same thing."

"Except," I stressed, "that it helped you decide to go for it."

Frannie pulled her Latin book out of her locker and slammed the door. "Okay, even for you, that's stretching it a little thin, don't you think?"

I wasn't going to argue. "This time, just make it five good things about Jeffrey. It'll give you a reason to take the next step. And if you can't come up with five things by seventh period, then that should tell you something, too."

"I barely even know him," she said again. "It's just a feeling, not an itemized list."

"Okay, fine," I told her. "Just don't come whining to me when you're eighty and don't have anyone to squeeze your boobs."

"Um . . . ew?"

"That's not an answer."

"Okay, okay, okay. I'll do it."

"Do what?" Jenn asked, just arriving at Frannie's locker with Belina. The two of them always picked her up on the way to sixth period.

I had to stifle myself. This was Frannie's thing to tell. Jenn and Belina both stared at her, and when she didn't say anything, they turned to look at me. I just raised my eyebrows and kept my mouth shut.

"Don't make us ask twice, 'cause you know you're going

to tell," Belina said. She always cuts through the crap to the truth of anything. Of course, she's also the only one of us with a boyfriend, so she can afford to be a little cocky.

Frannie shook her head. "I'll tell you on the way to class."

"What did you get her into this time?" Jenn asked me, but they were already walking away.

"You're going to like this one," I told them. Jenn glanced back with this very puzzled look on her face. Then again, that's her normal expression. She's much smarter than she looks (she's got that typical blond Barbie kind of thing going on), but smart isn't the same as quick.

I went in the opposite direction, toward geometry, my first period of the day without Frannie. Ethan Schumacher fell in step with me out of nowhere.

"Hey hey," he said. "What's going on?"

"Hey, Ethan."

"Listen, the GSA's doing a tarot card–reading booth for the carnival. Interested?"

"No thanks," I said.

Ethan was president of Roaring Brook High School's Gay-Straight Alliance and was always trying to get me involved. He was a perfectly nice person but seemed to think that being gay meant we were supposed to have all kinds of things to talk about, which we never did.

"You should come to another meeting," he told me for the millionth time.

"Maybe I will," I answered for the millionth time.

I couldn't blame him for his persistence. At the one meeting I'd ever gone to, it had been about ninety percent well-meaning straight kids and Ethan. He was slowly working up the queer membership, but I just wasn't interested. It wasn't like I had a jam-packed social calendar, but somehow, Frannie and I managed to fill a large percentage of our time with each other, and the idea of using the GSA as a dating service was (a) kind of gross and unethical, and (b) not going to happen anyway, given the current membership.

A little less than an hour later, I was sitting next to Frannie again. She slid me a folded piece of paper just after Mr. Hartley turned his back to the class and started writing on the board, something about the stock market crash of '29.

I unfolded Frannie's list and started reading.

1. *We would look good together. Beautiful babies, too (no, I'm not actually thinking about that seriously, so shut up—but we would look good together).*
2. *He does all kinds of good causes. Green Up Day, etc., etc.*
3. *He's a junior, so he's not graduating this year and going away somewhere.*
4. *He's a vegetarian.*

I looked over at Frannie and pointed at number four with my pencil. She shoved the paper back into my hand so Melissa Carpenter, who was trying to see without looking like she was trying to see, wouldn't see. Then Frannie grabbed my notebook and scribbled something on the page. Mr. Hartley rounded the corner into the Great Depression and kept going. Frannie slid my notebook back.

I support vegetarianism, even if I don't practice.

It didn't completely make sense, but enough that I had to let it pass.

5. *You and I said we were going to go for it if anything came up.*

That item wasn't actually a "good thing about Jeffrey," but it was a perfect opportunity for me to write back

So why aren't you going for it? What's keeping you??

She blacked out the question before Melissa could get a look at it and then didn't write anything in reply. I couldn't blame her for not having an answer. The fact that she didn't was kind of the point. The point being, we all need a little help sometimes, and maybe that was why Frannie and I had come into each other's lives in the first place.

Cue the flashback. The screen goes wavy and blurs out, then comes back into focus on swirling fall leaves, with an exterior shot of Roaring Brook High School.

It was a year and a half earlier. I was one of those kids no one ever wants to be, the ones who get moved across the country just days before starting high school. In my case, it was from Athens, Georgia, to Roaring Brook, Illinois, and it felt something like this:

Welcome to your new life, Marcus. This is a school full of people who all know each other. You don't know any of them. They all already have enough friends, thank you very much. Oh, and you're queer. Ready? Go.

Forget the school; I didn't know a single person in the whole state except my grandmother and father, who'd moved here with me. Not to mention that I was barely just starting to figure out who *I* was. I'd basically come out to myself that summer, so it was a less than optimal time to not have anyone to talk to, but there it was, and there I was. And then there she was.

Frannie rescued me on the second day of school. She just struck up a conversation in the cafeteria line. I think it was the first time anyone at that school said something to me that wasn't a question, as in, *Where you from? Do you have the answer to the equation? You want fries, honey?*

"Don't take the fries." She whispered it at my shoulder, like some kind of spy. I guess she was trying to be polite to the cafeteria lady, who at least called me honey.

I looked at the floor, playing it cool because she was whispering to me but also kind of excited because someone was *talking* to me. I saw a pair of vintage buffalo sandals and these two petticoats she was wearing as a skirt, and I thought, Cool.

"Do you have any little boxes of cereal instead?" I asked the cafeteria lady. When I turned away with my Frosted Flakes in hand, Frannie was standing there waiting for me. I liked her style right away—she wasn't anyone's clone, but she wasn't trying too hard, either. This girl had taste. It wasn't like anyone else's taste, but it worked. And she had this very friendly face, too—the kind that can stare at you without making you mad or uncomfortable.

"I don't really like fries, anyway," I said to her. "But thanks for the heads-up."

"Frannie Falconer." She said it just like that, which could have been weird but wasn't. I responded in kind.

"Marcus Beauregard."

"Beauregard?" Unlike most people, she got her mistake right away. "Oh. Right. Sorry."

Usually, everyone repeats my name like I picked it out myself or something. There's no good answer you can give to the question, *"Beauregard?"* I didn't have to say anything; she just got it. It was the first conversation we ever had without actually having it. The first of many yet to come.

Maybe it was fate. Or maybe our mothers got radiated by the same alien experiment when they were pregnant with us. Or it was a long-lost-twins-switched-at-birth kind of thing. Whatever it was, we snicked together like two refrigerator magnets that day, and no one's looked back since.

Flash forward and Frannie's dropping me off at home a year and a half later.

"Tomorrow, you're going to talk to him," I told her as I

got out of the car. I still hadn't managed to get anywhere with her on the Jeffrey thing.

"Whatever. I'll pick you up after dinner." We were going to study for a quiz later at her house, which was way more comfortable than mine and always had better snacks.

"I'm serious!" I yelled. She pretended not to hear and drove away.

Inside my own house, I could hear my grandmother singing in the shower, something about yellow roses. I snarfed some peanuts from the freezer, where my father kept them, and went back to my room. A few minutes later, she knock-knock-knocked. Always three.

"Marcus? You home?"

"Come on in, Patricia."

I've never called her grandma in my life. Patricia Beauregard, my father's mother, is what some people might call "young at heart" and what other people might call "crazy." Anyone who's ever seen or read *The Divine Secrets of the Ya-Ya Sisterhood* will have some idea of the kind of person she is: a blender full of proper Southern debutante, modern older woman, and ex-hippie.

She leaned into my room far enough to show the towel-turban on her head and one bra-strapped shoulder. "Hey, sugar, how you doing?"

"Fine," I said, trying not to look. I love the woman, but I love her more when she's dressed.

"I'm leaving soon. You and your dad can order a pizza. I already made a salad and some iced tea. That gonna be okay for you?"

"Sure, thanks."

Patricia eyeballed me, squinting without her glasses. "You got plans tonight?"

"Just studying at Frannie's."

She made this mouth-clicking sound of hers. "You two are so cute together. You ought to have her over here more often. She's welcome anytime."

"I know. Thanks."

Tidy doesn't exactly run in our family, and the furniture's about as old as I am. Patricia paid for half of everything, so I didn't want to tell her how uncomfortable our house was if you weren't used to living in it. I let it slide, along with everything else—like the fact that she thought Frannie was my girlfriend.

In the year and a half since we'd moved here, and more specifically, since I'd started thinking of myself as gay, I had shared that piece of information with my father, with Frannie, and with anyone else at school who cared to know. The one person I hadn't come out to was Patricia.

Coming out to Dad had been amazingly stress-free. He was fine about it; bland is probably a better word. I really don't think it bothered him that much, although he can be hard to read. Either way, telling him wasn't a big deal. For some reason, though, Patricia felt like another matter. I just couldn't bring myself to change her idea of who I was. She'd caught me lying once about some candy I'd stolen from the grocery store and I always remembered how disappointed she seemed in me and how terrible that disappointment made me feel. This was a completely different kind of lie, but the risk felt that much bigger. Now, even though I'd never said so, Frannie was my girlfriend where Patricia was concerned, and I was trapped in this stupid game of charades I couldn't stop playing.

Dad and I talked about it later, after he came home.

"If you want me to tell her for you," he said, "I will, but—"

"No," I said. "Never mind. Thanks."

The only thing that ever changed in this conversation was the amount of time it took me to come back to the same conclusion: I wanted to tell Patricia myself. Someday. Maybe on her deathbed, if I could put it off that long.

"What is a quark?" Dad said to the TV.

We were parked in front of *Jeopardy*, the closest thing he and I had to father-son bonding. I watched it with him all the time and usually held my own, too. Dad's some kind of trivia genius, but I can get him on pop culture and geography. He's got science and history buckled down. Everything else is up for grabs.

His job is something with computers and engineering and plastic packaging. One of these days, I'm going to have to find out what it is, exactly. Other than *Jeopardy*, he and I don't have a whole lot in common. The same is true between him and my grandmother. If Patricia is mocha almond fudge swirl on a sugar cone, then Dad (whose name is Patrick, after her) is a dish of vanilla. I'm somewhere in between.

It's hard to say which side of the fence all my chromosomes fall to. I never knew my mom. She took off before I can remember, which of course opens the door to all kinds of homophobic pop psychology about absent mothers and gay sons. I can't speak for anyone else, but for myself, slap a BORN GAY sticker on my chest and move on. End of discussion.

"What is Papua, New Guinea?" Dad said.

I shoved him with my shoulder. "I knew that one."

"You're too slow on the buzzer," he said. He's more competitive than most people would guess.

The phone rang a single time. That was Frannie's signal that she was about a block away. I stood up and grabbed my backpack, then heard her honk out front.

"See you, Dad. Gotta go."

"Who is Thurgood Marshall say hi to Frannie for me and be home by eleven, please."

"No prob," I said. Then I headed out the front door to go spend the rest of the evening with a normal family.

♀ Two "So, did you talk to him yet?"

These were Marcus's first words as he slid into Chirpy's passenger seat when I picked him up for our quiz study session. He hadn't even closed the door yet. (Chirpy, by the way, is my car—a bright green Beetle, which has a particularly fluty alarm. It's kind of like driving a cricket. You know—only bigger.)

So, anyway, there we were. It had been exactly five hours and forty-three minutes since I had told Marcus about my crush, and he was already demanding to know whether I had gone for it.

"Shh!" I whispered. "Close the door. There's a major update. I'll tell you the whole story."

He closed the door. "What? What? What's the story?"

His hazel eyes were all wide. He's so cute when he's gullible.

"I haven't talked to him yet," I said. Then I pulled away from the curb.

"Um, that story lacks a little something." Marcus drummed his fingers against the window.

"Give me a break," I told Marcus. I mean, school was over. What did he think I was going to do? Go over to Jeffrey's house dressed in a sheet of Saran Wrap and ask him if he wanted to "cook something up"?

"If I give you a break, this is going to end up like the talent show." Marcus fiddled with the radio, like he always does. I can't program anything, so Marcus is in charge of tech support—like the station buttons on the radio, my alarm clock CD player, and creating shortcuts on my computer desktop. Now he pressed a button and Fabulous Condescension blasted through the car—broadcasting from one of the indie stations in Chicago.

"Marcus—how could I have won the talent show? I don't have any talent!"

"I just didn't want that Glenn guy to win it again. Besides, you have plenty of talent."

"Look, I know you think that me giving Mr. Welton and Miss Snead style makeovers onstage would have blown everyone away. But I'm telling you, they never would have gone for it." I sighed as I turned into my family's gated community. I can never figure out if the bars and walls are supposed to keep people out or keep people in—like maybe families live here because they're afraid that all of these enormous houses built from the same five floor plans might make their children go crazy and try to storm out in a mass exodus of individuality.

Marcus jabbed at the radio, changing the station. Reggae poured from the speakers. "Look, it's not just the talent show." *Jab*—disco. "It's the art contest." *Jab*—NPR. "It's the poetry magazine." *Jab*—electronica. "It's Derek Johannsen—"

"I thought you said that Derek was a drug dealer waiting to happen."

"He's just an analogy!" *Jab*—eighties Madonna. Marcus let the radio rest. "An analogy of your unwillingness to go for it."

I pressed my lips together. I really hate it when I can't think of a good comeback. But I knew that Marcus was right.

The truth was, I wanted to talk to Jeffrey. I really did. I mean, I've liked a lot of guys before. Marcus always teases me about my Hottie of the Minute. But the guys I usually like always turn out to be losers. Like Ronald McHauser. And Derek. And Colin Jeffers—who was tossed out of school for trying to steal one of the computers from the lab. And Randy Neel—who I thought was totally hot until he shocked everyone by becoming a father last semester . . . to two babies by different mothers, both of whom were in my gym class. And I'm not even going to get into Andy Gardener, Felix Rack, and Damien Barbieri. Let's just say that they're all better forgotten.

But it wasn't until Drew Tiller that I decided I needed to get over myself. Jenn and Belina warned me that Drew had a reputation as a nut job, but I didn't listen to them. I thought he was the hottest guy on earth, and Marcus agreed, even though he said that he thought Drew was really only good for "viewing purposes." Anyway, so two months ago, I went to a party with my girls and had a drink or two and started chatting up Drew. It turned out that he had a dog—a beagle—and he was crazy about it. I love dogs, so we talked about that for a while. The conversation was going well until someone turned up the stereo.

"Whoa," I said to Drew, "this music just got really loud."

"What?" Drew frowned. "I can't really hear you; this music is too loud."

"Is this better?" I shouted.

"Hold on a second," Drew said. Then he picked up a baseball bat that was lying in a corner of the rec room, walked calmly over to the stereo, and smashed the crap out of it.

That was pretty much the end of the party.

"I told you that boy was crazy," Belina said as I drove her home later that night.

I sighed.

"Is Drew on the baseball team?" Jenn asked suddenly.

Belina flashed her a look.

"It's just that he had a really good swing . . ." Jenn explained.

"Drew has been kicked off of every sports team at RBH." This was Belina's boyfriend, Keith, who was sitting beside her in Chirpy's backseat. "He's not for you, Frannie, trust me."

"You should be glad this happened," Belina went on. "Now you don't have to waste any more time on that kind of crazy."

I glanced at Belina in the rearview mirror just in time to see her snuggle closer to Keith. I rolled my eyes but couldn't help smiling a little. It's funny—taken on their own, Belina and Keith are both kind of intimidating smart-asses. But when they're together, it's like something melts. It's sweet—and not in a vomitous way, either. Just in a nice way.

"Belina, you were right," I said. "You too, Keith. And I think the one thing we've all learned tonight is that my taste in guys totally sucks."

Nobody said anything after that. What was there to say?

Mercifully, Marcus has never to this day teased me about that incident with Drew. I think he realizes that it was actually pretty scary.

Anyway, since then, I've been on the lookout for a different kind of hot guy. I decided that I needed someone sweet and thoughtful . . . you know, in addition to being really cute. And it all came together for me one day when Jeffrey Osborne read this poem in an all-school assembly. The poem was called "The Candle and the Flame," and Jeffrey read it in this beautiful, calm, deep voice. And I started thinking . . . wow. I mean, I knew Jeffrey a little bit from last year's play. I'd been the wardrobe mistress, and he'd had about two lines, so we hadn't actually bonded much, although I was sure he knew who I was. But when I heard him read that poem, things shifted for me. I thought, Here's a guy who reads poetry. He cares about animals. He's smart. He's sweet. He looked out at the audience with those earnest blue eyes and said, "I hope you'll all consider signing the Amnesty International petition." His eyes locked onto mine for a second, and I felt like he was looking through my skull and into my soul. And that was when I knew. He was The One.

But ever since then, I'd been lying low. Here was the problem—how could I let him know that *I* was The One for him? Talk about pressure! I wanted the first time I talked to him to be perfect. I wanted to come up with something witty and clever—yet sensitive—that would blow him away. I knew that Marcus was right, that this wasn't brain surgery and I should just say hi . . . but somehow, it just seemed like hi wasn't going to cut it.

Marcus sighed. "Look, Frannie, just say hello to the guy. You've got nothing to lose."

"Nothing but my dignity."

"Okay, so you don't have *much* to lose."

"Gee, Marcus, I wonder why I kept this a secret from you. What *possible* reason could I have had for not telling you about my crush on Jeffrey Osborne?" I shook my head. "I'm drawing a blank!"

"I'm just trying to be helpful," Marcus huffed.

He actually sounded kind of hurt, so I put the brakes on the sarcasm and sighed. "I know. You're right—I'll do better."

"Good." Marcus brightened.

Okay, I feel the need to interject a little something here. I love Marcus. He's like my queer guy brain twin. But sometimes he can be relentless—like a dog with a bone. He'll gnaw and gnaw and—*grr!*—gnaw some more. Talk to Jeffrey, talk to Jeffrey—I, Marcus Beauregard, *command you* to talk to Jeffrey!

On the other hand, I totally knew why he was fixated. Marcus doesn't have a boyfriend. And it isn't going to be easy for him to get one, either. Boring Brook, Illinois, isn't exactly a mecca for gay pride—especially when you're in high school. So instead, Marcus wants me to have a boyfriend so that he can go out on vicarious dates, hear vicarious gossip, spend time putting together vicarious outfits, blahbie, blahbie, blah. I mean, when I had that one stupid date with Ronald, Marcus was all over it. He wanted all the pregame drama and the postgame wrap-up, even though he thought that Ronald was basically something ripped out of a display at the Museum of Natural History.

"Home sweet home," Marcus said happily as we pulled up in front of my house.

"Oy." I grabbed my green fake-fur messenger bag (made it myself to match my car. Not that my car has fur . . .) and we walked into the kitchen through the back door. My parents were sitting at the table with my sister, Laura, and her boyfriend of three years, What's-his-name. The four of them looked like they were on a double date.

"Frannie, you're home!" My mom grinned at me. "Marcus! Do you two want to join us for a snack?" There was a big plate of my mom's double-fudge brownies in the middle of the table. I swear, my mother thinks she's Betty Crocker. Mom works full time for an interior design firm, but she's also the best housekeeper I've ever met—she makes Martha Stewart look like a lazy slob. Mom's favorite hobby is Swiffering. I looked up at the kitchen clock. It was ten past seven, which meant that Mom had whipped up these brownies the minute she got home.

It's borderline psychotic, if you ask me.

"None for me, thanks," I said, simultaneously patting myself on the back for sticking to my diet and planning to sneak a brownie later, when nobody was looking.

"Marcus?" Mom prompted.

My dad held out the plate.

"Thanks, Mrs. Falconer," Marcus said as he took one. "These look delicious."

I rolled my eyes at him. There's something about my parents that makes Marcus turn into Eddie Haskell from *Leave It to Beaver*. Gee whiz, Mrs. Falconer, I thought sarcastically. These tasty treats look scrumptious!

"Laura was just telling us about the fund-raiser she's planning with her sorority," Dad said as Marcus went crazy, making yummy noises over the brownie.

"It's for the local battered women's shelter," Laura explained. She lives at home but goes to college nearby. She's one of those people who takes a full class load and does about eight zillion activities, all while maintaining a 4.0 GPA. "Did you know that in this country, a woman is abused every nine seconds?"

"You're amazing," What's-his-name said, gazing at Laura like she was some kind of goddess incarnate and pulling her close for a hug.

"No, *you're* amazing," Laura replied, cuddling him.

This made my mom and dad look at each other with this love-you-cuddle-bug glance, and my dad put his arm around Mom's shoulders while she sighed happily.

Okay, now do you have the picture of what my family is like? It's nauseating. I'm surrounded by superwomen. It makes my natural—well, Marcus would call it "artistic inclination" but most people call it "spazziness"—seem even worse by comparison. I looked at Marcus for support.

"This is the best brownie I've ever tasted," Marcus said, his eyes locked on the treat in his hand. "How do you do it?"

"I never use a mix," Mom replied.

"It doesn't pay to cut corners," Dad put in. That's basically his life philosophy.

"Marcus and I are going upstairs," I volunteered. "We have to work on a project." I didn't bother mentioning that it was a boyfriend project. Of course, we would study for our quiz, too—eventually.

"Don't work too hard," Dad joked. This was a joke, because my father doesn't believe that it's *possible* to work too hard.

"We won't," I singsonged.

"May I?" Marcus lifted his eyebrows at the plate of brownies.

"Take as many as you like, sweetheart," Mom said, her

blue eyes twinkling. The easiest way to get my mother to love you is to compliment her cooking, so basically she thought Marcus was a little piñata of joy.

"*Nuestras pasteles son tuyas pasteles,*" Laura said. Whatever that meant. Laura speaks Spanish, and sometimes she just throws these things into conversation. That's why I take Latin—it's a dead language, so I never have to speak it and make other people feel like jerks when they have no idea what I'm talking about.

"God, you're amazing," What's-his-name said to my sister.

"No, *you're* amazing," Laura countered, and then the whole round of cuddling started all over again.

"Ooo-kaaay," I said, walking out the door. "We'll check you guys later."

"Dinner is at eight!" Mom called after me.

"And don't be late!" Dad rhymed.

"It's a date!" Marcus joined in, and I glared at him. "Sorry," he whispered as we walked up the stairs to my room. "Reflex."

"God, Marcus, maybe we can just trade families," I griped as I tossed my fake-fur bag onto my unmade bed and shut the door. My room is the only one in the house that Mom doesn't touch. I convinced her a long time ago that if I kept the door closed, we could all just pretend that it was as tidy as the rest of the house, which would be easier than arguing about it. "Sometimes I think they love you better than me, anyway."

"Oh, come on," Marcus said as he tidied my bed and then sat down on it gingerly. "They're so nice. And you have the best house—"

"If you're into neutral tones from the Crate and Barrel catalog," I shot back. Stabbing a finger at my computer, I booted up and flopped into my desk chair. "You have no idea what it's like to live with the Perfects." Okay, this was only partially fair. I do love my mom and dad. And they really are sweet and supportive and all that stuff. It's just that sometimes I feel like I was switched at birth. My parents are totally into hard work, cleanliness, and clothes from J. Crew, and Laura's just like them. But I'm totally into movies, hanging out, and clothes from my favorite store, Buy the Pound, where they actually put the used clothing on a scale and you pay a dollar for each pound of stuff. "I mean, seriously—Mom and Dad have been together since they were seniors in high school, and Laura's been with What's-his-name—"

"Steve," Marcus prompted.

I rolled my eyes. "I *know* his name is Steve," I snapped. "That's not the point. The *point* is, he could be anybody. Laura has always had a boyfriend—from the minute she set foot in high school, there has always been a guy by her side. And if she ever breaks up with this one, there will be another one waiting to take his place. This is a family of perfect love—and I can't even *talk* to Jeffrey Osborne!"

"You will talk to Jeffrey," Marcus said confidently. "Laura hasn't got anything you haven't got."

"Are you kidding?" I demanded, typing in my favorite web address. My sister and I are polar opposites. I inherited my dad's beaky nose and my mom's plump curves, while Laura got the opposite package—Dad's tall, slender form and Mom's soft, feminine features. Also, I've got Dad's swarthy Mediterranean skin and dark hair, while Laura is like Mom—blue eyes, blond hair. Plus, Laura has perfect skin, perfect grades, and never seems to spill anything on herself.

Marcus flipped idly through a copy of *Vogue* that had been lying half under a throw pillow on my bed. "I'm speaking from a purely technical standpoint."

That was when I glanced at the screen and made this tiny, tiny, we're talking *microscopic*, little tooth-sucking noise.

Marcus was all over it. "What?" He looked up at me like a vulture eyeing prey.

"Nothing." I minimized the screen.

"Like hell." Marcus leaped off the bed and wrestled the mouse out of my hand. The window I'd been looking at reappeared. "It's the school's closed chat room." He sounded kind of confused.

"Yeah, you know. . . ." I tried to make it sound like, Hey, no big deal, lots of people hang out in the school chat room. The fact that I always refer to it as Dorks-dot-com shouldn't suggest that I never go there myself.

Marcus looked at me, his hazel eyes boring a hole in my skull. "Why would you hang out here?" It wasn't really a question. It was more like he was trying to figure it out for himself.

He looked back at the screen, and we saw it appear at the bottom of the page at the same time:

<<JEFFO: Still looking for volunteers for Green Up Day. Takers?>>

Marcus narrowed his eyes at me. "You sly dog," he said admiringly. "Have you been chatting Jeffrey up online?"

"No." This was the truth.

"No? You mean you don't actually talk to him? Then what are you—"

I shrugged. "Jeffrey hangs out online a lot. I like to see what he has to say."

Marcus stared at me. "So you just sit here 'listening in' on his conversations?"

"Yeah."

"Okay, that's borderline creepy."

"It's covert intelligence-gathering," I corrected. I could hear the defensiveness in my own voice. "It's reconnaissance. It's research so I'll know what to say to him when the time is right."

"I said it was *creepy*," Marcus repeated. "I didn't say it

wasn't brilliant." He thought for a moment. "But can't he see that you're in the chat room?"

"Well, you can change your screen name as much as you want," I explained. "See? Right now, I'm whoosie1988, but I use a different name every time I log in."

"It just gets creepier and more brilliant," Marcus said.

"Thank you."

"So—do you know who these other people are?" Marcus asked, squinting at the names that were scrolling across the screen.

"I think a lot of them are from the International Club," I said.

"International Club?" Marcus repeated.

"Jeffrey's Canadian." As I'd learned from eavesdropping on his conversations.

"Canada? Didn't we annex that along with Puerto Rico?" Marcus asked. "Who's Lola227?" he added as the name scrolled across the screen next to the comment <<J, you and I can handle greening.>>

I grimaced. "I'm pretty sure it's Astrid."

"Oh no, she di-en't," Marcus said. "Get in there."

"And say what?"

"Say anything!" Marcus's eyes glittered, and for a minute, I thought he might just lunge at my keyboard and start typing away himself. "Say hi. Say, 'I'll be at Green Up Day if you make it worth my while.'"

"Are you nuts?"

"Look, he doesn't even know who you are," Marcus said, pointing to whoosie1988 onscreen. "You could be anyone from Arnold Schwarzenegger to Melissa Carpenter," he said, naming this girl in our history class with a serious case of BO who's always trying to eavesdrop on our conversations. "It's perfect, don't you get it? This way if you say something dumb, you can just exit, then come back with a different screen name and try again, and he'll never even know the difference."

My fingers hesitated over the keyboard. "I don't know. . . ."

"Francesca Falconer, as my grandmother would say, it's time to poop or get off the pot." Marcus's usual faint Southern accent stretched into his grandmother's drawl. To tell the truth, Marcus's imitation of Patricia is frighteningly dead-on.

I bit my lip, thinking. He was right. This was my golden opportunity, and if I didn't take it, then I didn't have any right to gripe about not having a boyfriend. "What should I say again?"

"Say, 'Hey, what's the deal with Green Up Day?'"

"I don't know. . . ."

"You can't let Astrid win!" Marcus cried.

"Okay, okay. Jeez. Take a Xanax." My fingers flew across the keyboard as I typed in the question.

I held my breath, waiting for the response. The cursor

blinked, and I realized I was counting silently. I had reached eleven when Jeffrey's screen name appeared again.

<<We're going to plant a peace garden over by the community center. We need all the help we can get.>>

"Ohmigosh!" I said. "Ohmigosh! It worked!"

Marcus chuckled. "See?" he said eagerly. "You're talking to him!"

"Now what?" I asked.

"Play hard-to-get," Marcus commanded. "Tell him you'll have to check your busy schedule."

I typed it in. It seemed like we had to wait forever until the response scrolled upward.

<<And possibly miss out on the chance to shovel dirt?>>

I squealed. "He's funny!"

Just then, Astrid piped in with <<Anyone want to get some pizza?>>

Marcus narrowed his eyes. "That wily little Wiener schnitzel," he snarled. "Okay, we're taking it up a notch. Tell him to meet you in one of the private chat rooms." I obeyed.

<<C ya in a minute>> was the reply.

A few moments later, Jeffrey and I were all alone in cyberspace, and Astrid was smoked sausage. My heart was starting to pound.

"Okay, go for it!" Marcus said.

Like it was just that simple. "What do I say?"

"What do you mean? Say anything!"

"You know I'm no good at writing," I told Marcus. This is true. English is my worst subject. My teacher, Ms. Fleiss, is always telling me to "write the way I speak." But whenever I do that, she writes *frag* and *run-on* all over my papers. So, whatever, I've just given up on the whole thing. "You're the writer. I have to rely on my in-person charm."

"Oh, for God's sake," Marcus griped. "Gimme the chair. Okay, so what do we know about him? Classes? Interests? Aside from Canadian politics."

"I don't know—he's a junior, so he must take health."

I hopped out of the desk chair and flopped on my bed as Marcus took over the keyboard. I propped myself up against the pillows as Marcus's fingers pounded the keys. "'How do you like health class?'" Marcus read aloud.

"No, no," I said. "Then he'll know that I know he's a junior."

"Intrigue without commitment," Marcus suggested.

I sighed. "Send."

<<JEFFO: You mean hellth class?>>

"Okay, now I'm going to ask him how he likes Ms. Hay—*if you approve*." Marcus was laying on the sarcasm.

"Just do it."

Marcus paused for a moment, reading, then laughed out loud.

"What's he saying?" I asked.

"He said that only Ms. Hay could make sex into something boring."

I sat up straighter. "That's what I said the minute I saw her—that they must have picked the most unattractive person on earth to teach sex ed as some kind of pro–teen abstinence thing!"

"I know," Marcus said, typing away. "This is perfect— you two were made for each other. Okay, now you're going to sign up for Green Up Day."

"What?" I screeched. "Oh no. No way."

Marcus turned to look me in the eye. "Frannie—this is going really well."

"Yeah?" My voice was a dare.

"So . . . you can't just hide behind a computer screen and hope that he'll fall in love with your emoticons." Folding his arms across his chest, Marcus leaned back in my chair. "You've got to talk to him in person."

I sat down on my bed, picturing Jeffrey's blue eyes fringed with dark lashes. He was so perfect in every way . . . and I was so . . . well, not. And now I was just supposed to start talking to him—in person? It just seemed like too much. Like the first word out of my mouth would make him see how imperfect I was . . . and the whole thing would be dead then and there. "I can't," I whispered.

Then Marcus said the last thing I expected him to say. "I'll come with you."

"What?" For a minute, I couldn't even speak. I mean, Marcus hates school-activity stuff. This was a really sweet offer. "I don't—"

"And I'll bet Jenn and Belina will too," Marcus went on.

That did it. I could face Jeffrey if I had my friends for backup. And I knew I'd never get a better offer. "Okay," I said finally. "Do it."

Marcus's fingers flew across the keyboard. "I'm telling him that you'll come . . . and bring a few other people for the heavy lifting."

"Perfect."

The response came right away. <<How will I know which one is you?>>

My heart thudded in my chest. Ohmigod, I thought, he's going to know it's me. Somehow.

"'I'll be the one in the red shirt,'" Marcus said out loud, typing away.

I blinked, not getting it. "What?"

"Let's tell Jeffrey you'll be wearing red," Marcus suggested, his hand hovering over the mouse.

"Oh . . ." For a minute, I wanted to say, *No, no, forget it!* But Marcus was staring me down. It was too late. I was on the brink of going for it . . . and I knew that Marcus was going to shove me over the edge, no matter what I said. "Okay. Yeah. Red."

Marcus typed it in.

<<JEFFO: M or F?>>

"That's ironic," I said. "What do you think, Marcus? Are we M or F? After all, you're doing all the typing-slash-conversational work."

"But you'll be doing the dating," Marcus pointed out. <<F>> he typed.

Marcus clicked send, and I flopped back on my bed pillows, overwhelmed by a sickly combination of excitement and dread.

So this is what going for it feels like, I thought.

Jeez, I feel like I'm about to barf.

"What am I doing here again?" I whispered to Marcus as we walked toward the rear yard at the community center. A card table had been set with snacks and drinks, and a bunch of people—about half of whom were from our high school— were milling around. I waved to Julie Miller, who was standing in a little knot of girls from the pep squad over by a wheelbarrow full of sod. Jeffrey was standing in a group next to hers, holding a clipboard and looking gorgeous in a navy plaid shirt and faded jeans. He didn't look my way, thank God. I wasn't ready for him to see my red T-shirt with EVIL GENIUS written across the front in sparkly letters—not yet. I still hadn't decided on the perfect opening line.

"You're here to start living happily ever after," Marcus said, just as Ethan Schumacher hustled over to us.

"Hey, guys!" Ethan chirped, grinning hugely. "Marcus, I should have known I'd see *you* at a beautification project."

Marcus looked bored. "I'm really into plants," he lied.

"Hi, Ethan," I said, feeling kind of sorry for the guy. I mean, Ethan is nice. He's kind of like a Jack Russell terrier or something—all crazy energy and misdirected affection. But Marcus basically thinks that Ethan is a big yawn. Not that it stops Ethan.

"Do you guys want to join our mini-squad?" Ethan asked. "We're in charge of digging up old bulbs."

"Actually, we've got some friends joining us," Marcus said.

"Oh." Ethan looked kind of disappointed, but he recovered. "Okay, well, you know where to find me!" Giving a cheerful wave, he trotted off.

"Frannie! Marcus!"

I turned to see Jenn trotting toward us, followed closely by Belina and Keith. I only got to feel about a split second of relief before I realized that something was horribly wrong.

"What the . . . ?" Marcus murmured.

"What are you wearing?" I asked as the group walked up to us.

Jenn and Belina exchanged looks.

"Jenn said we were supposed to wear red T-shirts," Belina explained.

I looked at Jenn, who looked confused. "Well, I asked you what you were wearing," Jenn explained in this don't-you-remember? voice. "And you said a red T-shirt and jeans. You just sounded so definite, I thought that was what we were all supposed to wear."

Belina looked at her.

"Like we're a team," Jenn went on. "You know—the red team."

"Mine's plaid," Keith put in.

"Plaid isn't a color," I told Keith. "You're wearing red."

"Okay, so we're all in red. Who cares?" Belina eyed me carefully. "Is there a *problem* with the red shirts?"

I hesitated. When I'd told my friends about Green Up Day, I hadn't actually explained the real reason we were going there. I'd just said something crazy about community service and getting involved, and they'd gone for it. But now we were all in red—how would Jeffrey know which one was me? It might have almost been comforting to be able to hide amid the red camouflage until I was ready to make my move with Jeffrey. But the bad news was that Jenn's shirt was tight in all the right places, and her blond hair was tied back in a perfect ponytail, while mine was sort of piled loosely on my head and fastened with a chopstick. Ohmigod, I thought frantically, what if Jeffrey thinks he was chatting with *her* and then gets disappointed when he finds out it was *me*?

Marcus stepped in to help me out. "No problem," he said quickly. "But now everybody's so matchy-matchy, except for me."

I glanced over in Jeffrey's direction and immediately had to rub my neck in a desperate attempt to pretend that I hadn't been looking in his direction because at that very moment, he was headed our way, clipboard in hand.

"You're wearing red too," Keith pointed out to Marcus.

Marcus looked down at his shirt. "It's *rose*," he corrected.

Keith shrugged. "Whatever, dude. It's in the red family."

"Hey, guys! Whoa—the red team!" Jeffrey held up his clipboard and flashed his super-white smile. "With one rose member," he said to Marcus.

"I'm wearing plaid," Keith pointed out.

"Okay," Jeffrey said, then glanced down at his clipboard. "Do you guys mind if I put you in mini-groups? A lot of people have started working already."

Marcus looked at me, but I was pretty much incapable of speech or movement at that moment. My brain was in overdrive, trying to process about a hundred thoughts at once: Please let him know it's me, oh, please don't let him know it's me, what is he thinking right now, is anyone else here in a red shirt, he looks so cute with that clipboard, is he smiling at Jenn or just smiling in general, does he remember that conversation we had last year about nineteenth-century hats, do I have anything on my face right now, etc, etc.

"Just let us know where you want us," Belina said as she shoved her hands into the front pockets of her carpenter jeans. That was when I noticed how huge her boobs are. Thank the God of Small Things that she's obviously with Keith, I thought, eyeing her red shirt.

"Let's see, I need one person to oversee rosebushes and four people to plant maples." He looked up at us. "Any takers?"

He looked directly at me and smiled, and I nearly had a heart attack trying to decode what it meant. He wasn't giving any signals that he was looking for someone in a red shirt. I felt like I was going to faint and wished frantically that I could read minds. Does he know it was me? Does he even remember our conversation?

"Your name is Marcus, right?" Jeffrey said, turning to Marcus. "Since you're in the rose shirt, why don't you take the rose garden, and the others can take the trees."

"Sure," Marcus said.

"Ooh, I love maple trees!" Jenn said happily.

Jeffrey grinned at her. "And I'm sure they love you," he said.

Grr! Stupid Jenn. Looking good in her red shirt and loving maple trees.

Marcus elbow-nudged me.

"I love maple trees too," I said quickly.

Jeffrey gave me an odd little smile. "Great," he said. He looked like he was about to say something else.

"Jeffrey!" someone called.

Oh, jeez, I thought, rolling my eyes. It was stupid Astrid. She was standing in the middle of a group from the International Club, waving a trowel.

"Be right there!" Jeffrey called. "Okay, guys, thanks so much for volunteering," he told us. "Let me know if you need anything." He hustled off.

I watched him go, wondering what on earth had just happened.

Two hours later, I was covered in mud, my back ached, and I smelled like manure. I never would have signed up for this if I'd known what a pain in the butt trees can be, I thought as I shoved more manure onto the pile at the base of the thin trunk. The chilly, wet spring earth was freezing against my kneecaps.

"Is it me?" Jenn asked. "Or is our tree crooked?"

"It's you," I snapped, even though our tree was practically growing sideways. Standing up, I opened a bag of mulch and tried to aim it at the base of the tree, but it landed all over my shoes. Damn it! I thought, kicking mulch out of my clogs. Damn you, Nature!

Jenn looked doubtfully over at Belina and Keith's tree.

They were already on their third maple, actually. Those two are just this amazing team. All of their trees poked straight toward the sky and were surrounded by a tidy ring of mulch, like they had been professionally landscaped.

"Do you two need some help?"

I looked up into Astrid's green cat eyes. Her cheeks were flushed pink, and she looked really pretty and healthy, in this sort of European Woman of the Forest way. What is she doing here? I wondered. Hasn't she had enough green-upping? Her mini-team had already finished planting a ring of shrubbery around the entire perimeter of the garden. What a show-off, I thought, despising her German efficiency.

I was just about to tell her that we had everything under control when Jenn piped up with, "Ooh, would you help us? I think our tree is all wrong."

"Sure." Astrid looked down at me with this do-you-mind? look on her face.

I felt this weird flash of protectiveness for my mound of mulch. I didn't want Astrid touching it. Especially since I didn't want Jeffrey to see what a bad planter I was. But I had to admit that our maple looked pretty sad, hanging there like a leafy seesaw. I shrugged and backed away from the mulch.

Faster than I would have thought possible, Astrid cleared the dirt and mulch from the roots, yanked the maple out of the ground, dug our hole about a foot deeper, and dropped in the tree—straight up. "There you go!" she said brightly.

"Oh, thanks!" Jenn said eagerly as she accepted the shovel and started dropping dirt in at the base. "Frannie, would you just hold the trunk straight for me?"

Astrid gave us a smile, then walked off toward the corner of the garden where Jeffrey was finishing laying a brick path with two other guys from our high school. I narrowed my eyes as Astrid picked up a brick and Jeffrey smiled at her.

Jenn followed my glance. "She is so helpful, isn't she?"

I glared at her. Helpful? She's stealing my man! "That's what she wants you to think," I snapped.

Jenn blinked. "Oh," she said.

I sighed. Poor Jenn. It wasn't her fault that I was having a horrible day. Actually, it was my own. I couldn't stop kicking myself for not walking right up to Jeffrey and telling him that I was whoosie1988. It seemed like every minute that passed made doing that more awkward and impossible.

My knees creaked as I stood up and looked at our tree. Poor little guy, I thought sympathetically. He's been through a lot today.

"Nice tree," Marcus said brightly as he walked up to us. Reaching out, he wiped a smudge of dirt from my forehead.

"Why are you so clean?" I demanded grouchily, eyeing his pristine rose-colored shirt.

"I was in charge of writing labels for the roses," Marcus explained.

"Hey," Belina said as she and Keith joined our group. "It looks like things are wrapping up around here."

"Is anyone else starving?" Keith asked. "We could head to Giant Sombrero for burritos."

Giant Sombrero is our favorite Mexican place. That isn't really the name of it, by the way. Its real name is El Rey del Sol—but it has a giant sombrero out front, so that's what we call it.

"I'm not sure Frannie is done," Marcus said.

"Oh, we're done," Jenn said confidently, giving our tree a leaf pat.

Marcus looked at me, his hazel eyes boring into me. "Are you?"

Belina toyed with one of her baby dreads. "Why are you guys acting all secret spy mission?"

"It's nothing," I said quickly. "Forget it." I glared at Marcus, wanting to kill him for suggesting this Green Up thing in the first place. This whole day had been a total bust. I'd had a miserable time, I'd nearly murdered a tree, and Jeffrey hadn't even noticed me. I'd had enough. "Let's get out of here."

Belina looked like she didn't believe me, but she knew

better than to press. "Okay," she said finally. "Jenn, let's put the shovels by the shed."

"I'll help you," Keith volunteered.

"What are you doing?" Marcus hissed as soon as the others were gone. "You aren't leaving here until you talk to him."

I shook my head. "I'm not talking to him now," I said. "I look horrible, capital horror."

"You're talking to him," Marcus said.

"No, I'm not."

"Yes, you are."

"You can't make me."

"Um, excuse me?" said a voice behind me. *The* voice. The deep, rich, poetry-reading voice. I stared up at Marcus, cringing. Please, no, I thought.

"Hi, Jeffrey!" Marcus gave me a smug smile. I could practically read the thought bubble over his head: Ha, ha. You have to talk to him now.

Taking a deep breath, I tucked a wayward strand of hair behind my ear and turned to face Jeffrey.

"Frannie Falconer," Jeffrey said.

My name had never sounded so beautiful. "Hi," I squeaked. What do I say what do I say what do I say? Damn it—two hours of kneeling in manure, and I still didn't have an opening line!

But then, Jeffrey did something incredible. He held out a small bunch of daffodils and said, "These are for you."

I stared at the flowers in his hand, completely speechless.

"Ooh! Look, Frannie—flowers!" Marcus said giddily. He sounded really proud of himself. "None for me?"

Smiling, Jeffrey pulled one out of the bunch and handed it to Marcus.

Marcus's eyebrows flew up in surprise. I guess he was really taken off guard by that move. "Thanks," he whispered. He hesitated a moment, then accepted the flower. I could feel Marcus looking at me, but I just couldn't tear my eyes away from the daffodils in Jeffrey's hand.

"You . . . are . . . whoosie1988, right?" Jeffrey asked. I looked up into his face. He was starting to blush, and he hesitated. "I mean . . ." He laughed nervously. "Maybe I'm making a huge mistake right now. . . ."

"No, no," I said quickly. Shaking my head, I took the flowers. This was unbelievable. I mean, it was the kind of thing that happened to people in movies or to my sister, Laura, or something—not to me. "I just can't—I mean, how did you know it was me?"

Jeffrey looked relieved, and he laughed. "Well—I guess I didn't. Not for sure. I was just . . . hoping."

He was hoping it was me! I thought dizzily. I looked over at Marcus, who looked like he was about to burst.

"Anyway," Jeffrey said, clearing his throat, "I wanted to thank you guys for coming out today. You were a huge help."

"I think I got more dirt in my hair than I did around my tree," I confessed.

Jeffrey smiled. "You look great," he said. "Brown's your color."

I thought I was going to die.

"We had a great time!" Marcus said brightly.

"So, uh—would you . . . would you like to have lunch together sometime?" Jeffrey asked. "I was thinking Monday."

"Oh, that's perfect!" I said quickly, looking over at Marcus. "We'd love to!"

A strange look flickered across Jeffrey's face, but he recovered. "Oh, uh, great. Okay, well, uh—" He ran a hand through his soft, wavy brown hair. "Look, I've got to—" He gestured toward the supply shed, and I knew he meant that he had to help clean up. He was in charge of Green Up Day, after all. "So I'll—I'll see you Monday."

"See you!" I grinned as he walked away. The minute he was out of earshot, I turned to Marcus. "How'd you like that move, huh?" I asked him. "He wanted to hang out with us, and I said yes to lunch, just like that!"

Marcus rolled his eyes.

"What?" I demanded. "Aren't you proud of me?"

"Frannie, you adorable moron," Marcus said, "he was asking you out. You just accepted for both of us when all he wanted was you."

I was still trying to absorb this information when Jenn bopped over to us. "Hey—flowers!" she said, eyeing the bouquet in my hand and then the single flower in Marcus's hand.

"Where did they come from?" Belina asked as she and Keith walked up.

"Jeffrey Osborne," Marcus said quickly—like he was the one with the crush or something.

"Oh, really?" The corners of Belina's mouth twisted into a wry smile.

"What are you smiling at?" I asked.

Belina shrugged. "Nothing," she said. "I'm just glad we could all be here to do this valuable community service."

"Frannie, you sly dog," Keith put in, holding up his hand for a high five.

Giggling, I slapped it.

"What?" Jenn asked. "What's going on?"

"Frannie's about to get it on with Jeffrey," Keith explained.

Jenn's blue eyes were wide. "You are?" she squealed. "He's so cute!"

"Good choice, Frannie," Belina said, her dark eyes shining.

"Yeah, better than your usual," Keith agreed. "Ow!"

Belina had just punched him on the arm.

I couldn't help smiling, though. This was it. Real romance. Involving me . . . for a change.

♟ Three

I was in the middle of making a Big Deal when Frannie came in to see me.

Big Deals are our biggest sellers. I've made so many, I can almost literally do it with my eyes closed: cut a brownie into four pieces (triangles, not squares), slice half a banana (wheels, not chunks) and scatter the pieces on top of the brownie, then add three scoops of ice cream (Very Vanilla, Chocopalooza, and Chocolate Chipmunk, or you can special order), then three toppings (hot fudge, peanut butter, marshmallow, or special order), whipped cream, pecan halves, mini–chocolate chips, and a paper flag that says SCOOPS! on top of the whole thing.

Scoops is the place where I work in the mall. It pays more than minimum wage, and the ice cream is great, but the uniforms are hell, as in, striped polyester shirts and these seriously humiliating hats they make us wear. Still, for me, it beats bagging groceries or folding sweaters at the Gap. Plus, you can have a friend here talking to you as long as they act like a customer.

Frannie sat down at the counter, ordered a hot chocolate, and held up two bags of clothes from Buy the Pound. "I need a consultation," she said. "I'm trying to figure out what to wear to lunch."

"I hope you got something for me too," I said, slicing a banana. "We want to make a good impression."

"Very funny," she said, smile-free. I had been giving her a hard time ever since she had accepted Jeffrey's invitation—for both of us, which actually seemed appropriate. The whole thing was starting to feel like a joint project.

"You're more into this than I am," she accused me.

"I don't know about *more* into it," I said.

"Okay, just as into it as I am."

"Let's just say I want this for you as much as you want it." I leaned into the freezer with my scoop. "What time are we supposed to meet him?"

"Tomorrow after fifth period," she said. "What about this?" I looked up from the freezer to see her pulling a striped men's business shirt with a white collar out of one of her bags of clothes.

"Very eighties," I said.

She looked at the shirt suspiciously. "Good eighties or bad eighties?"

"If anyone can pull it off, you can," I said, which was true, in a good way. "But with a skirt, not pants," I added.

"Definitely," she said.

I don't know why Frannie comes after my fashion advice. Compared to her I'm a total yawn, all jeans and T-shirts and sweatshirts. Still, I like that she asks.

"I vote no," said Tina, one of the waitresses, who had just come over to pick up an order. Like everyone else at Scoops, Tina found other people's personal lives infinitely more interesting than her job. "This is some kind of date, right? Stripes are a bad idea." Which was an ironic thing to say, given the uniform she was wearing. (I think they're intended to make customers feel extra-attractive in comparison so they'll be comfortable buying lots of ice cream.) Outside of work, Tina wore all black, to go with her piercings and heavy eyeliner, even though her personality was kind of Disney Channel. Frannie and I referred to her as Goth in a Box.

Frannie had started to put the shirt back in the bag again, when Margaret, the assistant manager, piped in from where she was at the register. "Hang on, Frannie," she said. "Let's see that again."

Frannie held the shirt up without even raising an eyebrow in my direction. She had learned a long time ago that there's no such thing as a private conversation at Scoops.

"Okay," Margaret said. "Now, if you unbutton the bottom two buttons, you could tie it off. That'd be real cute."

Frannie smiled politely. "I'm not really the midriff type. I was thinking more half tucked, with a corduroy skirt."

The way Margaret pursed her lips said everything about how different their tastes were. She's about twice our age and divorced but likes to be part of the group. That's the other thing about this job—you end up connected to people you'd *never see* together anywhere else.

After Margaret filtered off to seat some customers and Tina went to serve the now-melting Big Deal I had made, Frannie dug back into the bag. She pulled out a big floppy cardigan sweater, like something a professor would wear.

"What about this?" she said.

"Well," I said. "It's not slutty. . . ."

She stuffed it back in the bag. "Do you know what you're going to wear?"

"Oh God, I don't know," I said. I picked up the next order ticket—a Saturday Sundae and a Raspberry Moo Shake.

"Liar."

"Probably jeans and that long-sleeved blue tee," I said quietly. I was embarrassed for anyone but Frannie to hear that I had already thought about it.

All of a sudden, Calvin was among us. He works the fountain with me and has the ability to appear out of nowhere. I could smell the cigarette break on him.

When you first meet Cal, you get one of three impressions:

1. Surfer
2. Stoner
3. Surfer-stoner

He's either the smartest dumb person I've ever known or the dumbest smart person. We called him Cal, not because of Calvin, but because it's short for California. I don't even know if he's ever been there. He just kind of *is* California, with the long blond hair, the mellow attitude, and the West Coast logic.

"You've got a math problem there, Fran," Cal said, then picked up an order ticket and went back to work.

"And this relates to math how?" I asked him. Cal almost always has a point; you just usually have to look for it.

"Well," he said, slowly, as always, "it's like this. Date equals two people, right? And date plus Marcus equals . . ." He stopped to think about it. "Not a date."

Before Frannie or I could respond, Tina was back in it again. "Cal's right," she said. "I mean, you like this guy, right? You should just go by yourself." She put a Root Beer Volcano on her tray and flew away, crossing paths with Margaret.

"Tina, those people at table three are in a hurry," she said, and then, "What'd I miss?"

Cal raised his hand unnecessarily to speak. "I'm just

saying Frannie's thing isn't a date if Marcus is there. No offense, man."

"None taken," I said. It's impossible to be offended by anything anyone says at Scoops, 'cause it's like working inside a cartoon.

Frannie shifted on her stool. "I don't know if I want it to be a date yet anyway. It's too early for that. Besides, what does that word even mean anymore? Dates are like this old-fashioned concept. Dates are—"

"Fruit?" I suggested.

"Yeah," Frannie said with a grateful smile my way. "Dates are fruit."

The only one who seemed to agree was Calvin, who nodded, although I'd give it a fifty-fifty chance that he was responding to some unrelated thought deep inside his head.

"Well, honey, you can call it what you want," Margaret said, sliding over to the cash register, "but a girl and a boy going out for lunch? That's a date."

"Or a boy and a boy," I said.

"But not a boy and a girl and a boy," Calvin said.

"Well, actually—" I started, but Margaret cut me off.

"Let's keep it PG, people." Which was an interesting thing to say, given what I knew about the reasons for Margaret's divorce.

Frannie watched the whole thing like a tennis match, back and forth.

"Anyway," I told her, "I think you're right. It doesn't have to be a date-date yet. You can go slow."

She started gathering up her stuff; we'd finish the fashion show later at her house. "You're just saying that 'cause you want to be there," she said.

"Correct."

"Well, good, because you're coming."

I took her ten-dollar bill for the hot chocolate and gave her a five, five ones, and a big chocolate chip cookie in change. She put the five in the tip jar.

"Tomorrow after fourth period," she said, and turned to go.

"Don't be nervous," Calvin called after her.

"I'm not," she called back without looking, but I saw her dump the cookie in the garbage on her way out.

At this point in the movie version, we cut to the next day with a slow fade. Maybe go into an overhead shot of suburban streets. The music comes up loud and the camera finds Frannie's car driving along. It swoops down so you can see us inside, bopping our heads to the sound track, which it turns out is coming from the car stereo. We're both obviously a little hyper. Cut to inside the car. Frannie looks in the rearview mirror and floofs her hair, then makes a face.

"You look fine!" I shout over the music.

She's still looking in the mirror. "What?"

I turn off the stereo. "You look perfect," I say.

And she did—just a little makeup, not too much. She had gone ahead with the striped shirt and corduroy skirt, too. They were just right, as in, casual enough so she wouldn't look like she'd dressed up for him, but nice enough so he'd notice. I had changed my mind about the blue tee and gone with a vintage short-sleeved madras plaid that Frannie had given me for my birthday, insisting I needed to have something besides a steady diet of T-shirts in my wardrobe.

"This is so stupid," I said. "Why am I nervous?"

She gave me a puppy dog look. "'Cause you love me," she said. "And because we're brain twins."

"Oh yeah."

Ever since Jeffrey had given Frannie (and me) those daffodils and asked her (us) out to lunch, it was like the stakes had gotten higher. And even though they weren't my daffodils or my stakes, for that matter, I couldn't stop my knees from bouncing up and down in the car. If she was the star of this show, then I was the nervous director standing behind the camera and biting his nails.

We pulled up to the curb outside of Disgusting Macrobiotic Café or whatever that place was called; I can't remember.

"All natural." I sighed. "I should have guessed."

"I didn't think you'd come if I told you," Frannie said.

"Are you kidding? I wouldn't miss this for anything. But we're stopping at IHOP for some real food on the way back to school."

She was barely listening. "Is this weird?" she said. "This whole thing is weird, isn't it?"

"No," I said. "It's lunch."

"Lunch with a guy who *thinks* he's been having private online conversations with me." Jeffrey was turning out to be a regular customer in the school chat room, so he was almost too easy to find. Our second chat with him had gone even better than the first, unless you counted how nervous it was making Frannie now.

"They *are* private conversations," I assured her. "Brain twins don't count."

"Technically, maybe, but still, ethically . . . I don't know."

"Listen," I said, "remember Great Adventure last summer? The guy in line for the log flume?" A little smile crossed Frannie's face. She had done some Oscarworthy flirting that day. She'd even used a British accent. "Just remember that feeling," I told her. "Like you've got nothing to lose."

"But that's the thing," she said. "I *do* have something to lose. I think I really like him."

I sighed. "Lucky."

That seemed to prop her up a little bit. She thought about it for another second, then sat up straighter. "You're right," she said. "I *am* lucky. This is a good thing. I'm being stupid. What am I so worried about?"

I figured I knew the answer to that one, but the whole point was to put her mind somewhere else. "All right, then," I said. "You ready to go in?" She nodded. "So, one more time: If you want me to talk more, look at me and touch your chin. If you want me to talk less, look at me and touch your lips." It was a new system I had come up with that morning.

"Isn't that supposed to be a come-on?" she asked. "Like if you touch your mouth, the guy's supposed to know you're interested?"

"Maybe," I said. "But if you want me to talk less, that means you *are* interested, so it doesn't matter."

She put a hand on my leg. "Thank you for being here."

"You'd do the same for me," I said.

"In a heartbeat," she said.

"Not that it'll ever happen."

"And we're focusing . . ."

"Sorry," I told her, and I reached for the door handle. "Let's go."

The inside of the restaurant was nicer than I expected. There were plants everywhere, clustered in the corners and hanging around the dining room, which was all glass and greenhousey. A little waterfall fountain gurgled near the front. It was all kind of beautiful, actually.

"Hey! Over here!" Jeffrey leaned out from behind a potted tree, where he was sitting in a booth. It wasn't until we got over there that we saw he had brought someone. "Do you guys know Glenn?"

Glenn Scarpelli was one of Jeffrey's more popular friends. He had that Italian thing going on, with the dark hair and cocky smile. At school, he was one of those hybrids—in his case, sports and theater. I was pretty sure he played baseball and soccer, and I knew he had been the lead in *Grease* when Frannie did costumes.

I was a little mad at Jeffrey for pulling this, which was hypocritical of me, except that I wasn't a surprise guest and Glenn was. Then, when we sat down again, it ended up me across from Jeffrey and Frannie across from Glenn. I couldn't think of any excuse why we should all stand up and start over, so I let it pass. Hopefully, Glenn would know enough to hang back and let the two of them be the center of things.

"So Jeff's told me about Frannie," he launched right in, smiling and waggling his eyebrows at her. "And you're Beauregard. The Southern guy, right?"

None of the responses in my head were helpful at this time:

1. Don't call me Beauregard if you don't know me.
2. When you say "Southern guy," why do you make it sound like it's a bad thing?

3. *Please* tell me you're not going to talk the entire time.

Frannie headed off my sarcasm and jumped in. "Marcus moved here from Georgia last year."

"Well, thanks for letting us come along," Glenn said to her. "Me and Marcus, I mean. I kind of thought this was supposed to be a date."

I felt Frannie's nails through my jeans where she was gripping my knee.

Jeffrey picked up his menu. "Get whatever you guys want. Lunch is on me."

"You don't have to do that," Frannie said.

"I know," he said, simple as that. "The burritos are really good, and the tempeh burgers. That's what I'm going to get."

I looked for *burrito* on my menu and recognized the words *tortilla* and *cheese*, along with a bunch of ingredients I had never heard of.

"I'll get the tempeh burger too," Frannie said. She and Jeffrey exchanged shy little smiles, then both went back to their menus, even though they had both supposedly decided what to order already.

"Frannie told me you really like this place," I said to Jeffrey, which wasn't actually true, but I wanted them to look at each other again. The problem was, Frannie turned to Glenn at that exact moment and asked, "Did you grow up in Roaring Brook?"

No, Frannie! my mind yelled. *Bad girl! Wrong boy!*

"We moved here when I was two," Glenn said. "I was born in Alaska, actually. . . ." I could already tell it was going to be an epic answer. He seemed like the type to use twenty words where just one will do.

"Where in Georgia are you from, Marcus?" Jeffrey asked me, and all of a sudden it was two separate conversations.

"Athens," I said. "Actually, Frannie was the first person I met here." Maybe I could at least get the topic back to her.

Frannie burst out laughing—at something Glenn had just said, I realized.

"That's hilarious," she said, twirling the straw in her water.

"Well, you lucked out, then," Jeffrey answered me, blushing just a tiny bit, with another shy-cutie look her way. And Frannie totally missed it.

If nothing else, Jeffrey was winning some best friend approval points from me. The hardest part of it was trying to forget what I already knew about him from the online chatting. As far as he knew, this was our first conversation ever. I had to keep reminding myself of that.

By the time we left, nothing really bad had happened, but nothing really good had happened, either. I spent more time talking to Jeffrey than Frannie ever did, and we all spent most of our time listening to Glenn. I drank a Coke and left hungry.

"You know, if you go out with Jeffrey, you're going to

have to eat vegetarian all the time," I told Frannie in the car.

"Hey, as long as he's nice and has cool friends, I'll be fine," Frannie said.

"Which cool friends would those be?"

"Oh, come on." She wiggled her fingers at the stereo so I'd know to turn it down for her. "I thought Glenn was great. And you have to admit he's funny. I love how uninhibited he is. Did you hear that thing he said about getting caught in the bathroom?"

"I guessed I missed that part," I said.

"And he's even good looking, almost as cute as Jeffrey."

"More my Jeffrey than yours so far," I said. "You've got to step up."

"Blahbie, blahbie, blah," Frannie said. "Seriously. It's fine. I'm kind of glad it was like that. Just little steps at a time. That way, I can ease into things with him, you know?"

I saw right through her. "You were still afraid to talk to him, weren't you?"

Frannie slapped the steering wheel. "What's up with that, anyway? Why is it so hard to talk to the people we like the most?"

"Uh, hello?" I said. "You don't seem to have any trouble talking to me."

"You know what I mean."

"You'll get there," I said. "The thing to think about now is what happens next."

"I already know what happens next," she said. "Can you come over tonight?"

"Back to the chat room?"

"He's usually there around eight-thirty."

I clapped. "Stalking boys is fun."

That gave me about five hours after school to write an overdue English paper, mow the lawn, and have yet another uncomfortable conversation with my grandmother. At dinner, she passed a bowl of succotash and just as casual as that, she said, "What words are the kids using for sex these days?"

Dad and I yelped at the same time.

"Momma!"

"Patricia!"

We never can get used to her little stealth bombs.

"I'm just wondering," she said, all wide-eyed and innocent, with a hand to her chest. "Honestly, you boys are so tightly wound. You're going to get ulcers, both of you." Dad filled his mouth with food and I got up to get something—anything—from the refrigerator.

Patricia cut into her pork chop and kept going. "We used to call it shagging. I never even heard the F-word until I was in college." Then, making some connection in her mind that I didn't even want to think about, she asked me, "How's Frannie, hon?"

With Patricia, it's never just a question. There's always

some decoding to be done. I guess that's where I get it. Frannie says I speak in code all the time.

"Fine," I said, which was my own code for, *Let's not go there, either.*

"I was thinking maybe you two might want to come out with me and Arthur this weekend. Like a good old-fashioned double date."

I had no idea who she was talking about, and apparently, neither did Dad. "Arthur?" I heard him ask.

"My new friend," she said. "I met him at the farmers' market."

Friend? Now *there* was some code. Suddenly, I realized why Patricia had sex on her mind, and then, just as suddenly, I had this whole new batch of unwanted images and thoughts.

"So what do you think, hon? Saturday night, maybe?" Patricia asked my back.

I leaned farther into the refrigerator. "Uhhh . . ." Milk, orange juice, pickles, mustard, canola oil, cream cheese, my grandmother having sex, please God, make it stop—

"Hon?"

"Uhhh," I tried again. "I don't know what Frannie's doing this weekend." It was a lame response, but it was all my mouth could come up with on its own since my brain was quickly shutting down.

"I thought you two always did Saturday night videos or something," she persisted.

Then I heard Dad cut in. "Momma, why don't you let Marcus see what's up, and he'll get back to you. How's that sound?"

Thank you, Dad. When I finally came back to the table, Patricia winked at me. "Oh, you're blushing. It's okay. I know you kids have better things to do than hang out with a couple of old farts." She wagged a forkful of pork chop and zucchini at me. "But you might have fun. Arthur and I know how to have a good time."

Yeah, I thought. I'll bet you do.

I'm not a prude. Not at all. Patricia was free to have all the wild, kinky senior citizen sex she wanted. I just didn't want to hear about it, know about it, or think about it. And on a side note, I wondered as I left the table, why was I always getting invited on other people's dates? I wanted one of my own, thank you very much.

When I told Frannie about it later at her house, she just thought it was cute. "Aww," she said, closing the door to her room. "Patricia wants to double date with us."

This was like a weird twist on the brain twin thing. Every time something annoyed me about my family, Frannie thought it was quaint or sweet or whatever, and vice versa with her family. I can never understand why she complains about them. The Falconers could have their own show on Nick at Nite. It would be called *The Perfects*, and it would be boring, because nothing bad would ever happen.

"Patricia wants a double date with someone who doesn't exist," I said to Frannie. "Namely, her straight grandson."

"Well, you know—" Frannie started in.

"Don't say it." She didn't have to. I already knew. If Patricia thought I was straight, it was only because I let her think it.

"Sweetie, I'm not saying it'll be easy to tell her. I'm not even saying that it should have happened by now, necessarily."

"But—"

"But you'll feel better if you do," she said. "I know it."

I rolled over on Frannie's bed and pulled a pillow close to my chest. "Do you see anything else in that crystal ball of yours?"

"I see another double date," she said. "For me and Jeffrey, and you and your new boyfriend."

"Right. Because there are so many gay boys at Boring Brook to choose from," I said.

"It doesn't have to be someone from school. It could be . . . Goatee Guy. You could get off your butt and ask him out once and for all."

"Well," I said, "For one thing, he doesn't work at the mall anymore. And for another thing, we don't even know his real name." Goatee Guy was the probably gay, definitely cute former assistant manager at Made in the Shades, where in the past year I'd bought not one but three pairs of sunglasses I didn't need.

"What happened to him?" Frannie asked.

"That's the point," I said. "You'll have to check the crystal ball again."

"Well, then, what about . . ." She trailed off.

I sat up on the bed and looked straight at her. "Yes? Who?"

"Well . . ."

"Exactly. So can we go online now, please? I already know what screen name you should use."

"What is it?"

"Tempeh Burger."

"Mmmm," she said. "Very sexy."

I got up and swiveled her chair so she was facing the computer. "It shows him you have a sense of humor. And he'll know it's you right away."

"Well, then why don't I just say Frannie?"

"Because then *everyone* will know it's you," I said.

"Oh yeah." She typed in *TEMPEHBURGER* and went in. Almost right away, she pulled her hands back from the keyboard. "There he is," she said. I looked down and saw that the first lines of chat had come in, including one from Jeffrey.

<<JEFFO: Yeah, well, that's 'cause everyone thinks they're edible.>>

Frannie still looked like she had been caught at something. "Uh, you know he can't see you, right?" I asked her.

Her response was a glare in my direction. "Just . . . tell

70

me what to say." She put her hands tentatively back on the keys while another line scrolled by.

<<LOLA227: Jeffo, you are so funny it makes me laugh LOL LOL. I wet my pants.>>

Astrid. Of course.

"Ee-ew," Frannie said. Then she stood up. "This is too much for me to handle. You go."

I could have told Frannie that no, in fact, this *wasn't* too much for her to handle and that she owed it to herself to keep going. But the alternate response meant I got to do a little of the driving. And I like to drive.

"What do you want me to say?" I asked, sitting in her place.

"Tell him I said hi. And . . . I had a good time at lunch. And I didn't know if maybe . . . um . . . I don't know. Maybe . . ." Her face brightened. "Should I ask him about going out again?"

"I have a better idea," I said, and typed in a private message to Jeffo.

<<TEMPEHBURGER: Hey>>

"That's good too," she said, and I hit send. He came back a second later.

<<JEFFO: T-burger? What happened to whoosie?>>

"He knows it's me!" Frannie sounded glad and surprised. "Good name choice."

"Told you so," I said.

<<TEMPEHBURGER: I like to change things up.>>

<<JEFFO: Cute>>

In the main chat room, Astrid wasn't giving up so easily.

<<LOLA227: Jeffo, where RU?>>

Frannie saw it too. "Go back to Germany!" she yelled at the screen.

<<JEFFO: Be right back.>>

"Auuugh," Frannie groaned. "He's talking to her too."

<<TEMPEHBURGER: I'm just here for a minute. Talk to you later.>>

<<JEFFO: No wait. Where are you off to?>>

"Genius!" Frannie said. She grabbed my shoulders and started rubbing them.

"So where do you want to tell him you're off to?" I asked her.

"The library. No, wait. Maybe it should be some kind of good cause, community-service thing."

"At nine at night?" I asked.

"See that?" she said. "This is why I need you." She bit her lower lip and shifted from foot to foot. "Okay, tell him my parents make me get off the computer after nine."

I made a wrong-answer-buzzer sound. "That doesn't seem—"

"I don't want him trying to chat me up when you're not around," she said. "Not yet."

I wasn't so sure this was a good idea, but I typed it in anyway.

<<TEMPEHBURGER: My parents have a death grip on my computer after nine. Ridiculous, but their house, their rules, etc. I just wanted to say thanks again for lunch.>>

<<JEFFO: Thanks to you too. I had a really good time. You looked amazing, BTW.>>

"All right," I said, "Jeffo's starting to show a little heat."

<<TEMPEHBURGER: Thanks. Not so bad yourself.>>

"Hey!" Frannie dug her thumbs into my shoulders a little too hard. I had just typed and sent the last response without checking first.

"Sorry," I said. "It just felt like we were getting into a rhythm. I got carried away."

"Well, put it back in your pants, Mr. Gigolo."

"I think I'm more of a pimp than a gigolo right now."

Frannie turned my head back to the screen. "Focus, please." Jeffrey's next line was already waiting.

<<JEFFO: Maybe next time just you and me?>>

"Yes!" I turned back to lock eyes with Frannie. "Okay, I'm checking with you about what you want to say, but you *are* going to say yes."

Frannie stared at the screen. "Ummm . . ."

"Why are you thinking about this? There's only one answer here," I told her.

"Maybe it's still too fast." She stepped back and sat on the bed.

73

"He's waiting," I said.

"Okay, okay. Fine." She flopped back and pulled a pillow over her face, just like I had done when the topic was me and my grandmother.

"Don't smother," I said. "Blue's not a good color for you."

<<TEMPEHBURGER: I'd like that.>>

<<JEFFO: I know you have to go. I'll talk to you at school.>>

"Wait!" Frannie bolted up. "Astrid's still back there. I can't leave yet."

"Don't worry about it," I told her. "You're exactly where you want to be. This is perfect. I'm going to say goodbye, okay?"

<<TEMPEHBURGER: See you tomorrow.>>

<<JEFFO: Gnight.>>

After I logged off, Frannie looked exhausted. "I can't take this pressure," she said.

"Sure, you can. You're totally on track. And he really is easy to talk to," I said. "I'll bet you guys will be an *and* by the end of the month."

"An *and?*"

"You know, like Belina *and* Keith. Frannie *and* Jeffrey." I thought that would make her smile, but she let out a big sigh. "What is it?" I asked her.

"Nothing," she said.

"*What?*"

74

"Well." She sighed again. "I'm going to have to do this on my own at some point."

"Omigod, you are so your father's daughter," I said. "Don't you think it's totally normal for friends to help friends with their relationships? I know you're nervous, but that's all it is—nerves. Jeffrey knows you and he likes you." I waited for her to look up at me. "He likes *you*. Okay? Just keep going. I swear you'll be glad you did."

"Unless he turns out to be a serial killer and hacks up my family in the middle of the night and steals my car."

"Right. But otherwise, you'll be glad even if it doesn't work out, 'cause then you can at least say you went for it."

"Yeah," she said. "File that one under *H* for *hypocrite*."

"We're talking about *you* right now."

Frannie sat on the edge of her bed, knotting up the blankets in her fists. I let her think.

"All right," she said finally. "But here's the deal."

"There's a deal?" I said.

"Yes. Next time something comes up for you, you positively, absolutely, no excuses have to go for it. Okay?"

I scoffed. "I can't agree to something that hasn't even happened yet."

"Marcus . . . "

We sat there doing brain wave karate, trying to stare each other down. Usually, I win every time, but she'd gotten me right where I was vulnerable. I looked away first.

Then I groaned and fake died onto the floor with my hands around my neck. "Fine," I choked. "You win."

"Such a drama queen," she said.

I lifted my head. "That's Mister Drama Queen to you."

I was happy for Frannie. I really was. So I just left it at that. It didn't make sense to tell her absolutely everything I was thinking. So what if I was a little bit jealous? What was she supposed to do with that? And so what if I wasn't just jealous of her for getting into Boyfriend Land, but also for getting there with Jeffrey Osborne? The only reason I felt that way was because I was kind of sort of *being* Frannie. It made perfect sense that I'd start to see him the same way she saw him. It was nothing. It would pass, I was sure. In no time at all, I'd stop thinking about Jeffrey like that, stop imagining what kind of kisser he might be, and stop wondering what he looked like naked.

Sure, I would.

♀ Four

My lipsticks stood lined up like little soldiers on my vanity before me, arranged from light to dark. Usually, I like the darker colors, but this occasion seemed to call for a more neutral shade. Sahara Shimmer? I thought, twisting it open. I smeared some onto my lips, which immediately seemed to disappear into my face. Too neutral. Tissuing it off, I reached for an unused tube of Lilac Breeze, a freebie cast off from one of Mom's department store makeup bonanzas. It had always seemed like a boring color to me, but I had already been through about thirty shades (did I mention that I have a problem throwing stuff away?), and I was running out of ideas. Actually, I thought as I put it on, it looks pretty good. It picked up the pink in the crazy paisley vintage blouse I had chosen after tearing apart my closet in the search for The Outfit. I'd finally settled on this pink, maroon, and apple green shirt, a black mini, black fishnets, and high-heeled boots. The effect was sort of Naughty Secretary . . . which wasn't exactly what I had been going for but wasn't bad, either.

See, I was going on a Date. I know, I know, no one dates anymore—but there was no other word for what this was. Jeffrey and I had been chatting online, and it had gone a little something like this:

<<JEFFO: Hey—what are you doing tonight?>>

"What am I doing tonight?" I said into the phone. "I should tell him I have plans, right?"

On the other end of the line, Marcus let out a groan. "Seriously, if you aren't going to pay attention, I don't know why I bother."

"What do you mean?" I demanded. "Isn't that one of the basic rules of keeping a guy interested—he has to think that you have a life?"

"Look, he's not just making conversation," Marcus explained. "He's asking you out."

I ran my fingers through my hair impatiently, giving silent thanks that I had Marcus around to translate. Belina and Jenn are absolutely no help when it comes to decoding these things. "So I should tell him that I'm available." It was a question, but it didn't really sound like one.

"Only if you *are* available." Marcus sounded kind of huffy.

"Am I?" Marcus and I have this standing Saturday night movie date thingie, and I knew that was what he was huffing about. We get together to watch crazy Indian musicals (Marcus's favorite) or Hong Kong kung fu (my usual choice) and pig out on Hawaiian-style ham-and-pineapple pizza. It's our thang.

Okay—truth: I wanted to go out with Jeffrey. Who wouldn't? I mean, pizza and a movie with Marcus was fun, but I could do that anytime. Quality time with the hottie of my choice wasn't usually on the menu. But I didn't want to say that to Marcus.

"I don't know, *are* you?" Marcus repeated.

Two could play at this game. "I don't know," I replied. "Am I?"

<<JEFFO: R U there? >> scrolled across the screen.

"Clock's ticking," I said.

"Oh, for God's sake," Marcus snapped. "Tell him you're free."

My fingers hovered over the keyboard. "But what about us?" I had to offer some kind of alternate hangage. "Do you want to have brunch tomorrow?"

"Ooooh, brunch," Marcus said sarcastically. "I just love sloppy seconds. Besides, brunch is so eighties, and you know I'm into anything retro."

"Okay, I'm telling him that I can't make it." I started to type.

"Don't you dare!" Marcus shouted. "Frannie Falconer, you will go on that date, and you will wear something low-cut, and you will dish up all of the details while we watch *Sholay* tomorrow night. Type it in."

So that's what I did.

<<Flava788: Sorry, stepped away for a minute. I'm free tonight. 7?>>

<<JEFFO: Cool. Oh, BTW, your friend Marcus is really cool and funny and everything . . . but I was thinking this would be just us. . . .>>

A few things flashed through me at that moment—a thrill that it was a real "date," as in the Scoops-crew-approved two-person date formula and everything . . . and a little, tiny, microscopic pang of jealousy that Jeffrey thought that Marcus was cool and funny. Does he think *I'm* cool and funny? I wondered.

I hit the keyboard.

<<Flava788: Sounds great>>

"Okay," I told Marcus. "It's on."

"Good," he replied. His voice was a weird combination of satisfied and hurt, and I really felt bad for ditching on our plans at the last minute. But wasn't that what he had told me to do?

Anyhoo, so Marcus and I firmed up our brunch plans, and then I hung up and started to get ready. And then I started to get nervous about the Jeffrey date. And *then* I started feeling like a jerk about the whole Marcus thing, like if I was a better friend, I would have insisted that we keep our plans. And *then* I started to think that maybe Lilac Breeze was making me look kind of yellow, and I was just about to tissue it off when Laura walked into my room.

"Pink or blue?" she asked. She was wearing low-riding black pants and a formfitting pink cashmere sweater and holding up a baby blue one that was exactly the same as the one she had on in every respect except for the color.

I wanted to say, *What difference does it make?* But I'm a nice person, so I actually said, "I think the pink really goes well with your skin tone."

"Really?" Laura asked, giving me a huge smile. I don't usually hand out compliments on her Banana Republic wardrobe, but I was in a good mood. "You're pretty dressed up," she said, eyeing my skirt. "What's the deal? Cute guy at the video store?"

"Actually, I have a date." I tried to sound nonchalant while still putting enough emphasis on the word *date* so that Laura would know it was important.

"Really?" Laura squealed. "With who?"

I fought the grin, but the grin won. "Jeffrey Osborne."

Laura waggled her eyebrows. "Ooh—I remember him." Laura had been a senior at my high school last year. "*Cute!*" She shoved aside a mountain of reject clothes and flopped down on my bed. "What are you guys doing?"

"I don't know yet," I said truthfully. "What are you up to?"

"Well . . . Steve is taking me for a moonlight picnic at Simms's Peak." Laura smiled dreamily. "You can see stars and all the city lights from there. Then we're going for chocolate fondue at the Melting Pot. They have a really cozy back room, with a fireplace and everything." She tossed her long blond hair over her shoulder and leaned back on her elbows, blue eyes shining.

"Wow," I said, feeling unbelievably lame. Suddenly, my date didn't even sound like a date at all. This is how most of my interactions with Laura go. Even when she's being sweet, she manages to make me crazy.

I heard a car stop in front of our house. Laura and I both rushed toward the window—but she got there first. "Yours," she said.

At that moment, I was all nerves. I had this weird urge to ask Laura to go out on my date for me—I was sure she'd do a much better job than I would. "Tell me that I look okay," I begged.

"You look great," Laura said.

She sounded sincere, so I decided to believe her. "Thanks." I gave her one last nervous smile and darted out the door. "'Bye, Dad!" I shouted as I thudded down the stairs. "Be back before eleven-thirty you can reach me on the cellie I won't do drugs or get into any trouble see you later!"

"Have fun!" Dad called from the living room as I busted

out the front door, successfully avoiding the whole awkward parent-date interaction heinousness. This is already going brilliantly, I congratulated myself silently. Just brilliantly.

"Hey!" I said as I headed down the front walk toward Jeffrey. He was walking toward our house, and my heart did this thuddy little freak-out when I saw him. He was wearing a soft slate blue flannel shirt over brown corduroys, and Timberlands. He looked clean and rugged at the same time, and it basically took all of my energy not to either (a) jump on him or (b) run back inside the house in terror.

"Hey," Jeffrey said warmly. He looked me up and down, then smiled.

Note to self: Naughty Secretary works. We both turned toward Jeffrey's car, and we reached for the door at the same moment, knocking heads.

Okay, this is the problem with modern culture: chivalry is in a coma. I mean, usually, you think it's dead—hardly anybody lays a cloak across a mud puddle or opens doors or stands up when a woman joins the table anymore. But every now and again it'll give a little death rattle, and someone will go to open the car door for you when you're least expecting it, and you'll end up giving your date an accidental head butt. Very romantic.

"Ooh," I said, wincing and rubbing my forehead. "Sorry."

"My fault," Jeffrey replied, blinking hard—to clear the stars from his eyes, I guess.

Then we both reached for the door again. This time, though, we didn't butt heads—we just kind of let out these nervous giggles; then Jeffrey stepped back and waved toward the door with this "go ahead" gesture, so I ended up opening my own door. Which was weirdly disappointing, in a way.

"So," Jeffrey said as he slid into the driver's seat. "Where are we headed?"

"Well, I know this great Cuban-Chinese place," I said, managing to make it sound like I'd just thought of it, when really, I'd racked my brain for almost two hours to come up with a place that had plenty of vegetarian options but where I wouldn't have to eat tempeh again. And the Cuban-Chinese place was cool—for one thing, the food was great, like spicy Chinese food with rice and beans and these awesome fried plantains. For another thing, the waiters were out-of-control surly. I'm talking, they practically threw the food at you, which was always good for a laugh. Plus, it's owned by our neighbor, who is a very nice man and has a super-cute pug named Zero.

Jeffrey grimaced. "Actually . . ." he said slowly, "I'm kind of on a boycott. I'm not eating any Chinese food until Tibet is free."

I sat there for a moment, trying to process what Jeffrey was talking about. Tibet? I guess this was one of his good causes. . . . Be sympathetic, I told myself, even though I didn't see how boycotting Cuban-Chinese food prepared in America by Mr. Wong who lived three blocks away was going to help anything. Then again, I'm really not up on current events, so . . . "Oh, right," I said, as though I had momentarily forgotten my own Chinese-food boycott.

"I was thinking we could hit the Polish food festival," Jeffrey said. "They've got these amazing dumplings. . . ."

I nodded like Polish food was the greatest thing since the creation of exfoliant, even though I didn't really know anything about it, except that it probably didn't involve tempeh. Which made it okay by me. "Sounds good."

"Great," Jeffrey said brightly.

"Great," I repeated.

We sat there, smiling blankly at each other for a moment, and I racked my brain to think of something clever to say. "Polish food," I started awkwardly. "That reminds me of a story. So this Polish guy and a Catholic priest are in a rowboat—"

Jeffrey's blue eyes were staring at me as though what I had to say was the most incredibly important thing ever, and suddenly I realized that he was the world's worst audience for a Polish joke. I mean, Jeffrey was the sweetest, most earnest person I'd ever met. He was in the International Club. He read poetry. He only ate things that were (a) vegetables and (b) not hurting Tibet. I didn't want to offend him.

"So what happened?" Jeffrey asked.

"Well . . . their ship went down, and they had to live in that lifeboat for forty days before they were rescued," I improvised. "But before anyone could reach them, the priest fell overboard and was eaten by a shark." Jeez, where did that come from? I wondered.

"Oh, that's so tragic," Jeffrey said, his blue eyes clouding.

Way to go, Frannie, I thought. Now you've depressed him. Perfect date material. What would Laura say? I wondered desperately. Something uplifting, I guess. I decided to tack on a happy ending. "Yes, but the Polish guy had been a criminal, and when the priest died, he decided to dedicate his life to doing good works. So it was kind of inspirational."

"Wow." Jeffrey shook his head as he started the car. "What an amazing story. There's a lesson in that."

"Yeah," I said, shifting uncomfortably in my seat. The lesson is . . . don't try to tell the most PC guy on earth a Polish joke, I thought.

Silence descended over the car as we started toward downtown. I snuck a sideways look at Jeffrey's profile and watched his hand on the gearshift as he drove. Mmmm. Who needs dinner, anyway? I thought. The view is delicious.

I could hear the tires humming as we drove, and after a few minutes, I decided I had to break the silence or I'd go completely insane. "So, uh . . . how did you become interested in Tibet?" I asked, grasping at straws.

"Well, I got into Buddhism a couple of years ago," Jeffrey said, downshifting sexily. "That was when I became a vegetarian. And that was when I started reading up on the plight of Tibet. You know, China has been doing the most horrible things to the blahbie, blahbie, blah."

Well, actually, he didn't really say "blahbie, blahbie, blah," but that was kind of where my brain tuned out his words and started searching for something intelligent to say on the subject. Tibet, Tibet . . . My dad always reads *National Geographic*, I thought. Hadn't there been a cover story on Tibet a while ago? I seemed to remember flipping idly through the article while I was waiting for Laura to get off the phone. . . . There were pictures of mountains and guys in robes. They must have been Buddhist.

Finally, Jeffrey stopped his diatribe about Tibet, and I said in my most earnest voice, "Yeah, I've always wanted to go there. I think I'd love to climb Mount Everest someday."

For a minute, Jeffrey looked confused; then he laughed. "I think you're thinking of Nepal," he said gently.

Crap! Nepal! *That* was the article I'd flipped through. "Oh yeah," I said quickly. "I just meant that I wanted to go to Nepal too. In addition to Tibet. It's all just so fascinating."

"Yeah, Nepal is interesting because they have all of these issues with the Sherpas," Jeffrey agreed, launching into some speech about Sherpa rights. Personally, I wasn't sure what a Sherpa was (isn't it some kind of yak?), but I was just glad that Jeffrey was talking about something.

I decided to just sit back and watch his full lips move as he explained the situation with Mount Everest and the

Sherpa-yaks. It was like hearing my grandmother speak in Greek—I only understood about every third word. It's funny—I'd always thought of myself as someone who cared about the world and the environment and all of that junk. You know, I'm a maniac about recycling, and I always snip up my six-pack rings so the squirrels won't get caught in them. But I was starting to realize that I had a long way to go if I wanted to learn to speak "Jeffrese."

Note to self, I thought, read this month's issue of *National Geographic*, and go online to find out more about Tibet.

One thing was becoming very clear: Marcus and I had a lot of research to do if we were going to make this relationship with Jeffrey work out.

"Well, here we are," Jeffrey said as we pulled up in front of my house three and a half hours later.

"Yep, here we are," I agreed.

Silence. Then my stomach gave a queasy lurch.

Why did I have to eat all of that kielbasa? I wondered miserably. It was not sitting well. Actually, it kind of felt like it had come alive in my gut, like that beast in the *Alien* movies.

Polish food: when good sausage goes bad.

I guess it was my own fault. The food festival had been more fun than I'd expected—and the food was great—so I'd kind of let down my guard.

The first thing I saw when we got there were these old people in crazy crinoline outfits, dancing to this bopping polka music. They looked like they were having so much fun that I tried to get Jeffrey to dance with me, but he wouldn't do it. Of course. Guys never do. Marcus once told me that he won't dance because he doesn't want to look like a dork, and I told him that was funny coming from a guy who dressed up as Stanley Kubrick (don't worry, nobody else has heard of him, either—he's a movie director and Marcus's hero) for last year's Halloween party, but he still wouldn't get his booty out there.

So Jeffrey and I ended up wandering around the booths filled with homemade crafts and different foods, and he kept explaining the significance of everything to Polish culture, which was interesting in the way that social studies is interesting. The fact was, the smell of the grilling sausages was driving me crazy. But I thought I'd better not order any. . . . I didn't know what Jeffrey would think. Finally, we stopped at a booth, and Jeffrey ordered a plate of pierogi. I'd never even heard of it.

"Try this," he said, holding out a small dumpling.

I eyed the food dubiously. "What is it?"

"It's delicious." The corners of his mouth tucked into a smile, so I opened my mouth. His fingertip touched my lower lip for a split second as he popped the pierogi inside.

The dumpling was warm . . . and it yielded gently as I

bit down, revealing creamy cheese and potato. "Mmmm."

Jeffrey smiled. "Better than tempeh," he said. "Right?"

"I love tempeh," I lied.

Jeffrey gave me a look, as though my nose had just grown about a foot. "Frannie, *nobody* loves tempeh." Then he laughed, which made me laugh.

"Okay, okay," I admitted finally. "The truth is, I'm not really a vegetarian."

"Really?" Jeffrey pretended to be shocked. "Because the way you've been eyeing the sausage stands all night totally made me think that you wanted to go get some tofu."

I laughed, but I could feel myself blushing.

"You want to try some?" Jeffrey cocked his head toward a booth, where spicy sausage was hissing on the grill.

I lifted my eyebrows. "Won't it gross you out?"

"No." Jeffrey shook his head. "You go ahead. I'll stick with these pierogi, though."

So once I had the green light, I went ahead and got a plate of sausage and fried onions, which was unbelievably delicious. Then we had some cheese-filled nalesniki, which are these crepe-like things, and some jablecznik, which is apple cake, and some sok, which is just fruit juice. The best part was, the food gave us something to talk about. I mean, sure, most of the conversations were just, "Mmmm, this is so good!" and, "Do you taste cinnamon in this?" but it was better than discussing Sherpas. And like I said, everything was great, and I was having a pretty good time . . . until the car ride home. That's when the kielbasa really kicked in.

My stomach let out a groan. "So!" I said brightly to cover the noise. "That was fun."

"Yeah," Jeffrey agreed. "It was." A smile played on his lips. "So . . . what are you doing tomorrow night?"

"Tomorrow night?" I squirmed in my seat and tried to subtly adjust the waistband on my mini. "Oh—just, uh, hanging out with Marcus. Doing our usual thing." A belch tried to crawl up my throat, but I pushed it back down.

"Mind if I come?" Jeffrey asked.

What? Oh my God, I thought as I shoved a damp hank of hair away from my face, Marcus will kill me if I invite Jeffrey along on our hang. Then again, maybe he would kill me if I didn't. This whole boyfriend thing had thrown me into a new zone with Marcus—so much for brain twins.

Now it was Jeffrey's turn to look uncomfortable. "I mean, if you think it would be weird—"

"No, no," I said quickly. My stomach started to burble away, and I realized that I was going to need a bathroom in about forty-five seconds or this car was going to lose its pine-fresh scent in a way that wasn't going to be pretty. Get out of car now, my brain said. Worry about consequences later. "I mean—yes! That sounds fun. Just come over around six."

"Okay, great." Jeffrey smiled.

That seemed to be it, and I was desperate to leave, but I was having a hard time making myself get out of the car. What if he's building up to a kiss? I wondered. What am I supposed to do? Is there some kind of cue I'm supposed to give? It was hard to even consider flashing him a come-hither look when my stomach felt like it was about to explode.

I waited another moment, but Jeffrey didn't lean toward me or anything. Then my stomach let out a lurch like I'd just fallen off a hundred-foot cliff, and my decision was made. "Okay, see you tomorrow," I said quickly as the pressure built against my tight miniskirt. "This was great—thanks again. 'Bye!"

"I'll call you!" Jeffrey shouted after me as I slammed shut the car door and hurried up the front walk.

I didn't even have time to give him a wave—I shoved my way into the house and made it to the downstairs bathroom— just in time. Okay, let's just say that I'd made the right decision. Even if I had missed out on a kiss, I never would have gotten another one if I'd stayed in that car three seconds longer.

Mom was standing by the sink, scraping something into the garbage disposal as I walked into the kitchen about fifteen minutes—no, I'm not kidding—later. She was still dressed in a navy blue business suit. "Hey, Mom," I said. "What's up?"

Mom gave me a smile. "Just finished dinner. I only got home about half an hour ago."

I checked my watch. It was ten-thirty. "Wow. Late!

Were you out on a hot date or something?" I teased, slipping into a chair at the kitchen table.

"A hot date with my computer," Mom replied with a laugh as she sat down across from me. "We seem to be spending a lot of time together lately."

I nodded absently. It was true—Mom had been spending a lot of time at work, even working on the weekends. Laura had actually made dinner twice last week. I hadn't really thought about it, but it was kind of unusual.

"Mom . . ." I said, propping my elbows on the table and putting my chin in my palms. "What was it like when you met Dad? Was it . . . was it love at first sight? I mean, did you click right away?"

Mom looked at me carefully. "Why are you asking?"

I shrugged, thinking about how hard it was for me to talk to Jeffrey. "No reason. Just wondering."

Mom sighed and sat back in her chair. "It was such a long time ago, sweetie. I hardly remember. . . ."

"Was it ever—you know—awkward?" I asked.

Mom smiled at me, but it was a faraway smile. "It's always awkward at first, when you meet someone new. You don't know what to say . . . they don't know what to say. . . . Then you get to know them, and you can hardly believe there was a time when you weren't finishing their sentences for them." She looked at my face carefully. "Is this about your date tonight?"

I twirled a thick chunk of hair around my index finger. "Kind of," I admitted. "I guess I just can't wait until I stop feeling nervous all the time."

Reaching out, Mom took my hand between her own. "I know that this is hard to believe, but you'll reach a point when you miss that nervous heart flutter. You'll miss the romance."

I nodded, even though I wasn't sure that what my mom was saying was true. I mean, that thing with the pierogi when Jeffrey touched my lip had been kind of romantic . . . but I'd have exchanged that in a heartbeat for being able to get rid of the jerk feeling I had after confusing Nepal and Tibet. "I don't know. . . ."

Mom shrugged. "Well, *I* miss it."

"You do?" That was news to me. "But you and Dad are so lovey-dovey."

"Mmmm." Mom drummed her fingers on the table once, twice, then stopped. "Do you know what Laura and Steve are doing tonight?"

I rolled my eyes. "Picnic under the stars and chocolate fondue."

Mom nodded. "You know they got that out of a book?"

"What?" I stared at my mom. "Are you kidding?"

Sheepishly, Mom reached into her briefcase and pulled out a red paperback with pink lettering. She shoved it across the Formica table at me. *The Romance Handbook*, the title screamed, *Revitalize Your Relationship in Just Five Weeks! Over One Million Copies in Print!*

Oh, that is *so* Laura, I thought. To do everything by the book! I started to giggle, but it got caught in my throat when I saw my mother's expression. Her blue eyes locked on mine—studying my reaction. I cleared my throat. "And . . . the fondue is in the book?"

Mom flipped through the pages. "'Chapter Three— Plan Your Perfect Date,'" she read aloud. "It has a whole list of ideas."

"Wow . . ." I said. And then, because I couldn't think of anything else to say, I said it again. "Wow."

"So—I was going to try it out on your father." My mother's eyes, which were usually a serious dark blue, were sparkling.

Hmmm, maybe I could pick up a few tips too, I thought as I plucked the book from her hands and flipped through it. The first thing I saw was "Chapter Six: Spice Things Up in the Bedroom!"

Whoa—that was way too vivid. I slapped the book closed. God—why couldn't I have been born in the for- ties? I wondered. Back when parents never told their chil- dren anything. But I didn't want to hurt Mom's feelings. "Um, sure, Mom," I said, trying not to sound completely grossed out. "Why not?"

Mom pulled the book back and turned the cover so that

she could look at it. "Why not?" she repeated softly, more to the book than to me.

I hauled myself out of my chair. "I think I'm going to bed," I said.

"Okay, sweetie," Mom said, tucking the book back into her briefcase. " 'Night."

Once I was in my room, I flopped on my bed and stared at my computer. Jeffrey would be home by now, I thought. I should see if he's in the chat room. But I didn't move. I just didn't have the energy to try to think of things to say to him.

I'll write him tomorrow, I decided, reaching for my phone. Once I've had a chance to look through *National Geographic*. I punched in Marcus's number and let it ring. Right now, I just wanted to have a conversation that was easy on the brain.

Why wait for tomorrow night to deliver the full report? I decided. Not that I'd get much of a chance then anyway, with Jeffrey coming over. So I really *have* to call Marcus now. Besides, I needed to tell Marcus that we had to get some polka music ASAP. Those beats were off the hook. And I knew that he was the only person on earth who would appreciate them the way I did.

♟ Five

"How about just plain cheese?" I asked. I was staring at the pizza menu on Frannie's kitchen table, trying to come up with something vegetarian. Jeffrey was coming over, and I knew he wouldn't eat our usual—ham and pineapple, aka pig and pineapple—and none of the veggies sounded good to me.

"Cheese . . . sure . . ." Frannie had a pan of blondie batter in one hand and was trying to open the oven door with a giant mitt on the other hand. Her mom would have probably made a whole dessert buffet if Frannie had asked, but she wanted to make these herself, even if they were from a mix.

I got up to help her. "Thanks," she said, and slid the pan into the oven, then set the timer. "Okay, now what?"

The clock said 5:58. Jeffrey was coming at six-ish. "Now we wait," I said.

Everything else was already set. We'd been to the video store and only rented one movie—*Sholay*. It's about two small-time crooks and a cop working together to get revenge on a big-time crook . . . in India . . . with subtitles . . . and musical numbers. I realized once that I like those Bollywood classics for the same reason I like the way Frannie dresses. Anytime someone can take a bunch of different elements that no one else would think of putting together and then make them work in some unexpected way, I'm interested. To me, that's art. It's surprising. It's strange. It's inspiring. It's all of the above.

Plus, we wanted to rent something we'd seen a million times just in case Jeffrey turned out to be a movie talker. I'm not a completely high-maintenance person, but I do have a few rules where movies are concerned, and no talking is one of them. It usually wasn't an issue at Frannie's house because it had always been just the two of us.

I couldn't help feeling a little pressure over the fact that Jeffrey was coming. I didn't mind so much since I had a lot of ideas about how I wanted it to go. Frannie and Jeffrey were moving past the neutral-ground phase of things and into the part where you start sniffing out each other's territory to see if you can deal with hanging out there. I wanted Jeffrey to see me as a permanent structure in Frannie's world. I also wanted him to think of me the same way Frannie thought of Glenn: as the cool best friend. And yes, if I'm being honest, I just plain old wanted Jeffrey to like me.

The doorbell rang at 6:10, about two seconds after Frannie's father happened to pass through the kitchen and into the foyer. "I'll get it!" she yelled, but we heard the front door open anyway.

Then Jeffrey's voice. "Hi, is Frannie home?"

Frannie froze. She stood just inside the kitchen door, listening with her eyes closed. It looked like she was praying that her father wouldn't say something like:

"Sure, come on in. You must be the reason Frannie's been buying so many new clothes lately."

Which was what he said. Frannie whipped out into the hall while I kept listening from the kitchen table.

"Dad, Jeffrey, Jeffrey, Dad."

"Nice to meet you." Jeffrey sounded polite, in a cute way. Not ass-kissy.

"Okay, Dad, thanks. We're all set. Come on in." Her voice got closer to the kitchen door. I could see the back of her head now.

"I'll be up in my office if you kids need anything."

Mr. Falconer's steps receded up the stairs while Frannie kind of shuffled backward into the kitchen with Jeffrey following. His hair was parted on the side, different than usual. Good different.

"Sorry about that," Frannie said. "He's so embarrassing sometimes."

"Don't worry about it," Jeffrey told her. "He seemed really nice."

"Oh . . . he is nice." She sounded a tiny bit defensive. "It's just, he's just . . ." She looked over at me. "We were thinking about pizza. Does that sound good?"

I waved the pizza menu at Jeffrey in greeting. "Just plain cheese okay?"

"Great," he said. "Do they have whole wheat crust?"

His shirt rode up as he slipped off his fleece pullover and I couldn't help noticing the line of hair that ran down from his belly button. I forced my eyes back to the menu. "Um, we can ask when we call."

We ended up ordering two mediums—ham and pineapple on white and Way Too Many Veggies on whole wheat. Then we sat down to wait for the delivery.

"Marcus and I like to get the food before we start the movie," Frannie said. "If that's okay." I liked that she said "Marcus and I," even though it was more my thing than hers.

While we sat there talking, I kept wondering what Jeffrey thought of the house. The foyer is two stories high, with a marble floor and a big open staircase. The kitchen, where we were hanging out, is like from a magazine. There's even a TV in the refrigerator. I remembered seeing it all for the first time, and how much I had thought it said about Frannie, and how wrong that assumption had been.

Once the food came, we went into the TV room and started the movie. I sat in the big leather easy chair. Frannie and Jeffrey took the couch. From my position, I could watch the TV *and* the two of them without being obvious about it. They both sat on the cracks between the outside couch cushions and the middle one, which was nowhere you'd ordinarily sit unless you weren't sure how close to get to the other person. I thought the matching shyness thing was a good sign.

Then, about fifteen minutes into the movie, Jeffrey started looking bored. He scratched his chin, smiled at Frannie, looked around the room, took another piece of pizza. All bad signs. I knew this movie wasn't for everyone, but now I felt self-conscious about it. It's one thing to watch some crazy esoteric musical with your best friend who you know is into it. It's another thing to watch while you're wondering if someone else in the room is wondering what kind of an idiot would choose a movie like this.

Half an hour in, Jeffrey got up to go to the bathroom right in the middle of a song. When Frannie reached for the pause button and Jeffrey said, "Keep going. Don't worry about it," that was all I could take.

"We can turn this off and do something else," I suggested as casually as I could. Frannie shot me a look, like, *Who are you and what have you done with my friend Marcus?* I'm not exactly known for stopping movies in the middle.

"Whatever," Jeffrey said. "I'm good either way." Although I'm sure he was just being polite.

After he left the room, Frannie turned and whispered to me, "I can't believe you just said that."

I couldn't believe it either. To me, the whole point of a movie is that it's supposed to be an uninterrupted experience. But this was Flexible Marcus, who I hoped was part of Cool Best Friend Marcus.

"It's fine," I whispered back. "Let's just have dessert or something."

She started closing up the pizza boxes and scrunching up napkins. "He's totally bored, isn't he?"

"Don't worry about it," I told her, even though I couldn't help feeling a little worried myself. Maybe *Sholay* had been a big mistake. Maybe we should have gotten a few new releases as backup. . . .

Maybe Jeffrey wasn't my boyfriend and I needed to not think about it so much.

Back in the kitchen, Frannie cut the blondies into huge squares and put them in bowls with big scoops of vanilla ice cream and hot fudge on top. She barely touched her own while Jeffrey and I mowed through ours.

"These are good," I said.

"They *are* good," he said.

"*Really* good," I said, and then wondered if that had sounded competitive. I hadn't meant for it to.

I saw Frannie stifle a smile. "Thanks," she said into her bowl.

"So what else do you guys do when you hang out?" Jeffrey asked us. I loved that he wanted to know.

What was strange, though, was that I couldn't come up with an answer. For all the time Frannie and I spend together, I couldn't quite think of how we filled it. Apparently, she couldn't either. We both looked at each other for a long couple of seconds and then burst out laughing.

"I don't know," Frannie said. "I guess we just . . . hang out."

"Watch movies, of course," I added.

"Do homework. Procrastinate from doing homework," Frannie said. "Eat. Talk."

"Play favorites," I said.

"Play favorites?" Jeffrey looked like he didn't like the sound of that.

"It's just a little game we have," Frannie said. "It's kind of dumb." I shot her a "don't even" look, and she quickly added, "But it's fun."

Jeffrey scraped some fudge off the side of his bowl with his spoon. "How do you play?"

"I don't know if *game*'s the right word," I said. "It's just questions. The more random the better. Like . . . favorite shade of blue?"

Jeffrey raised his eyebrows at Frannie, as in, you go

first. I noticed his nice blue eyes and hoped I hadn't just set her up to say *that* was her favorite shade. It would be overkill if she did.

"You know that color of sky near the horizon just before it gets dark?" Frannie said. "I'd like a shirt that color."

"Good answer," I told her, a little relieved. Then we both looked at Jeffrey.

"Oh, uh . . . I don't know," he said, shrugging. "There's this color called 'ocean' in the Fritz Fielding catalog. It's nice." He smiled at Frannie. "And actually, I do have a shirt that color."

Wow, I thought, how semi-queer of you. Although it did make its own kind of sense now that he mentioned it. Jeffrey always looked like something out of a Fritz Fielding catalog, all muted tones and natural fibers and well groomed but not overgroomed . . . and hot, but attainable.

"What about you, Marcus?" he asked me.

This was all going much better than the movie. Everyone looked relaxed.

I thought about my answer for a second. "I really like that steely gray-blue color, like on—"

Frannie pointed at me with her spoon. "Mrs. Pasternak's car!"

"Exactly."

Jeffrey sat up straighter on his kitchen stool. He seemed kind of amazed by us, which I was privately loving. "You guys are like—" he started.

"Brain twins," Frannie and I said together, and all three of us cracked up. Jeffrey's stool tipped back and he stumbled off it, which made us laugh even harder. I'd never seen him so loose. It was sexy on him. I always imagine my own face to look kind of circus freaky when I laugh hard.

But it was happening. We were bonding, all three of us. I was going to be the CBF (cool best friend). This was good. It was all good.

And I realized something else just then. Something about the way Jeffrey asked questions, the way he expressed an interest in Frannie, in both of us: he wanted people to like him. Better yet, he wanted *us* to like him. You'd never think Jeffrey Osborne worried about that kind of thing because (a) everyone already did like him and (b) he just seemed so quietly confident all the time. I loved seeing this new piece. It made him less perfect . . . which made him more perfect.

Which was why, during our recap on the phone later that night, I suggested Frannie go online and talk to him some more.

"Nooo," she said. "It started off so sketchy tonight, but then it got pretty good by the end. I just want to quit while I'm ahead."

"Quit?" I said.

"You know what I mean." Which was true but didn't mean that I agreed with her.

"*Or,*" I said, "you can move things forward. You know, get past that phase where you need an excuse to talk to each other even though you just said good night an hour ago." This was exactly the phase Frannie had never gotten past with a boy. It seemed worth pushing for.

She cleared her throat. "Wouldn't that count as coming on too strong?"

"My new opinion is that he can take it."

I heard her adjust the phone to the other ear, probably flipping over on her bed. "How do you have such strong opinions about all this? It's not like you're exactly . . . experienced."

Coming from someone else that might have stung a little bit. "I don't know," I said. "Maybe I was a straight girl in a past life. Or a more experienced gay boy." Or, I thought, maybe this was my thing—helping people do for themselves what I would never able to do for myself. I pushed the thought away.

"And maybe Jeffrey was your boyfriend," Frannie added. "In the Renaissance or something."

"And maybe it's time for you to stop changing the subject," I said.

She groaned, as in, *You're right, but I don't want to think about it.* "He's probably not even online," she said. "He couldn't have been home for more than—"

"He's in the RBHS chat room right now," I said.

Her voice went up a step. "Does that mean *you're* in the chat room?"

"Unofficially," I said. "I haven't logged on. But I do have a screen name for you. Nicenite, with an *n-i-t-e*."

"That's cute," Frannie said. There were a few seconds of silence, and then she said, "No. You know what? I'm going to take the rest of the night off. I really want it to happen, but this stuff exhausts me. Maybe I just have to go in short spurts."

"Oh, come on," I said, not sure why I cared so much. "It'll be like saying good night on the front porch, just without the kiss. It won't take any energy at all, and I'll be right there with you. If you want me to be."

She thought some more. "You're probably right," she said, and I was already logging in for her with the new name, Nicenite.

"Good," I said.

"And it definitely couldn't hurt to say good night or whatever."

"Exactly." I found Jeffo, typed in, *Hi again*, and hit send.

"But I'm just not up for it," Frannie concluded.

"Huh?" My fingers froze.

"I have to take a shower. I'm tired. The cat died. Insert excuse here. I don't know."

Jeffrey's response scrolled by.

<<JEFFO: Nicenite? I agree.>>

Looking back, it seems like I could have easily explained to Frannie that Jeffrey was already on the scene and why. At that moment, though, a little spike of panic—

or something, I'm not sure what—blocked out my common sense. I didn't know what to say, so I didn't say anything.

"Talk to you tomorrow?" Frannie asked me. "And don't forget I have a dentist appointment so I can't pick you up. I'll see you after first period."

"Uhhh . . . okay."

And she hung up.

And there I was, alone with Jeffrey for the first time. My fingers hung about an inch over the keyboard, my heart thumped, and my brain churned out two competing messages:

What are you doing? Are you crazy? Don't even think about it. Just make up some excuse and get out of there. Nothing good can come of this. And stop thinking about Jeffrey. Think about something else. Think about nuns. Nuns crocheting. And eating cottage cheese.

What are you doing? Are you crazy? Don't even think about leaving now. Just get in there and say something. It would be worse for Frannie if you ditched now than if you just had a quick little conversation and then left. And stop thinking about nuns. Think about Frannie. Think about your best friend and what's best for her. Now go.

Somehow the right side of my brain was louder and more convincing than the left. I put my fingers back onto the keyboard. I closed my eyes, took a breath, and focused on what I had to do. *Frannie and Jeffrey. Frannie and Jeffrey. I'm Frannie. Okay. Go.*

<<NICENITE: Thanks for coming over tonight.>>

<<JEFFO: Thanks U2. Is it ok for you to be online? Your parents around?>>

<<NICENITE: They are. I should probably be quick.>>

There was a long pause and then he said:

<<JEFFO: I was just thinking about you.>>

Well, *that* was a good sign. For Frannie.

<<NICENITE: Me too.>>

<<JEFFO: I was thinking how I wanted to XX you tonight.>>

Whoa.

I sat back from the computer. XX? Did Jeffrey want to kiss Frannie or *porn* her? I knew the answer, but just thinking about it made my stomach swirl. No one had ever told me they wanted to XX me or anything me, for that matter. This was the closest thing to boy-on-boy action I'd had in a long time. And by long time, of course, I mean since I was born.

Not that it was my action, technically. Or even boy-on-boy, technically. More like boy-on-boy-who-thinks-it's-boy-on-girl. I had the strangest mix of feelings I've ever had—an exact tie between good and bad.

Good: he wanted to kiss Frannie.

Bad: Frannie wasn't here.

Good: the way it excited me-as-Frannie when he said it.

Bad: the way it excited me-as-myself when he said it.

It was like borrowing thrills from someone else's life. Or stealing them. That's how it felt to the left side of my brain. The right side—the stronger side, the bully who told the left side to shut up or else—was having a shamelessly good time.

<<NICENITE: I wanted to XX you too.>>

<<JEFFO: There's always next time.>>

<<NICENITE: If I didn't hate those little smiley emoticons, I'd type one in right now. >>

<<JEFFO: You mean like this? :) :) :)>>

<<NICENITE: You don't seem like the logo type.>>

<<JEFFO: I'm full of surprises if you know where to look.>>

<<NICENITE: Wow. Is there a logo for blushing?>>

<<JEFFO: I'll see what I can come up with.>>

Whatever doubts I had about doing this, there was no denying that it was going great for Frannie. Meanwhile, my own pulse was about twice normal. The whole roleplay thing was blurring around the edges, so I was relieved and sorry at the same time when Jeffrey changed the subject to something more ordinary.

<<JEFFO: Hey, I meant to ask—is it too early to draft you for STF at the carnival? >>

<<NICENITE: STF?>>

<<JEFFO: Our booth for Int'l Student Club. We're raising money for Heifer Int'l.>>

I Googled Heifer International as fast as I could. At the top of their web site, it said, *Ending Hunger, Caring for the Earth*. Very Jeffrey. I felt weird about saying yes for Frannie, but saying no seemed like a worse idea.

<<NICENITE: Great cause. Yeah sure.>>

<<JEFFO: Thx! No one else wants to do it with me.>>

I couldn't help myself, and I wrote:

<<NICENITE: Well, I do . . . wink wink.>>

<<JEFFO: Now I'm the one who needs the blushing logo.>>

A little siren went off in my head, and the Common Sense Department made an announcement to all sides of my brain: *STOP WHAT YOU ARE DOING. YOUR WORK HERE IS THROUGH. GET OUT. NOW.* If I didn't wrap things up and soon, someone was going to lose her virtual virginity. Or his. Whichever.

<<NICENITE: Hey, my mom is calling me. I better go. Thanks again for coming over. I had a really good time.>>

<<JEFFO: See you tomorrow, Nicenite.>>

I flopped down on the bed all smiles. There was plenty NOT to smile about, but I couldn't help it. First of all, "Frannie" had been honest, funny, and just a little edgy, which frankly couldn't hurt. I felt like I had done my job and done it well.

Second (and this is the more screwed-up part), I liked how excited he made me feel. I knew I deserved more than a crush on a straight boy, but right now that's what I had, crumbs for a starving man. And as long as I kept Frannie's interests first in line, then none of this had to be a problem.

Of course, there was still the matter of catching her up on what had happened. It was too late to call now, so I'd have to get her when she came to school after her dentist appointment in the morning. Between first and second period. At her locker. Most importantly: before Jeffrey got to her.

This would be a good place in the movie for everything to speed up into super-fast motion. The numbers on the clock in my room start changing rapid-fire. Maybe there's some kind of hard-driving music to add tension. The sun pops up; I get ready for school; I catch the bus; students race around the halls in a blur; I go to my first class. . . . Then it slows down to normal, just long enough to show how bored everyone is, contrasted with me looking anxiously at the clock . . . which then speeds up again. It spins around another forty-five minutes and then goes back to normal just as the bell rings for the end of class.

I jumped up and beat everyone else out into the hall. Jeffrey had second-period gym on the other side of the school, but still, there were no guarantees here. I took the stairs two at a time, headed for Frannie's locker.

"Hey, Marcus!" It was Ethan Schumacher, coming right at me.

"Hi, Ethan, I can't—"

"Just real quick," he said. "You've got to come to the next GSA meeting. I'm officially begging. Guys are a complete endangered species at those things. I'm drowning in estrogen."

I kept walking. "What about Nicole?" Nicole was aka Peter Mintley when she wasn't out, which was most of the time at school.

"Estrogen by intention," Ethan said.

"Carlos?"

"GSA meets at the same time as yearbook. He's not coming." Ethan lowered his voice to a confidential volume. "And Brendan Thomas isn't ready yet."

Just then I saw Frannie come around the corner at the far end of the hall. I yelled and waved. She waved back and started opening her locker.

"Gotta go, Eth."

He kept pace with me. "We meet Mondays after school, in room 108—"

"I know, I know," I said, desperate to shake him off. I stopped walking. "Fine. I'll be there."

"Great, because . . ." Oh God, he was still talking.

And then—and then—I felt a hand on my shoulder from behind and heard Jeffrey's familiar voice. "Hey,

Marcus," he said, and kept going, straight toward Frannie.

Close up on my throat as I swallow hard. Exaggerated sound effect: *Gulp*.

"Later, Ethan."

"See you then!"

"Jeffrey, wait up!"

The most I could hope for now was to get to Frannie at the same time as him. After that, I had no idea what I'd do. I caught up just as he reached her. He had barely gotten out the *ing* in *good morning* when I blurted, "Frannie, we have to get to stats early to set up for that project."

I could see Frannie knew right away that something was up since there was no project. She played along beautifully. At first.

"Oh, right," she said. "So I guess we better go."

Jeffrey looked confused. "Um, okay. Catch you at lunch?"

"Sure." I answered for her.

"Sure," she echoed.

"Oh, and thanks again for volunteering," he said.

There it was. I could only imagine Frannie's thoughts. *Thanks for volunteering? For what? The Polish food festival? For having you over?*

I stood at my locker with Jeffrey between us, where he had his back to me. I nodded subtly at Frannie and mouthed "no problem" while I pretended to work the lock.

"No problem," she said. Her eyes flicked over to me again, and when Jeffrey turned to look, I scraped my nose on my locker door, trying to disappear.

"Are you okay?" he asked her.

"I'm fine," Frannie said. I could hear the fake smile in her voice.

"No one ever wants to do STF," he said, "But it's actually a lot of fun." The boy's got a voice that makes you want to slide right down inside his throat. No wonder he can get people to do things.

I glanced over at Frannie and pointed at my wrist. Time to go.

"Do you know what time it is?" she asked.

Doink!

Jeffrey pointed at her vintage Swatch. "Is your watch broken?"

Doink!!

"Oh yeah, it is." Frannie folded her arms. "I just really like to wear it. Anyway . . ." Then she laughed for no apparent reason, which wasn't so good. Then she snorted, and I knew I had to step in.

"Frannie, are you ready? It's ten after." I could barely look at Jeffrey. "Sorry to drag her away," I told him. "But we really have to set up for that thing."

He flashed his Jeffrey Osborne smile, the one that went so well with the voice. "No problem. I'll see you guys at lunch."

As he walked away, I looked into my locker again, wondering if it was possible to get in and close the door behind me. Too late. Frannie grabbed my arm and started pulling me down the hall.

"What the hell just happened?" Her voice had that upbeat-but-tense quality, as in, *Darling, I think I'm going to have to kill you.*

"It's ninety-nine percent good," I said, trailing along beside her. "Depending on how you look at it."

"Go on."

I chose my words carefully. "Put it this way. You and Jeffrey had a *really* good chat online last night."

She stopped dead in the hallway. Erica Blevins actually bumped into her, and Frannie barely got out a "sorry," she was so intent on me. I motioned her off to the side.

"Okay," she said slowly. "Tell me everything he said and everything I said."

I pulled the chat transcript out of my back pocket. "Actually, I printed it for you."

She took the paper and read it at least twice on the way to class without saying a word. I felt like a puppy, waiting to see if she'd pat me on the head or roll the thing up and smack me with it. Just as we got to the door for stats, she stopped short again and smiled at me.

"We had such a good talk."

I exhaled for the first time in about a minute. "See?"

The second bell rang. "Okay," she said with her hand on the doorknob. "You're forgiven. But just this once."

Forgiven? I wasn't exactly asking for forgiveness. This had turned out pretty well for her, after all, but I didn't push it.

She turned and whispered to me now since we were in the middle of a crowded classroom. "Just please don't be me without me around anymore. My nerves can't take it."

"Don't worry," I said. "Neither can mine. It won't happen again."

I even thought I meant it.

"Frannie and Marcus, do you mind if I start class?" Mrs. Duke and most everyone else was looking at us. We slipped into our usual spots in the back, where Jenn was saving us seats. Once Mrs. Duke started lecturing, Frannie scribbled something and tilted her notebook for me to see.

One question. This carnival thing. What did I volunteer for? What's STF??

I shrugged. All I knew was that it had something to do with a good cause. Jenn leaned in and read the note, then shrugged too, not that she had any idea what this was all about.

I scribbled back an answer.

Dunno. STF = Save the Ferrets?

♀ Six

"A skirt, definitely." Jenn's voice sounded positive, so I cradled the phone between my shoulder and neck and started sorting through the pile of clothes on my bed. Skirt, skirt, skirt . . . Okay, I had a green-and-black plaid kilt, a couple of minis, a long maroon velvet thing, two crinolines that I liked to throw together sometimes, a sarong, and a fifties poodle skirt that I'd stolen from last year's production of *Grease* and never worn. Where to start?

"Who wears a skirt when they're volunteering at a carnival?" Belina demanded. "Frannie—go casual."

My girls were on a three-way call, giving me some pre-Jeffrey fashion therapy. Not that it was helping much.

Every time I pictured Jeffrey's smile or his warm blue eyes, I got a fluttery feeling in my stomach, and my brain stopped processing things—like whether my striped orange-and-green shirt and flowered skirt were a brilliant ensemble or seriously hideous together. I'd just stand in front of my mirror, thinking, Clash? Not clash? Clash? Not clash? Then an image of Jeffrey would flash through my mind, and I'd space out for a while. . . .

It wasn't helping that I had to dress for some mystery activity that Marcus had signed me up for. Of course, as Marcus would point out, a date is a date. Still, I couldn't decide whether I wanted to kiss him or kill him.

"Go with jeans," Belina prompted.

"Jeans?" I wasn't sure. I mean, I hardly ever wear jeans, under any circumstances. It's not that I have anything against them—except that they tend to fit me weird and make me look like a dumpy housewife impersonating a high school student. All I had was one pair that I'd found in a Dumpster on the campus of Saint Xavier Boarding School at the end of the term last year. Marcus and I liked to pick the trash there at the end of the semester because the kids were rich, and they always tossed out tons of great stuff before heading back home. I started digging around in the bottom of my closet, searching for the jeans, as the argument continued in my ear.

"But Frannie has great legs!" Jenn insisted.

"She's got good boobs, too," Belina pointed out. "She can wear something low-cut."

"She should wear her hair up, then," Jenn said. "To accentuate her neck."

"No, down," Belina snapped. "Otherwise there's too much emphasis on her nose."

"Um, *hello*? I think you just turned a corner into not helping." I blew out a sigh. "And I can't find the jeans." I was starting to get irritated. How could someone who buys her clothes by the pound have nothing to wear?

"Black pants, then," Belina suggested. "You have a hundred pairs of those."

"Purple is the new black," Jenn chimed in.

"Jenn, I wouldn't wear purple pants even if I owned them," I said patiently. "My butt would look like two giant eggplants in a catfight."

"I love your butt!" Jenn cried. "Mine's so tiny."

I rolled my eyes. Jenn has a real gift for compliments. "Okay, everyone," I said into the receiver. "Thanks for the help—I think that about wraps things up here."

"So what are you wearing?" Belina asked.

"I have no idea," I told her. "See you guys at the carnival."

"Don't you want to hear what *I'm* wearing?" Jenn asked Belina as I clicked off.

I dug around for the jeans one last time, but it was no go. They had disappeared. The only thing at the bottom of my closet was an old pair of purple cowboy boots. I'd bought them at a flea market a few months before because I fell in love with the flowers stitched on the sides. Hmmm, I thought as I held one up. They're a little bit country . . . a little bit rock and roll. . . .

Oh, who am I kidding? I chucked the boot back into the closet. Jeffrey would think I was nuts if I wore those. I definitely got the sense that he thought I was kind of borderline insane ever since the whole movie-night-with-Jeffrey evening.

Which, if I tell the truth about it, was kind of disappointing. I know that not everyone is tuned into Marcus's and my wavelength . . . but I somehow thought that Jeffrey would be. After all, he's a sensitive guy. He's not hung up on being trendy, and he does his own thing. But it hadn't turned out that way. He'd hated *Sholay*, and he hadn't even bothered to hide it.

And to tell the truth, it kind of bothered me.

I really hate it when you try to share something with someone and they just stare at you like you're nuts. That was part of what I loved about Marcus. You could say something like, "The way the afternoon light is shining on that trash can is really beautiful," and he would know what you were talking about. He wouldn't feel the need to point out that trash cans aren't beautiful, that they're just trash cans, made of green plastic and overflowing with broken and rejected objects. He would see the light too, and he would agree. . . .

Stop it, stop it, stop it! I told myself. Don't compare Jeffrey to your best friend. And *don't* do that thing where you pick out every little flaw in a guy and then tell him to get lost before you've even given him a chance. Jeffrey's great. He's sensitive, and smart, and sweet. So what if he doesn't like Indian musicals? Besides, he could have just been having an off night, or maybe he was nervous or something. I know I was.

But you know what really bugged me about the whole thing? I could see how hard Marcus was trying to help me out. He wanted the date to be perfect *so badly* that when it wasn't, I almost felt more disappointed for him than for myself.

"Hey, Frannie," my dad said, yanking me out of my thoughts. He was standing in the doorway to my room, this half-amused, half-confused smile on his face. "Doing some cleaning?"

I looked down at my cluttered bed and sighed. It is a sad, sad commentary when a father thinks his teenage daughter might actually be spending a Friday night cleaning out her closet. Although I could see why he'd gotten that impression. I'd spent the last hour tearing through my closet, tossing all of my clothes into three piles: "maybe," "no," and "no way." Basically, my room looked like a landfill. "Just trying to find something to wear," I told my dad.

"Ah." He nodded, like I'd just said something perfectly rational. My dad is a man of few words, but he does have an amazing ability to humor people.

"I have a date," I said. For some reason, I felt like I needed to offer him an explanation. Because he was still standing there, I guess.

"Yeah," Dad said slowly. "I do too." He sighed heavily. "Your mom has this book. . . ."

I nodded. *The Romance Handbook."*

Dad looked at the ceiling. "Tonight it's chapter one: 'Relive the Magic.'"

"Well . . . that sounds like fun," I said in my most encouraging voice as I twirled a chunk of hair around my finger. "Everyone likes magic."

"We're supposed to re-enact our first meeting," he said darkly, folding his arms across his chest.

Whoa. "So . . . you're going to a church potluck supper?" I asked, lifting an eyebrow.

Dad nodded miserably. "And we're supposed to pretend that we don't know each other at first. Mom is insisting that we take separate cars."

I didn't know what to say. "Sounds really . . . magical."

Dad snorted. "Two cars to one supper," he repeated. "Do you know how much gas costs these days?"

"Well . . ." Only my parents could take a handbook on romance and use it to create the world's most unromantic evening. I decided to change the subject. "What's chapter two?" I asked.

"'Recapture a Sense of Spontaneity.'" Dad sighed again. "Next week, Mom wants us to just drive into Chicago. With no plan!" There was horror in his dark eyes. My dad is heavily into planning. "She doesn't even want to make dinner reservations because that isn't 'spontaneous' enough."

I winced in sympathy. Poor Dad, I thought. He has to humor so many people in this family. "Does it get any better?"

"Well . . . chapter six looks pretty good," Dad admitted.

Oh, *ew*—the parental sex chapter! I had to force myself not to clap my hands over my ears and sing lalalalalala at the top of my lungs. Instead, I let out a nervous giggle that made me sound like a crazed cricket.

Dad leaned against the door frame. "So—where are you and Marcus off to tonight?"

"I'm not going out with Marcus," I told him, picking a blouse out of my "maybe" pile and studying it. "I have a *real* date, with that guy who came over the other night. Jeffrey." No to you, red satin shirt, I thought, tossing it aside. I regret to inform you that I will never find your missing button. Go make someone at the Salvation Army happy.

Dad rolled his eyes. "Women," he said in this jeez-you're-all-alike kind of voice.

I looked at him. "What's that supposed to mean?"

"You just love to have two guys fighting over you." Dad gave me a knowing smile.

A giggle bubbled up at the back of my throat, but I swallowed it. Wait a minute, I thought. Is Dad joking? Actually, I wasn't sure. Dad's humor is usually deadpan. . . . Then again, he looked pretty serious right now. "Dad, you know Marcus isn't interested in me—he's gay."

"*What?*" Now Dad looked like his eyes might just pop out of his head and roll around on the floor. Apparently he hadn't been joking after all.

But how could my own father have not noticed? I mean, I knew the minute I met Marcus that he was as gay as the Easter parade. Don't get me wrong—he doesn't wear European clothes or talk with a lisp or carry around a Lhasa apso named Trixie like queer people on TV. He's just . . . so . . . *gay.* I can't explain it. Maybe it's because he's interested in old movies, or because he doesn't follow every fashion trend, or because he isn't afraid to order Frosted Flakes with a grilled cheese sandwich. Not that any of these things are automatic "you're gay," signals. No, I decided, it was more that I hadn't felt uncomfortable around him. I'd known right away that he wasn't checking me out. And I'd known that the fact that he wasn't checking me out wasn't some kind of dis, either. I guess it's just a vibe.

"How long have you known?" my dad asked.

"From day one," I told my dad, suddenly wishing that I hadn't brought up this whole subject. Where is Mom? I wondered. I guessed she was still at work. My dad doesn't usually just come and start chatting with me, and it was kind of freaking me out. And the subject matter wasn't helping, either. Even though I always think of my parents as pretty open-minded people, you never really know how someone of their generation is going to react to the whole queer thing.

"Wow," Dad said, folding his arms across his chest.

"Yes?" I prompted.

"It's just . . . interesting."

"What's so interesting about it?" I demanded, maybe a little sharply. The thing is, I know that being queer isn't easy for Marcus. Not like it's some major disadvantage or challenge or whatever—but things are harder for him than for an average guy. And if my dad was going to say one single thing—

"It's just . . . interesting that you can never really know what's going on in someone else's mind," my dad said finally, the words spilling out of him slowly. "If someone chooses not to tell you something, how would you ever know it? You'd think you could guess, but . . ." He shook his head.

Wow. Deep thoughts, by Dad. I knew that there was something to what he was saying, but I just couldn't wrap my brain around it. After all, I had a date—or whatever it was—in two hours, and I still needed to find an outfit. But my dad was still standing in my doorway, staring off into space, as though mesmerized by the workings of his brain.

But at least he wasn't a homophobe. That was a relief. Marcus is so in love with my family, I knew it would just kill him to think that my dad didn't approve of him.

I cleared my throat, which sort of snapped Dad out of his reverie. "So, uh—I'd better get ready," I hedged.

"Oh, sure." Dad looked like he wanted to say something else but stopped himself and just nodded, smiling. "Well, I'm sure you're going to have a great time with Jason."

"Jeffrey," I corrected.

"Jeffrey," Dad repeated. "Right, right. Have fun with Jeffrey."

"Thanks, Dad," I told him. "Have fun at the potluck."

Dad gave me a final smile and loped down the hallway to his bedroom. It was funny to think about it, but I definitely got the impression that Dad was kind of disappointed that Marcus wasn't interested in being my boyfriend after all. The whole idea made me giggle. I mean, maybe he and Mom had been planning our wedding behind my back. It's funny how everyone is so eager to couple us up. Because we're so alike, I guess.

I yanked an orange miniskirt out of the closet and held it up. Does orange send out "I care enough to volunteer" signals? I wondered. I chucked it in the "maybe" pile and tried to quiet the nerves in my stomach. At least this is a group thing, I told myself as I pulled a pair of red velvet pants from my closet and tossed them in the "no" pile. That should take some of the tension away.

Besides, we'll be working the STF booth, I told myself.

Whatever that is.

The school carnival was already buzzing when I got there. It was a cool night—the first traces of the waning April chill hung in the air as the sun started to set. The decorations committee had strung white fairy lights between the booths, and the football field lights were on. People were running around adding finishing touches to booths, and someone had fired up the grill—the scent of cooking meat hung in the air, reminding me that I had forgotten to eat dinner. Oh, well, I thought as I looked around for Jeffrey's booth. Maybe I can take a break from collecting tickets or whatever and run and get myself a burger. A veggie burger.

"Francesca!"

Looking over, I saw Marcus's grandmother, Patricia, standing with a group of old ladies in outrageous hats.

Patricia herself was done up like some kind of color-blind bag lady—she had on two feather boas—bright purple and fuchsia twisted together—an orange hat with cherries on the brim, a brilliant green dress, red pumps, and glitter eye shadow. I'd seen her in some pretty wild outfits before—including, once, a purple bustier and leather pants—but this really took the cake.

"Hey, Patricia," I said.

"Hey, girl!" She gave me a huge, brilliant grin. "Look at you! You're just as pretty as you can be!"

"Thanks." I smiled warmly, glad that my outfit had already received a thumbs-up. I'd struggled for an hour and forty minutes, trying on everything in the "maybe" pile—then trying on the "no" pile, just in case I'd missed something. I was about to start on "no way," when I decided that I had to pick something or I'd be late, so I went with a clingy black V-neck sweater and vintage sil-ver-and-peacock-blue cigarette pants. It was kind of bor-derline dressy casual, which—given that I had no idea what Marcus had volunteered me to do—seemed the safest bet. And it was kind of low-cut, so I knew that Belina would approve. "Um . . . love your outfit too," I told Patricia, because I felt I had to say something.

Patricia let out this huge belly laugh. "Oh, now, go on!" she said, giving her outfit a twirl, so that I got the full effect. I hadn't noticed the big yellow bow in the back.

"The Wailing Grannies and I are here to do a little a cappella. Gonna rock this place! Right girls?" she called.

The Wailing Grannies let out a cheer, and one of them said something that sounded like "Bust out the beats!"

"I didn't know you were in a singing group."

"Well, it's sort of a combination singing group and drinking club," Patricia confided. "Once we do our thing, it's Miller time!"

The Wailing Grannies let out another cheer.

"Bust out the beers!" one of them said.

"Which brings me to my question," Patricia went on. "Have you seen Marcus? He's our ride home tonight."

"Uh, no," I said, relieved that this was actually the truth. I wasn't sure that Marcus would be thrilled to find out he was the Wailing Grannies' designated driver. "But if I see him, I'll let him know you're looking for him." More like warn him, I added mentally.

"Thanks, darlin'!" Patricia chirped. "And let him know that I'm going to dedicate our first song to him."

"I sure will."

With a quick wave, I left the Wailing Grannies behind and started to prowl the booths. Most of them were pretty typical—dunking booth, bottle toss, balloon pop, blahbie, blahbie, blah. . . . Where was the Heifer International/Save the Ferrets booth?

Suddenly, a guy dressed as a pirate jumped out in front of me and shouted, *"Gar!"*

I let out a shriek.

"Sorry, sorry!" Jeffrey flipped up his eye patch and smiled at me, his warm blue eyes crinkling at the edges. "Sorry—I didn't mean to scare you."

I took a deep breath, trying to clear the adrenaline that was now pumping through my body. "No, no—*I'm* sorry," I said, feeling totally girly and lame. "It's just . . . I always scream during a pirate attack."

Jeffrey tipped his tricornered hat back on his head and planted his fists at the sides of the wide belt he wore over a long, raggedy pirate coat. "I'm not a pirate," he said, grinning. "I'm a Central High Buccaneer."

"Oh." I nodded like it made sense that he was dressed as our rival school's mascot. Play along, I told myself. Clearly this has something to do with STF. . . .

"Come on over," Jeffrey said, waving me toward a nearby booth. Astrid was already there, looking glamorous in a green off-the-shoulder sweater worn over slim black pants.

She smiled when she saw me. "Hello, Francesca."

"Hi, Astrid." Grr. How long has she been here? I wondered. That was so like Astrid, to show up at the booth early just to sneak in some extra time with Jeffrey.

"I think I stuck your costume under here," Jeffrey said, reaching under the table.

Costume? That was when I looked up and saw the banner. "Shoot the freak?" I said out loud. Please tell me that those words don't mean what I think they mean. . . .

"Yeah—didn't Astrid do a great job with the sign?" Jeffrey asked as he held out something to me that looked like a plastic suit of armor and a black bodysuit. "I decided that you should get to be the St. Thomas Fighting Knight. I've got on padding, but some of those paintballs can wing you pretty hard." He smiled and patted his chest. "The armor should protect you pretty well, though."

"What's Astrid going to be?" I asked, thinking, Please, Lord, let her be the Springfield Fighting Duck. . . .

"I'm the ticket taker," Astrid said brightly.

Great, I thought. That's the kind of job you get when you actually do the volunteering for yourself. Frannie, I thought, that could have been you.

"Anyway," Jeffrey went on, "the idea is that you and I will just run around in here—through the bales of hay— while people shoot at us. Anyone who hits us gets a Heifer International T-shirt . . . but we've only got about thirty of them—so we really have to try hard not to get hit."

"Oh, don't worry about that," I told him, smiling through gritted teeth. Marcus Beauregard, you are a dead man, I thought.

"You can go get changed in the girls' locker room," Jeffrey said. "Astrid and I still have a little more hay to set up."

I definitely did not like how easily "Astrid and I" tripped off his tongue. I mean, I knew that Jeffrey and I had been hanging out lately . . . but I still didn't feel like he realized that he was The One. So don't blow it, I told myself. Act cheerful. Act like you got *yourself* into this. "Okay!" I chirped, like getting shot at with paintballs was a dream come true. I gripped the plastic armor and headed for the locker room.

Just as I was about to push my way through the door, I spotted Marcus walking past the cotton candy booth. He took one look at me and scurried in the other direction.

"Come back here!" I shouted, darting after him. I finally caught him by the collar and he stopped in his tracks.

"Let go, let go!" he begged. "You know I hate it when my clothes get stretched out."

"Oh, boo hoo, Marcus," I snarled. "Do you know what STF is?"

"I just found out," he admitted, "and I am so, so, sorry. . . ." He tried to look like he meant it, but I could tell that a little smile was peeking out at the corner of his mouth.

"This is so not funny. I have to wear a plastic suit of armor!"

"Well," Marcus said, stifling a giggle, "at least you have a date. And metallics are really in this year."

I narrowed my eyes at him. "Five words, Marcus: payback is a bitch."

"Um, I think *payback* is one word," he said. He was really grinning now.

"Go ahead, dig your own grave," I snapped. Then I turned and stalked off as Marcus cracked up. "And by the way—Patricia and the Wailing Grannies are looking for you."

The smile dropped off Marcus's face. Ha, I thought. You deserve that, Marcus Beauregard. That and a whole lot more.

"Whoo-hoo!" Jeffrey shouted as he jumped from a bale of hay. Pete Keynes took aim, but the paintball whizzed past Jeffrey's tricorn and splattered yellow against the backboard. "Gar, gar, gar!" he said in his pirate voice. "You'll never catch Buccaneer Bob, you scurvy scum!"

Pete loaded another ball into the gun and let fly, but Jeffrey ducked away just in time.

"Next," Astrid shouted as Pete put down the gun and Melanie Johnson stepped forward.

"Fran," Jeffrey whispered to me, "you've got to run around a little more."

I looked up at him. I was crouched behind a tall bale of hay, and I hadn't moved for the past ten minutes. "I thought I wasn't supposed to get hit," I said.

"Well, yeah," Jeffrey admitted. "But you know, you have to give them a chance." He gave me an encouraging smile. "Just try it. It's really fun." Just then, Melanie shot him in the arm. "Ow! Crap!"

"A winner!" Astrid shouted. Only her accent made it sound like "veener." A cheer went up.

Why couldn't I have gotten her job? I wondered miserably. She got to sit there looking gorgeous, while I was stuck wearing someone's old Halloween costume and eau de sweat. Seriously—the girl was starting to work my nerves.

I stood up as Jeffrey smiled at me. "Well—that's why you run around, right?" he said cheerfully, rubbing the spot on his arm where he was splattered with blue paint.

Lurching awkwardly in the armor, I started to lunge around between the bales of hay as Stuart Jenks loaded up the gun. That was bad news—I knew that Stuart and his dad went hunting a lot. He's the only kid in school who actually drives a pickup with a gun rack on the back. . . .

I lurched harder.

Oh my God, I thought as I stared at the crowd lined up at our booth. There had to be fifty people waiting for a turn to shoot at us and another thirty or so just standing around watching. Marcus was in the line—about ten people back—and he grinned, giving me a little wave. Narrowing my eyes at him, I dropped my visor.

"Prepare to meet your holy grail!" Stuart shouted as he aimed at me.

"Crap!" I dove behind a bale of hay as Stuart missed.

"That's great, Fran!" Jeffrey shouted. "Isn't this fun?" He turned toward Stuart. "What's the matter, matey? No match for a buccaneer?"

I GI-Joed toward another hay bale as Stuart unleashed a paintball at Jeffrey, barely missing his tricorn. Stuart tried another shot at my feet, but he didn't get anywhere close. He had to hand over the gun to Mr. Carter, the phys-ed instructor and soccer coach.

"You ruined our undefeated season!" he shouted, shooting at my shin.

"Ow!" The paintball drove into my plastic shin guard, which stung against my leg. "Jeez!"

"Another veener!" Astrid shouted. The crowd went wild.

"Frannie!" I heard Jenn call from somewhere in the crowd. I scanned the line. She, Belina, and Keith had joined Marcus in the line. Belina waved madly as Marcus whispered something in Jenn's ear. She giggled.

"Perfect outfit!" Jenn shouted to me. "Metallics are really in this year."

"Now aren't you glad you didn't wear a skirt?" Belina yelled.

I waved at them, flashing a huge, fake smile. "Kill you all later!" I hollered.

"Keep moving!" Jeffrey called to me. "Keep moving!" He darted up onto a bale of hay, then leaped off it, crowing madly.

I decided to follow his lead and run around like a maniac. It was hard to move in the armor, but that actually turned out to be something of an advantage, as it forced me to run in a weird, lurching, zigzaggy way. This is great practice in case I ever find myself trapped inside a video game, I told myself. And think of all of the calories you're burning.

Just keep lurching.

"Gar, gar!" Jeffrey said, slapping me on the back. "You did great!"

After three hours, it was finally over. I shoved back my visor with a paint-smeared silver glove. My hair was stuck to my scalp, and I don't even want to think about what I smelled like. I'd been hit eleven times, and I knew I was going to be sore and bruised up the next day. But the way Jeffrey was looking at me right then . . . Well, suddenly, the pain and sweat and stink seemed very far away. "Yeah?" I said breathlessly.

Jeffrey nodded, then looked away. "Uh—how much money did we earn, Astrid?"

"Five hundred thirty-five dollars," Astrid said, tucking her pale blond hair behind her ear. She crossed one slim black-clad leg over the other, dangling an elfishly pointy green suede mule from her toes. God, I hate your stupid European shoes, I thought. Go to an outlet mall! Shop normal!

"Five hundred thirty-five dollars?" Jeffrey crowed, as though she had just said "a hundred million." It didn't seem like that much to me. Note to self, I thought: If I ever have to get shot at again, demand more money.

"Hey, Jeffo!" Glenn called as he strutted over to our booth. "How'd you make out?"

"Five thirty-five," Jeffrey called.

"Wow!" Glenn looked really surprised. "That's more than twice as much as anybody else."

"For real?" I asked.

"Thanks to you, Lady Lancelot," Glenn said, sitting on our booth's table.

"Well—what can I say?" I replied. "A lot of people want to shoot at me, I guess."

Glenn laughed. "I know that must have been really fun," he said sarcastically. "Not every girl would agree to run around like an insane chicken while people shot at her. But it was really sweet of you to do it. . . ." He glanced at Jeffrey.

"Oh yeah," Jeffrey agreed. "Very sweet. Really, really sweet."

Astrid glared at me, and suddenly I felt a whole lot better. "Well, it was a lot of fun," I lied. "Besides, it's for a good cause."

"See? That's the spirit!" Glenn said. "I'm sure that Jeffrey can't wait to find some way to thank you." He waggled his eyebrows.

I felt my neck grow warm. I could think of about a million ways that would work just fine. . . .

Jeffrey nodded. "Absolutely. In fact . . ." He reached for the box under the table. "You did such a good job not getting shot that we have a few T-shirts left over. Do you want one?"

"Oh, thanks," I said. I blushed a little, accepting the shirt. Actually, it wasn't bad. It said HEIFER INTERNATIONAL in small letters on the front left, and had a picture of a cow on the back. It was about forty zillion sizes too big for me. "I can wear it to sleep in."

"Then you can think about Jeffrey in bed," Glenn said.

Jeffrey looked like he was about to die, and I blushed a little more. Not so much because of Glenn's comment, but because I felt kind of like a fraud. I mean, the truth was, I'd had a horrible time wearing the hot, stinky armor and getting shot at. And I hadn't even volunteered on purpose. In fact—I hadn't volunteered at all. That was Marcus, in the role of Frannie.

On the plus side, though, Jeffrey seemed to like me better than ever. I thought. So I must be doing this girlfriend thing right. . . .

"So," Astrid said suddenly, "I'm hungry. Does anybody want to get something to eat?"

"I'm in," Jeffrey said.

"Me too," Glenn agreed. "Frannie?"

I bit my lip. I knew that Marcus would say that I

should go for it—especially if Astrid was going. And I was starving. But on the other hand, I was completely wiped. I needed about three weeks' worth of hot bath and soft bed. Besides, our date had already gone well this time—you know, from Jeffrey's point of view—and anything more would probably just mess it up. "I think I'll pass," I said. "I'm exhausted."

Glenn looked like he might insist, but Jeffrey just said, "I totally understand."

"Well . . . 'bye," I said awkwardly.

Jeffrey kind of leaned toward me, and I thought he was going to kiss me right there, but it turned out that he just wanted a hug. But I wasn't expecting that, so I ended up giving him a weird little kiss kind of under his ear.

"Ooh," he said in surprise, touching his neck where I'd kissed him. Then I was so embarrassed that I had to scurry away as fast as possible.

Oh, just get me out of here, I thought as I headed toward the girls' locker room. I just want to take off this stupid armor, find my friends, gripe to them, and go home. . . .

"Francesca—just the woman I was looking for." Patricia stepped right in my path, smiling like crazy. She had two bright red spots on her cheeks.

"Oh, hi, Patricia." I smiled wearily. "How did the performance go?"

"Pure crap," Patricia said cheerfully. "But the drinking went great."

I laughed.

"So, did you ever find my grandson?"

"Well—not exactly," I hedged. The truth was, Marcus had managed to nail me with the paint gun. Right on the butt. Is he ever going to get it, I thought.

"You know, I was wondering," Patricia said, her hazel eyes twinkling as she swayed slightly on her feet. "I have this new gentleman friend—Arthur. He's a businessman from Chicago, but he's a lot of fun. I was wondering if you and Marcus might like to double date with us sometime? Maybe next Saturday?"

I opened my mouth to say no. Of course not. For one thing, Marcus and I aren't dating . . . but I knew that Patricia seemed to think we were, and I know that Marcus kind of plays it off with her because he can't deal with telling her the truth.

But then it hit me—what on earth could be worse than going on a double date with your very own grandmother? Answer: Not much.

It was perfect. Perfect payback.

I smiled. "Patricia," I said, "we'll definitely be there."

♟ Seven

"No," I said to Frannie. "I'm not saying it's going to happen; I'm just saying that if we weren't friends anymore, I'd be the one eating lunch alone the next day."

"It's never going to happen," she insisted.

We were both in our rooms on the phone, and I was getting sorry that I had brought this up. I wasn't even sure why I had, except that if you spend as much time on the phone as we do, everything comes up eventually.

I tried again. "My point isn't that something is going to happen. My point is just that you have backup I don't have. That's all."

"Please," she said. "If you get hit by a truck, I'm going to go off and be a nun or something."

"A nun with a boyfriend," I reminded her.

"He's not my boyfriend," she came back.

"He's pretty close to being your boyfriend," I said. "Besides, 'Sister Mary Frannie' just doesn't sound as good as 'Frannie Osborne.'"

"I'm not changing my name."

"When you get married—"

"Right."

"To Jeffrey—"

"To whoever."

"Jeffrey, who isn't your boyfriend."

"You just said he's pretty close to being my boyfriend."

"Good. I just wanted to hear you say it."

"Omigod. You're impossible," she said.

"Talk to you later?"

"Call me if you see him."

"As always," I said, and we hung up.

Frannie and I had a new system. If one of us saw Jeffrey online, and we weren't already with each other or on the phone (which we usually were), I'd call her or she'd call me, and we'd go into a three-way chat: Jeffrey on his computer, Frannie on the phone in my ear, and me, invisible, at my computer, making suggestions and typing in Frannie's half of the conversation. It was way less bizarre than it sounds and way more fun. Frannie and I had great flow where Jeffrey was concerned. At some point, of course, she was going to have to wean herself off me, but so far, she didn't feel ready, and I didn't push it. I was having too good a time for that.

About an hour later that same night, I was surfing around, looking at movie previews online and waiting for my homework to do itself, when I clicked over to the chat room for the umpteenth time and found that Jeffo had logged on. I picked up the phone and dialed Frannie's cell.

Voice mail answered on the first ring. She was probably talking to Jenn or Belina or both. "Hi, it's Frannie. Leave a message. Be original."

And I hung up.

Something like silence filled my room, except that there was a big unspoken question hanging in the middle of it: *Why did I just do that?* I never hung up on Frannie's voice mail. I always left some kind of message—a random question, or a little smoochy sound, or at least a quick "hi call me later"—but not this time. And since I wasn't sure I wanted to know the reason why, I picked up the phone again. My thumb found the redial button while my eyes stayed glued to the computer screen.

"Hi, it's Frannie. Leave a message. Be original."

"Hey, it's me. Ummm . . . what's the worst movie ever made? Later."

And I hung up again. Without mentioning Jeffrey.

Technically, I hadn't broken any rules. Frannie had asked me not to chat Jeffrey without her, and I had stuck to that promise. It was tempting sometimes, but so far, I'd been good.

Maybe I could just go into the chat room and look around, I thought. As long as I wasn't being Frannie, that wasn't against the rules either. I might even learn a thing or two that she could use later. It was all so convincing (in my head) that I went for it, and logged on as Stanley.

Jeffrey was still there, along with a bunch of screen names I didn't recognize and one that I did.

<<JEFFO: It just seems like a shorter school year could save some major resources.>>

<<LIFE_SUX: Whatever>>

<<WA-HOO!: Bring down the school, save fossil fuel!>>

<<JEFFO: Or maybe just close it down for the winter?>>

<<LOLA227: I agree with Jeffo completely. He should be president. Rock on, Jeffo!>>

Rock on? Apparently, Astrid's shoe collection wasn't the only thing about her that was stuck in the nineties. I was embarrassed for her and a little glad for Frannie.

<<JEFFO: Wow, thanks. What's the little symbol for blushing?>>

What's the symbol for blushing? I couldn't believe it. That was what I had said to him before. Jeffrey had just stolen my line—or Frannie's line, depending on how you looked at it. And . . . maybe not stolen. Maybe it was imitation, as in, the sincerest form of flattery, even if he *had* used it on Astrid. It wasn't like Astrid posed a threat to Frannie anymore. At least, she probably didn't . . . but probably wasn't the same thing as definitely.

Cue the thought bubble. In the movie, it kind of blossoms out of my head and floats above me like a mini-cartoon on the screen:

Dear Advice Wench: My best friend told me not to impersonate her when she's not around, and I really wasn't planning on doing it again, but now I'm in this situation where I could do her more good by ignoring the request than by following it. What should I do? Signed, Queer and Conflicted.

Dear Q&C: Normally, I'd say you should let your friend solve her own problems because really, isn't that more empowering in the end? But for you, I'll make an exception. Go for it. Signed, Advice Wench.

And then, like an idiot moth to a flame, I flitted straight toward Jeffrey before I could remember why it was such a bad idea. In about two seconds, I logged off as Stanley, logged back on, and sent Jeffrey a private message.

<<HI_IT'S_ME: Hi. It's me.>>

He responded right away.

<<JEFFO: Hi me.>>

<<HI_IT'S_ME: Am I interrupting anything?>>

Translation: Are you talking to Astrid?

<<JEFFO: That depends. Is procrastination something that can be interrupted?>>

<<HI_IT'S_ME: Definitely. You don't want to put that off. You'll just have to do it later.>>

<<JEFFO: I'll take my chances if you're sticking around.>>

<<HI_IT'S_ME: I'll bet you say that to everyone.>>

<<JEFFO: Not everyone.>>

<<HI_IT'S_ME: Good.>>

<<JEFFO: Just the girls. (Kidding.) Just you.>>

That one barbed me a little as a non-Frannie, non-girl person. It made feel *almost* weird enough to stop what I was doing. Almost . . . but not quite.

<<HI_IT'S_ME: What are you procrastinating on?>>

<<JEFFO: U.S. History. I got an extension on this paper and it's still not ready.>>

<<HI_IT'S_ME: I know what you mean. Why do I ALWAYS wait until the last minute?>>

<<JEFFO: Uh—because you're human?>>

<<HI_IT'S_ME: Suppose so.>>

<<JEFFO: You ARE human, right?>>

<<HI_IT'S_ME: Ha ha.>>

<<JEFFO: Cause you seem almost too perfect.>>

I smiled right at the screen. Jeffrey thought that I was— that Frannie was—almost too perfect. If Frannie were here, she'd want to answer with something like, "No, I'm not."

<<HI_IT'S_ME: Thanks.>>

<<JEFFO: Was that a dweeby thing of me to say?>>

<<HI_IT'S_ME: Uhhh . . . nope. It made me feel really good.>>

<<JEFFO: Good. I think some people think I'm too intense.>>

<<HI_IT'S_ME: Too intense? What does that even mean?>>

<<JEFFO: That's what I'd like to know. I guess I'm just a little neurotic.>>

<<HI_IT'S_ME: Now you're surprising me.>>

<<JEFFO: How?>>

<<HI_IT'S_ME: You seem so . . . not neurotic.>>

<<JEFFO: That's what I'd say about you.>>

<<HI_IT'S_ME: Liar.>>

<<JEFFO: I mean it.>>

My mind was racing and excited and at the same time relaxed in a really unexpected way. I was so much more comfortable with this stuff as Frannie than I ever would have been with my own not-quite-boyfriend. A big part of it was about not having to think. I didn't worry about every little word; I just said whatever came to mind, and somehow, it all seemed to come out right.

At the same time, though, not thinking was what had gotten me this far behind Frannie's back in the first place.

It was frustrating, because I was somewhere I absolutely should not be, but still, all I wanted was to keep going.

When I couldn't stand the mixed feelings anymore, I forced myself to say good night and log off. It was some kind of psychic move, I guess, because the phone rang about thirty seconds later.

"I know what you did last summer," Frannie said.

My heart thumped involuntarily. "What?"

"Worst movie ever," she said. "*I Know What You Did Last Summer.* I hated it."

Then I remembered the question I'd left on her voice mail. "You hate slasher movies in general," I said. "That doesn't mean it was the worst movie ever made."

"Hey, choose your own," she said. "That one's mine."

"We could do a whole bad-movie fest. The Worst of Hollywood, this Saturday night."

"Nice try," she said. "We've already got plans, as if you didn't know that."

This was a perfect topic to help me get away from my guilty feelings, so I glommed onto it. "You know," I said, "this double-date thing with Patricia is way more than the paintball thing deserves. I'm going to owe you some payback when this is over."

"Oh no no no," Frannie came back. "Double date with grandma and the man friend is worth the exact same number of points as a night of paintball hell. I looked it up."

"Grandma and the man friend," I said. "It sounds like a bad TV show."

"And you're this week's guest star!" she crowed.

"You're actually looking forward to this, aren't you?" I asked. It was amazing how quickly I could fall back into normal conversation with her.

"Of course," she said. "Aren't you?"

"Oh, please."

"How do you know you won't have a good time?"

"I don't know" I said. "I must be psychic."

Later that night, wide awake in bed, everything started to weigh down on me. This whole thing had been a kind of lie to Jeffrey from the beginning, and now it was spilling over onto Frannie as well. I couldn't take back what I had done, and even worse, I wasn't sure I wanted to. With all the places in the world where it's not okay to be queer, it's more than easy for me to get hooked on the ones where I can just be myself without having to think about it. I'd always felt that kind of freedom around Frannie and now was feeling it in these conversations with Jeffrey too, no matter how high that sent the irony meter. What did that say about me, if I felt like my own best self when I was pretending to be someone else?

My only refuge was the fact that things were still on track with Frannie and Jeffrey. At least there, I had done some good work. It seemed more important than ever, too, because amid everything else, I was starting to see Jeffrey Osborne as the seriously nice, funny, and good person he was. Good enough for my best friend.

A few nights later was the big double date. At six that Saturday, a giant American car of some kind pulled up in front of the house. Dad, Frannie, and I were waiting on the couch while Patricia put on her finishing touches.

"Manfred is here," Frannie whispered in my ear. That was our new shorthand for Arthur Goldstein, aka The Man Friend, now aka Manfred.

Patricia came into the living room and gave us a twirl. "How do I look?"

"What is Uzbekistan?" Dad said to the TV, not that it counted. They had *Jeopardy* repeats on the weekend, and we'd seen this one before.

"You look fabulous," Frannie told her.

"You really do, Momma," Dad added without looking up.

She had on a pair of stretch jeans tucked into black cowboy boots, and a denim shirt with red lassos embroidered on the shoulders. Her hair was pulled back tight in a silver ponytail that made her look younger somehow. She did, in fact, look great. The whole Western thing, though, was giving me a bad feeling. All Patricia had told us was that we should dress comfortably.

She waved at Arthur through the living room window. His

face lit up when he saw her. He looked very Texas himself—definitely shopped at Big and Tall. He had on jeans and an open-collared shirt and oh yes, a big gold chain around his neck. When the doorbell rang, Frannie practically skipped across the floor to get it. She was loving this already.

"What is *Breakfast at Tiffany's*?" I grumbled at the TV.

Dad nudged me. "Good one."

A big Texas voice boomed from the doorway. "You must be Frannie. Just as pretty as Patricia said."

"Well, thank you." I could have sworn she threw in a little twang of her own.

Dad turned off the TV and we stood up as Frannie led Arthur inside. He filled the room with his take-charge energy. "Don't tell me," he said. "Patrick and Marcus. Real good to meet you." I tried not to show the pain on my face when he shook my hand.

"Good to meet you too," Dad said.

We looked around. Patricia had disappeared in the confusion. I knew she wanted to make an entrance. That's the Southern belle in her. "Be right there," she called out, as if on cue.

"So where are you all headed tonight?" Dad asked Arthur.

"I think that's supposed to be a surprise," he said, jabbing Dad with his elbow just as Patricia came in. "Oh my," he went on. "Two gorgeous ladies and two lucky gentlemen. You sure you won't join us, Patrick?"

"Patrick isn't invited," Patricia said, coming out of her second fashion twirl of the evening, this one for Arthur. "Tonight's a double date. No room for a fifth wheel. Sorry, honey." She reached over and grabbed Dad's chin affectionately.

"No problem," Dad said. It was the most jealous of him I'd ever been.

"So y'all have already met?" Patricia said.

"We have," Frannie answered for us.

"Isn't he divine?" Patricia leaned into Arthur and put her skinny arms as far around his middle as she could get them. He was a good foot taller than her, too, but you could just see how they clicked together.

Well, good for Patricia, I thought.

"Where are we going?" I tried again on the way to the car. "Line dancing or something?" It was supposed to be a joke.

"I thought you were making this a surprise," Arthur said to Patricia, and my heart sank.

Frannie smiled even harder, if that was possible. She tried a little do-si-do with me on the lawn, but I wasn't buying.

There are plenty of gay stereotypes I fit into, but "good dancer" is not one of them. In that department, I'm a shame to my people. A drunk baby ostrich with no sense of direction. Two arms and two legs that never know what the others are doing. A natural disaster, set to music.

"Marcus thinks he doesn't dance," Patricia told Arthur.

"Marcus *knows* he doesn't dance," I said in return.

"Come on, honey, it'll be fun." Patricia joined Frannie and started shimmying around me, bumping hips and pushing me across the yard. I wondered how many neighbors were watching and went straight for the car.

The inside of Arthur's ride smelled like leather upholstery, pine air freshener, and cigar smoke. I was hoping for a nice long (or maybe endless) drive, but that didn't pan out. Arthur got us onto I-94 and back off again somewhere west of downtown Chicago in some kind of record-breaking time. We pulled into a strip mall, generic looking except for the big pink-and-red neon sign that flashed LINE 'EM UP! . . . LINE 'EM UP! . . . LINE 'EM UP!

"You kids are going to love this place," Patricia said. "And the food's great. The ribs are to die for."

"Sounds good to me," I muttered to Frannie.

"Ribs?" she asked.

"No," I said. "Dying."

She took my arm and leaned into me affectionately as we crossed the parking lot. "I just have one word for you," she whispered. "Paintball."

"I thought you were going to say payback."

"That too."

Inside, the cowboy music was thumping. I could feel it on my cheeks. The place was huge. There was a restaurant in the back, and here in the front, a giant dance floor, where hundreds of people were kicking and stepping and turning and whooping, all in perfect unison.

Frannie started bobbing her head. "Looks fun!" she shouted. I tried to shoot lasers out of my eyes at her, but she wasn't paying attention anyway.

"Let's get a table!" Arthur said. We followed him back to a quieter spot. Our booth had a giant set of steer horns on the wall overhead. As soon as we were settled, Patricia scrootched against me to get back out again.

"Come on, Frannie, let's tinkle." Frannie followed her obediently away, leaving me and Manfred alone at the table.

"What do you think?" he asked me, looking around.

"It's, um . . . a very big place," I said.

"Don't worry. We'll have you kickin' up dust before you know it."

The waitress showed up, saving me from the sarcastic comment I was about to make to a man who, after all, seemed like a very nice person, even if he had just driven me straight to cowboy hell. Arthur ordered two Cokes and two rum and Cokes. I was staring hard at my menu when Frannie and Patricia came back.

"Let's go, boys. These songs aren't going to dance themselves," Patricia said.

"Sure, they will," I said into my menu. I hated being the boring one, and that was just one more thing to be annoyed about.

"You guys go ahead," Frannie said. "I'll work on the party pooper here."

Arthur took Patricia's hand; Patricia let out a whoop like I'd never heard before, and they headed to the dance floor.

"Come ooo-on," Frannie said. "As long as we're here."

"You can lead a horse to water," I told her.

"But I can't make him dance, I know," she said, mock dejected. I'm sure she wasn't surprised. The girl's never seen me shake an ounce of booty. Finally, she gave up and went over to the dance floor by herself. I watched while she stood on the sidelines, bopping and making little kicks and studying everyone else's movements. I still didn't want to dance, but I felt just a little guilty and a little jealous. She looked like she was having fun, even standing alone.

Then this lanky cowboy came up and said something in her ear. Frannie looked unsure and checked back my way. I waved her on with both hands. Dance your feet off, girl. Just leave me out of it. She shrugged and followed him onto the floor, where they got swallowed up right away.

I didn't see them again until a few songs later, when the crowd spit them back out. She and the cowboy were sweaty and grinning when they got to our table. Patricia and Arthur, meanwhile, were still going at it somewhere. And if they had slipped away to make out in the parking lot, well, I just didn't want to know about it.

"Now, *that* is fun," Frannie said collapsing back into the booth. The cowboy sat down tentatively, on the edge of the seat. He was tall, with dark hair and smoky dark eyes under a straw cowboy hat. He got my attention.

"How you doin'?" He shook my hand across the table. "You guys want something to drink?" I'd already finished my Coke, and Frannie's, while they were dancing.

"I'll have a Jones Cola if they have them," Frannie said, "or a Coke. He'll have the same. Thanks."

"Jones Cola?" he asked.

"She gets them at Smoothie King in Roaring Brook," I said. "It's the only place that sells them, but she's always on the lookout for something else." I wondered if Frannie picked up on my code, as in, *Aren't we just overflowing with options tonight?*

"I'll have to check it out sometime," he said to Frannie, which I think was a little code of his own. Then he sauntered off to get the drinks.

"Nice butt," I said, watching him walk away. Frannie shushed me, as if anyone could hear us over the music.

"Don't worry," I said. "I won't tell your other boyfriend."

"It was just dancing," Frannie said. "Besides—"

"Jeffrey isn't your boyfriend yet." I finished her sentence.

"No. I was going to say, besides, I asked you to dance first."

"I'm not complaining," I told her. "I'm just glad you have a playmate."

She turned in the booth to face me. "Just so we're clear

here, if you tell Jenn or Belina I was dancing with the Sundance Kid, I will drag you back to this place every Saturday for the rest of your life. They'd never let me live him down."

"What are you talking about?" I said. "He's hot."

"Yeah, just the kind of ranch hand I want to show up at the prom with."

"Besides, you already have a potential prom date," I said.

"That too," she said.

Sundance came back with three glasses clutched in his noticeably big hands. "Just plain Cokes, sorry," he said, and then sat down with us for a while. It turned out he was a sophomore at the College of the Midwest; originally from Oklahoma; didn't come to Line 'Em Up very often but loved country dancing; and no, he had never heard of the band Coogie Fuji, which was something I entirely made up just to see what he'd say. Frannie stepped on my foot under the table when I did it, but he passed the test and didn't try to pretend to know anything.

Patricia and Arthur finally came back to the table, and the five of us kept talking. Sundance was a big hit with both of them, and I had to fight off a chronic case of irrational jealousy. It wasn't like I *wanted* Patricia to think Frannie and I were a couple. Just the opposite. But still . . .

When a slow song started, Sundance turned to Frannie. "You wanna learn how to two-step?"

Frannie shrugged her shrug. "Sure."

Patricia and Arthur were already on their feet. She leaned over before they walked away and said in my ear, "You're going to lose your best girl." For some reason, that made me mad too.

"She's not my girl!" I shouted at all of their backs, but only because I knew they couldn't hear me.

⚲ Eight

"Hey, Marcus," I said as I hopped onto a pink-and-chrome counter stool at Scoops.

Marcus frowned up at the clock, which has an ice cream cone in place of each number—you know, because "it's always ice cream time at Scoops." Anyway. "Aren't you early?" he asked. I was supposed to meet him here in another half an hour, at the end of his shift.

"Yeah—about that—" I didn't quite have time to get out, "Please don't kill me," because in the next moment Jeffrey had walked up to the counter.

"Marcus!" Jeffrey flashed Marcus a huge smile as he slid onto the stool behind mine. "I didn't know you worked here."

For a moment, Marcus just stared at Jeffrey. His mouth dropped open. Then he snapped it shut again. His face flushed pink, and my heart sank for him. "Hey, Jeffrey," Marcus said finally. "What a surprise."

I gave my best friend a half wince, half smile that I hoped he understood was an apology. Marcus hates it when people from school see him in his polyester uniform. Actually, I think he looks adorable in his pink-and-white-striped soda fountain hat, but Marcus says that it makes him feel like he's wearing a peppermint stick on his head, like he belongs on a Christmas parade float or something. So he keeps his Scoops job on the double DL.

Anyway, I know that Marcus is kind of sensitive about it, and I didn't want him to think that I was just being thoughtless by bringing Jeffrey here. It had been an honest-to-God accident. "I just happened to mention to Jeffrey that I was meeting you here—" I started.

"Hey, Marcus!" Rajeev Gupta and Makonnen Kalorama were waving from across the restaurant. They were sitting at a huge corner booth with Astrid and Glenn.

"Your hat ees so cute!" Leila Manais called. She's French, so she can get away with saying stuff like that. I gave Marcus a weak smile as he sliced into a banana like he was tearing out its guts.

"Wow—everybody's here!" Marcus said brightly. "What's everybody doing here, Frannie?" His eyes flashed dangerously, like he wanted to smash a scoop of ice cream on my head.

"Sorry," I mouthed silently as Jeffrey scanned the menu above Marcus's head. But Marcus didn't notice. His eyes had flicked back to Jeffrey, watching him intently as he skimmed the list of flavors. Marcus looked like he was trying to use laser vision to bore into Jeffrey's skull and read his thoughts. That made me feel even worse, because I was almost sure that I knew what Marcus was thinking— Does Jeffrey think I'm lame because I'm stuck wearing this stupid outfit? Is Frannie embarrassed to be my friend? Does the International Club think I'm a jerk? Poor Marcus. I never should have let Jeffrey come here. . . .

"We decided to do something fun for our International Club meeting," Jeffrey explained absently. "Hey—" His eyes landed on Marcus's, and his grin widened. "Maybe we'll have all of our meetings here from now on!"

Marcus turned from pale to green. His face was really working the whole kaleidoscope of horror colors.

"Oh, ho, ho, Jeffrey, you kidder," I put in quickly. "You don't want the International Club to gain a zillion pounds, do you?"

"Yeah, man, mix it up." This comment was from Cal, who was putting a scoop of vanilla into a root beer float. "Maybe you guys could go bowling or get your tarot cards read."

"Jeffrey, this is Calvin," I said.

"Nice to meet you." Jeffrey smiled.

"Jeffrey!" Astrid called from the booth. "Come here zo ve can order!"

Jeffrey nodded, then turned to me. "Coming?"

"In a sec," I told him.

He gave us all a little wave and headed off to join the rest of the ICers. "I'm sorry, I'm sorry, I'm so, so, sorry," I whispered to Marcus the minute Jeffrey was out of earshot.

Just then, Goth in a Box—Tina Tamarino—slapped an order on the counter in front of Cal. "Since when are you in the International Club?" she asked, snapping her gum, looking at me darkly from underneath black sparkly eye shadow. "I need a Colonel Custard butterscotch sundae."

"Hey, is that the guy you're dating?" Cal asked me.

"Isn't he cute?" I said.

"Are you actually going out with him?" Tina asked.

"Can we have a moment here?" Marcus snapped, looking miserable. "Frannie, you know that working here is my secret identity."

I felt a flush creep up the back of my neck. Jeez, I'd already apologized. What did he want from me? "I'm sorry."

"What would happen to Superman if Lois Lane went around telling everyone that he was really Clark Kent?" Marcus demanded.

"He'd probably be a lot less confused, dude," Cal suggested.

"Stay out of it, Cal," Marcus growled in this very un-Marcus way.

Whoa. Part of me couldn't help thinking that Marcus was really overreacting. I mean, it wasn't like he needed to impress Jeffrey or anything. *I* was supposed to be the one who felt self-conscious. Still, another—bigger—part of me totally understood. In a way, Jeffrey was *our* project. We both wanted him to like us. "I know. I didn't mean for this to happen," I said in a low voice. "I didn't suggest coming here, I swear. See, Jeffrey asked if I wanted to hang out after school. I told him I was meeting you here, and then . . ." Well, and then Jeffrey had invited the whole IC to hang out at Scoops.

Marcus narrowed his eyes even more. "So—you were just going to blow me off?"

"No—of course not!" God! Didn't he know me at all? It was almost like Marcus was *looking* for a fight. "I'm not supposed to meet you until later, *remember*?" I ran my fingers through a hunk of hair . . . and got stuck.

Cal frowned. "Is that a new hairstyle?" he asked.

"No," I said with a groan as I tried to extricate my hand from my hair. "New gel. I'm trying to go all natural—but that seems to translate into major frizz." It was also making my head itch, but I didn't want to get into it. The products had been Jeffrey's suggestion. I should have known better than to take hair product advice from a guy.

Marcus looked annoyed. "Can we stick to the subject?" he demanded.

"What was the subject?" Cal asked.

"People, table three needs water; table six needs sundaes; and Tina, a very rude man is waiting for Colonel Custard to get him with a silver serving dish in the ice cream parlor, so let's have a little less chatting and more working, okay?" Margaret twisted her pink-frosted lips into a smile. "Don't look now, hon," she said to me, "but a certain blue-eyed cutie is looking your way. Is that the guy?"

I smiled and waved at Jeffrey. "That's him."

"What's *Glenn* doing here?" Marcus demanded as he flung a scoop of ice cream into a dish. "Don't tell me he's from Canada too."

"No—he's from Alaska, remember? Jeffrey just asked him if he wanted to come along at the last minute," I explained. Actually, I think Glenn had kind of gotten railroaded into coming, just as I had.

"So you and Jeffrey are *actually* going out?" Tina repeated, like she was some journalist for *Goth Beat* who wanted to make sure she had her story straight.

"Yeah," I told her. "I guess."

"You guess?" Cal repeated. "What's up?"

"Is he one of those tongue-all-over-the-face kissers?" Margaret wanted to know.

I winced. "I don't know."

"You don't know?" Tina repeated, her dark eyes narrowed.

Marcus made this snorting sound, which I chose to ignore.

"If you haven't kissed the guy," Cal put in, "how can you be sure that you're really going out?"

"That's what I'm saying, Cal," I said, a little sharply. To tell the truth, his comment stung. Of course, there were reasons that Jeffrey and I hadn't kissed—first, I'd nearly exploded at the Polish food fest; then we'd hung out as a threesome with Marcus; then there was the whole STF thing. . . . But still, it did seem strange that he'd never made a move.

"They've hung out a bunch of times," Marcus said loyally. "And they've been on a real two-person date."

Tina pursed her lips. "It *sounds* like going out."

I was grateful to Tina for saying that, even though she didn't really sound convinced.

Cal wasn't impressed. "When a guy is interested, he goes for the kiss."

"Don't listen to them, Frannie," Marcus said as he drizzled butterscotch over a sundae. "This is just like the time that they all told you not to go for the guy who worked in the sausage store."

"I'm telling you," Tina said crinkling her nose, "that guy had a really weird smell."

"That was good advice, man," Cal insisted. "And Frannie, all I'm saying is, maybe you need to clear things up."

"Yeah," I said slowly. I had to admit, Cal had a point.

"Well, don't look now," Margaret said to me, "but some blond girl is moving in awful tight to your man."

I didn't even have to look. I knew it was Astrid. "Okay, I gotta go," I said quickly. "Marcus, I'm sorry—I'll make it up to you later." I scurried over to the International Club booth and squeezed in on the end, next to Jeffrey and across from Glenn, who grinned at me. He was sitting underneath a picture of a giant sundae that seemed to be attacking the Grand Canyon. Whoever did the interior decorating at Scoops definitely had an original sense of style.

Jeffrey smiled at me as I sat down, and a queasy little butterfly fluttered through my stomach. Why haven't you kissed me? I wondered, feeling kind of like I was back in eighth grade. What am I doing wrong? But I managed to smile back weakly, and Jeffrey turned his attention to the conversation.

"No, the problems with Eritrea are a lot more complicated than that," Makonnen was saying.

I nodded and made a little *hm* sound, like I knew all about it. Of course, meanwhile, I was scanning my brain. . . . Eritrea, I thought. Skin disease or African nation? I wasn't a hundred percent sure—but I knew it was one or the other. Oh, man, I thought. What have I been *learning* in school? Why don't they teach us these things?

"What's *your* opinion, Frannie?" Astrid asked me. This little smile played at the corners of her mouth, like she knew I wasn't sure what Eritrea was. Hate her. It only made things worse that she'd recently gotten a super-cute pixie-style haircut, and I was sitting there with an all-natural sticky frizz ball on my head.

Okay, say something that covers both skin diseases *and* African nations, I thought. I shook my head sadly. "Makonnen is right—Eritrea *is* complicated. So many people are suffering—"

"That is so true, Fran," Jeffrey said warmly, like I'd just said the most brilliant thing in the world.

My stomach fluttered again. I'm a genius, I thought. A genius who has no idea what she's talking about.

"The situation between Eritrea and Ethiopia is very much like what's happening between India and Pakistan," Rajeev put in.

Okay, now we were getting somewhere! Eritrea *was* an African nation! I gave myself a little mental pat on the back as the other International Clubbers debated the matter back and forth. Sometimes hanging out with Jeffrey and his friends felt a little like being a contestant on *Jeopardy*. It was kind of thrilling to feel like I finally had a few points.

Tina delivered a table's worth of ice cream goodies, waggling her shaved-off-then-painted-back-on-again black eyebrows at me. I sipped my water as she handed me a one-scoop sundae with a napkin wrapped around it.

Unwrapping it slowly, I held the napkin under the table and peeked at it. Sure enough, there was a note: *Astrid looks like she wants to kill you! Smooch, M.*

I looked over at Marcus and he grinned at me. My head felt light with relief. . . . At least he wasn't mad at me anymore.

And it seemed like I'd finally done one thing right, I thought. Actually, that whole Eritrea thing reminded me of Marcus's little Coogie Fuji test the night before. I have to admit, I admired Sundance for telling the truth and not trying to play it cool. I guess you have to be the kind of guy who doesn't care about cool if you're going to go around wearing jeans and cowboy boots in Chicago, right?

Actually, I'd had a great time the night before. I hadn't realized that line dancing would be so much fun! I mean, nobody cares if you suck or anything—so I'd really let loose, dancing and whooping and hollering like a maniac. Why not, right? I was never going to see any of those people again. Except for Patricia and Manfred, and they'd been hollering just as loudly as I was. Besides, I knew that Marcus would never tell anyone about what an idiot I'd made of myself. He'd be too embarrassed for me.

Just thinking about it made me giggle.

Suddenly, I realized that everyone at the table was staring at me.

Omigosh. Had I just giggled *out loud*? I cleared my throat, hoping desperately that we hadn't been discussing world famine or something. Jeffrey was staring at me with an expression I couldn't read, and a knot of nerves tightened across my chest, making it hard to breathe. Please tell me that I haven't done something that's going to take my future-smooch-probability rating down to zero, I begged silently.

"I agree with Frannie," Glenn said after a beat of silence. "The UN *is* a joke."

"But it *could* be so important if the leadership were effective!" Jeffrey argued.

This set the club off again.

I smiled my thanks at Glenn, who winked. Leaning toward me, he whispered, "I wasn't sure about Eritrea, either."

I laughed, and the knot of nerves across my chest loosened a little.

"So," Glenn said after a minute, "seen any good movies lately?"

I shrugged and took a bite of my mini-sundae. Mmmm. Marcus knows just what I like—a half scoop of Chocopalooza and a half scoop of vanilla, hot fudge, whipped cream, and three cherries—no nuts. "Well . . . Marcus keeps dragging me to these film festivals. So I just saw *Persona*."

The left side of Glenn's mouth ticked up into a smile. "And?"

I rolled my eyes. "I hate going to movies that make me feel dumb," I confessed. I tried to sneak in a little scalp scratch. God, my head was itching horrendously.

Glenn laughed. "Oh, man," he said with a grin. "Nobody *ever* admits that they have no idea what that movie is about."

"*Thank* you," I said warmly, digging into my sundae. "Marcus loved it, but I didn't get it at all. I *hate* having to use my brain when I see a movie. I just want to laugh and have a good time. It's not like I'm looking for extra things to get depressed about."

"Give me kung fu any day," Glenn agreed.

"Marcus loves kung fu." Hey! There's something Marcus and Glenn have in common, I thought. I knew Marcus thought Glenn was kind of annoying, but I was really starting to like the guy. It would be so great if my best friend and Jeffrey's best friend got along. I started picturing them having animated talks about directors while Jeffrey and I made out on the couch. . . .

Without thinking, I tried to twirl a piece of hair around my finger. My finger got stuck again.

I tried to play it off, but Glenn noticed, of course. "Are you using some new kind of gel?"

I sighed and glanced in Jeffrey's direction. He was talking to Leila, so I leaned forward and whispered, "It's all natural."

Glenn nodded. "I switched my shampoo once because Jeff suggested this biodegradable crap," he admitted. "It totally made my scalp itch."

"I have that problem, too!"

Glenn laughed, and then I giggled, which made him laugh harder. Then I let out a little snort, and it was all over for the both of us.

Just then, Marcus walked over to our table. He had his pink-and-white hat and apron tucked under his arm, and he frowned at me as Glenn and we brought our giggles under control. "Hey, everyone."

The International Club chorused a hello.

"Sit down with us," Jeffrey said, gesturing to the booth.

There was space next to Glenn, but Marcus motioned me over, so everyone had to scooch around the horseshoe until Glenn was at the edge of the seat and Marcus was sitting next to me. That wasn't so bad, though, because my leg was pressing against Jeffrey's. He didn't move away, either, which I took as a good sign.

For a moment, nobody said anything.

I was feeling the pressure. I guessed that whole UN debate had come to a close. Okay, we needed a new topic. . . . "So . . . uh . . . Marcus and I went out with his grandmother and her boyfriend last weekend," I said brightly.

Silence.

"We went line dancing," I elaborated.

More silence. Everyone looked like they had no idea how to respond. Jeffrey, in particular, was giving me an odd look.

Marcus sighed.

Okay—is that or is that not a good conversational opener? I mean, any normal group of people would laugh and demand details, right? Going line dancing with your grandmother—that has to be funny, right? Right?

Glenn took pity on me. "Where'd you go?"

"This crazy place called Line 'Em Up," I told him.

"Oh, Line 'Em Up," Glenn said, giving Jeffrey a knowing smile. "That place has gay night on Thursdays." He winked at Jeffrey. "You're going to take me there next week, right Jeffrey?" he asked in this mock-flirty tone.

Jeffrey laughed awkwardly.

Ooh, I could practically feel Marcus's blood boiling at the gay joke. Crap. I always just assume that people know Marcus is queer . . . but ever since that convo with my dad, I've realized maybe it's not as obvious as I thought. "Don't be a jerk, Glenn," I told him.

Glenn looked surprised. "Okay," he said after a moment. "Sorry." He reached out and touched my hand lightly with long, slim fingers. His palm felt warm over my hand. For some reason, it didn't strike me as strange that he had his hand on mine . . . it just seemed like a friendly gesture. But when I looked up at Marcus, I saw that he was glaring at Glenn's hand as though he were about to rip it from the end of Glenn's arm and chuck it behind the ice cream counter. Reflexively, I pulled my hand away.

Marcus stood up. "Frannie and I have to get going," he announced. Actually, I think he might have considered just walking out and leaving me there if he hadn't been counting on me for a ride.

"Oh, right," I said quickly. "I forgot we have that— thing. Okay, everyone, well, this has been a blast!" I stood up. My leg felt cold once it wasn't touching Jeffrey's any- more. "See you tomorrow!"

Jeffrey flashed his super-white smile at me. "Thanks for suggesting this place, Fran."

"Sure." I hesitated for a moment, then retreated with- out even giving Jeffrey a special little hug or anything. To tell you the truth, I didn't think about the fact that I'd blown my chances at kissing Jeffrey—again—until it was too late. I just trotted after Marcus as the International Club waved and shouted goodbyes after us.

"How can you *stand* that guy?" Marcus raged as we stormed through the mall toward the parking lot. "He's a homophobic jerk!"

I winced. I mean, Marcus had a point—Glenn's comment had been pretty bad. Still, I knew he could be a nice guy. . . . "Maybe he didn't mean it the way it sounded," I suggested.

Marcus stared at me like he'd just been stabbed in the back and found me holding the dagger.

I could feel my face flushing. "I mean, *you'd* make the same kind of joke. So would Ethan Schumacher—he's always kidding around about hitting on guys, and he's head of the GSA!"

"Uh, this just in, Frannie—Ethan *is* queer, and so am I," Marcus snapped. "I'm not some good-looking frat boy wannabe who thinks it's okay to call people faggot."

"He didn't call you that."

"What's the difference?"

I sighed. Marcus was right, and I knew it. Stupid Glenn. Why did he have to make that joke just as I'd found a little glimmer of hope that he and Marcus might actually get along? "Well, at least he backed off when I called him on it."

"Ooh, yeah, let's give him the Nobel Peace Prize." Marcus's voice was dripping sarcasm.

I decided not to say anything else. There were too many thoughts crowding my brain. For a moment there, when Glenn was touching my hand, I'd felt the rage coming off Marcus like a torch radiating heat. But it had seemed so out of proportion. . . . And then there was the way he'd overreacted when Jeffrey and the other ICers had shown up. . . . It was almost like Marcus was *jealous* or something.

I snuck a sideways look at my best friend and watched his jaw muscles as they worked angrily. He *is* jealous, I realized suddenly. He thinks he's losing me, and he's jealous. Suddenly, all of my annoyance faded away. I wanted him to know that he had nothing to worry about. But I couldn't think of the right thing to say—somehow "You'll never lose me to Jeffrey" sounded so presumptuous on so many levels that I could never have let the words out of my mouth—so I just slipped my hand into his.

Marcus didn't look up. He didn't look at me; he didn't speak. He just wrapped his fingers around mine, and we walked through the mall together in silence, hand in hand.

I was actually feeling happy. That floaty kind of happy, where you feel totally comfortable, as though everything is all right and nothing could go very wrong.

That didn't last long.

We were just passing Totally Stuff, this store that sells lots of useless crap—like blue sparkly CD holders and bowls that say BITE THIS! on them—that I always have to buy a ton of, when Marcus stopped dead in his tracks.

"What is it?" I asked.

"Don't look," he said. Then he tried to change directions, but he was still holding my hand, so he ended up yanking me around like a Mylar balloon.

"Ow," I griped, twisting to see. "What is it?"

"I said, don't look," Marcus repeated. He pulled on my arm, but I dug in and didn't budge. "Trust me," he begged. "I'm saving you thousands of dollars in future therapy bills."

That did it. Of course I had to look—so I craned my neck just in time to see my mom and dad walking out of Intimate Pleasures. My dad was holding a giant red bag, and Mom was giggling. My eyes darted over the display in the Intimate Pleasures window—a see-through black teddy trimmed in red feathers.

I felt the Chocopalooza crawling up the back of my throat.

Damn you, chapter six! "I think I've been struck blind," I said.

"I *told* you not to look," Marcus said. His voice was half scolding, half sympathetic. "I'm just surprised we didn't see my grandmother and Manfred walking out with them."

"Oh my God," I said, rubbing my temples. "I actually just wondered what was in the bag."

"Don't think about it," Marcus commanded, wrapping an arm around my shoulders. "Don't ever let those thoughts dirty your brain."

"Let's pretend this never happened," I suggested.

"We'll never speak of it again." Marcus drew an X over his heart and looked so serious that it actually made me smile.

I looked up at him for a moment. "I'm so glad that I'm here with you," I told him finally. I really meant it.

Marcus ran a hand through his shaggy hair, like he always does when he's not sure what I'm talking about. "What?"

"I mean—Belina would have tried to give me a lecture about older people's sexuality," I explained. "And Jenn . . . I don't know. She just would have thought it was cute that my parents were at Intimate Pleasures. Anyone else would have tried to pretend it was totally normal and nothing to be embarrassed about."

Marcus nodded solemnly. "But I'm totally grossed out."

We both laughed, and that was when I knew for sure that everything was all right between us. I mean, we were so on the same wavelength—it made sense that Marcus might feel a flash of jealousy. But he had to know that I just couldn't function without him. With a sigh, I pressed my forehead against his chest, feeling the rough fabric of his polyester Scoops shirt against my skin. "Thank you," I said. "That's just what I needed right now."

Laughing, Marcus touched my hair. He lifted a limp lock, then let it drop. "Frannie," he said after a moment, "let's get you home so that you can wash this goo off your head."

"Marcus . . ." I gazed up into his warm hazel eyes. He was smiling his real Marcus smile—the one that shows off his dimples. "You always know just what to say."

Nine

This next scene opens with a tracking shot. The camera moves slowly through my house, like it's looking for something. Pass through the living room, where Dad is parked in front of the TV. Continue into the kitchen. Patricia is sitting at the counter and talking on the phone. You can only half hear her voice behind the music on the sound track, which is ominous but cheesy, like something out of a sequel to a sequel to a slasher flick.

Now we're in the hallway. It's dark, except for one light coming from a room at the far end. The camera accelerates toward it, moving in for the climax. It reaches the end of the hall, swings around the corner and through the door. There's a big screech of music, all high-pitched and synthesized. . . .

But instead of some chain-saw-mangled body, there's just me sitting there, typing away at the computer with this silly grin on my face. Cut to a tight close-up of the computer screen, where the chat scrolls by.

<<FRANNO: Okay you go.>>

<<JEFFO: Ummm . . . favorite time of day?>>

<<FRANNO: Eleven to twelve at night, just when everything is getting quiet. That's when I can really think. You?>>

<<JEFFO: I like the transitions—night into morning, afternoon into evening, that kind of thing.>>

<<FRANNO: Sunsets, sunrises . . . nice. Favorite planet?>>

<<JEFFO: Planet Frannie.>>

<<FRANNO: Subtle. But you get extra points for kissing up.>>

<<JEFFO: I thought you didn't keep score in this game.>>

<<FRANNO: We don't.>>

<<JEFFO: Speaking of kissing up—nice screen name.>>

<<FRANNO: So you noticed. Imitation: the sincerest form of flattery.>>

<<JEFFO: And the nearest thing to schizophrenia. You're not going to boil my bunny rabbit, are you?>>

<<FRANNO: "Fatal Attraction," right? I thought you weren't so into old movies.>>

<<JEFFO: I'm not, but everyone knows that one.>>

<<FRANNO: Hmmm. Boiled bunnies. I like a man with a well-hidden sick sense of humor.>>

<<JEFFO: Then I guess you're in luck.>>

Somehow, somehow, SOMEHOW, I had convinced myself that it was okay to keep having these unauthorized conversations, like the seal on my promise to Frannie had already been broken and there was no harm in continuing. Yeah, right.

Jeffrey, I was learning, had layers. There was First Impression Jeffrey, who was the one I knew from school, all popular, quiet, serious, and politically correct. But there was also Funny Jeffrey, Insecure Jeffrey, Able to Play the Games of Life Jeffrey, and who knew what else, but I wanted to find out . . . Jeffrey. The more of these conversations I had, the more I wanted to have them. They were my junk food, my bad TV, and my drug of choice all rolled into one. All of which is an explanation, not to be confused with a rationalization or an excuse for what I was doing. But I had those too.

My rationalization was something like this: Everything was still on track. Jeffrey was more into Frannie than ever. Frannie was happy. Whatever I was doing, it seemed to be helping.

And if I had to pick one excuse, it was the fact that sometimes, Jeffrey asked Frannie questions about me. I don't know anyone who could have resisted hanging around for that.

<<JEFFO: Where's Marcus tonight?>>

<<FRANNO: He was here for dinner but then went home.>>

<<JEFFO: Can I ask you something?>>

<<FRANNO: You can ask, sure.>>

<<JEFFO: What does Marcus think of me?>>

<<FRANNO: He thinks you're the best guy I've ever hung out with, not counting himself.>>

<<JEFFO: I'll take that as a compliment.>>

<<FRANNO: You should. So while we're on the subject, what do you think of him?>>

<<JEFFO: I think he's the best guy you've ever hung out with, not counting me.>>

<<FRANNO: Ha.>>

<<JEFFO: Seriously, he seems like a really good friend. I like him a lot.>>

I couldn't resist. . . .

<<FRANNO: What about him?>>

<<JEFFO: He's your brain twin for one thing. How could I NOT like him?>>

<<FRANNO: Good point.>>

<<JEFFO: What about Glenn?>>

<<FRANNO: What about him?>>

<<JEFFO: What do you think of him?>>

What *did* I think of Glenn? Now, that was a two-part question. Part one: I think Glenn is a homophobic attention hog who should go back to Alaska and take Astrid with him while he's at it. Part two:

<<FRANNO: I like Glenn a lot.>>

<<JEFFO: How about Marcus? To tell you the truth, Glenn thinks M doesn't like him so much.>>

<<FRANNO: What makes him think that?>>

<<JEFFO: Just a vibe, I guess. Although I think M barely knows him. Maybe the four of us should do something again—?>>

<<FRANNO: Let me check it out with M first. I don't want to force anything. Everything's kind of changing fast these days.>>

<<JEFFO: Understood. We'll see how it goes. I'd never want to come between you guys.>>

Okay, how much was I loving Jeffrey right now? Talk about giving all the right answers. This was Not Alienating the Best Friend Jeffrey, my favorite so far. At the same time, though, I could feel myself slipping more and more of my own agenda, or thoughts, or whatever into the conversation. I needed to pull back a little, I thought. But before I could respond, Patricia interrupted.

"Knock, knock, knock."

With a flick of the mouse, I switched the screen over to

Word, then turned to see her standing in my door wearing a skirt and a blue lace bra.

"Patricia!" I looked away again.

"Oh, lighten up, sugar. It's just like a bikini top. You wouldn't get embarrassed about that." I didn't bother to correct her. "Anyway, Frannie's on the phone."

My chest tightened. "What? I didn't even hear it ring."

"Doesn't mean it didn't happen. You want this?"

I looked over at Patricia just long enough to take the phone. "Thanks." I waited for her to leave the room, then quickly nudged Jeffrey off.

<<FRANNO: I have to go. Will you be online later?>>

<<JEFFO: Sure.>>

I closed my door, took a deep breath, and put the phone to my ear. "Hey."

Frannie's voice was tinged with stress. "Jeffrey's talking to some other girl online."

"How do you know?" I asked. Somewhere in the back of my mind, I recognized how ironically funny this would be . . . if it were happening to someone else.

"I was watching him in the chat room, but then he just dropped out," she said. "Now he's been gone for a long time without logging off."

"He could be doing anything."

"Well, exactly."

"Did you send him a message?" I asked, praying that the answer was no.

"Uh, hello? Not my department. That's why I'm calling you. Can you come over?"

Could I? Should I? It was hard to concentrate on anything but the problem itself: *Do not let Frannie find out that she has just been chatting with Jeffrey.*

"Why don't we just do it over the phone, like always?" I said. Yes, that was good. "I'll try sending him a message right now if you want."

Frannie paused. It was almost eerie. "I'll come to you," she said. "See you in a second." The click on the line was her goodbye. I sat there with the phone still on and my tongue against the roof of my mouth, which was as far as I had gotten toward saying, "NO!"

Factoring in the distance between Frannie's house and mine, along with her usual driving speed and the adrenaline that was no doubt pumping through her system, that meant I had . . . zero time to figure something out. A few options crossed my mind:

1. Tell Jeffrey there's a rampant computer virus spreading around and he needs to shut down his system indefinitely, or at least for the rest of the night.
2. Turn off all the lights and pretend no one's home when Frannie gets here.
3. Fake it.

Option number three won out by default. Before you could say, *"Auuuughhhh! Help me, help me, somebody help me!"* Frannie was in my room and panting over my shoulder. I logged back into the RBHS chat room as slowly as I could without seeming weird about it.

"There he is." She put her finger to his name on the screen. "See if you can find out who he was talking to."

"You don't even know for sure that he was talking to someone," I said, which was true but still felt like a lie.

"Just go," she said, starting to rub my shoulders. "Go, go, go."

I typed in Franno and hit enter.

"Um, okay, that's good," she said. "Like Jeffo. Cute."

"All right," I said. "We're just going to ease in here."

<<FRANNO: Hey there.>>

<<JEFFO: Welcome back>>

"Welcome back?" Her fingers stopped rubbing. I held off a nervous laugh.

<<FRANNO: Miss me?>>

<<JEFFO: You know it.>>

"Oh, that's good, right?" she said. "Now ask him if he was talking to someone."

"Not so fast," I said.

<<FRANNO: What are you up to?>>

<<JEFFO: Same as before.>>

Frannie didn't say anything, but I could feel the gears

turning in her head. I wished she would sit down and stop looking over my shoulder. I'm pretty sure my face was turning red.

<<FRANNO: Homework?>>

<<JEFFO: Yeah. Listen, I was thinking about what you said.>>

<<FRANNO: US History?>>

<<JEFFO: Yes, but hang on. I mean about you and Marcus.>>

"Wha-at?" Frannie's voice had that faraway quality. So did my brain. I couldn't think of a thing to type and Jeffrey kept going.

<<JEFFO: If things are sketchy with you guys right now, maybe you should blow me off Saturday and just hang out with him. I'll do something with Glenn.>>

Any other time, I would have thought that was sweet. Right now, though, Frannie was staring at me in a way that could have blocked out the sun, much less any deluded little crushes in the room.

"What have you been. . . ?" She didn't have to finish asking. She already knew. "How much have you been talking to him?" she asked instead. Her face was perfectly still. I couldn't read her expression at all.

"Frannie," I fumbled, "I . . . I'm sorry."

"Has it been you the whole time . . . posing as me? Or something else?" Her voice got higher as she said it.

"It's always been me as you," I said. "I would never—"

"Ha!" She cut me off. "Don't even."

I turned in my chair to face her as she walked away from me. "No, I'm serious," I said. Even now, it bothered me she would so quickly assume I had forgotten our friendship. "I know how this might sound," I told her, "but I would never do anything against you."

"Oh, really?" she said. She looked over at the computer for a second and then right into my eyes. "And you told him things are *sketchy* between us? Why would you do that?"

The fact was that I hadn't said that to Jeffrey. He had interpreted it from our conversation, but somehow that distinction felt meaningless right now. This was only getting more complicated as it went on.

Then the computer toned with another line of chat coming in.

<<JEFFO: Hello? Still there?>>

Frannie groaned with frustration. "Just tell him—" but then she changed her mind. "Just . . . get up for a second." The bossiness of it hurt, and she sat down at the computer like I wasn't even there anymore. The lump in my throat started to ache.

<<FRANNO: Really sorry; I have to go again. Sorry.>>

<<JEFFO: No prob. XO. Night.>>

<<FRANNO: Good night.>>

Even Jeffrey's little XO—the one she never would have seen if this hadn't happened—felt incriminating. I said the only thing I could think of.

"I'm sorry."

She ignored the apology. "Tell me something. How many times have you talked to him?"

"Not that many."

"How many?"

I had to think about it, and she saw that right away.

"More than you can say. Unbelievable." She went to the door but stopped with her hand on the knob. "I feel so stupid," she said. "I feel so, so stupid."

"Why?" I asked.

"Why?!"

Maybe it was a dumb question, but I honestly didn't know the answer.

"Mostly because I trusted you," she said. "But also because this makes me even more of a . . . whatever. An idiot, as far as Jeffrey is concerned."

"He doesn't think that, Frannie. He likes you. A lot."

"Thanks for the update. Anything else I should know?"

"I didn't do this to hurt you," I said, trying not to sound aggressive.

"Yet look what happened. Funny how that works out." She was getting heavy into the sarcasm, and it was starting to piss me off. I think more than anything, I was mad at the situation, but right now it felt a lot like being mad at Frannie.

"For the record," I said, "this all started with you."

"What does *that* have to do it?"

"Maybe not everything, but it does have something to do with it."

"It's got *nothing* to do with it. For the record." She practically spit it at me.

"You're not even trying to understand where I'm coming from," I told her.

She pointed at the computer again, as if that closed her case. "Understand what? I didn't make you have those conversations behind my back, Marcus."

"That's right, Frannie, you didn't," I told her. It was all starting to spill out of me, including some things I hadn't realized until I said them. "You stayed at your usual safe distance and did everything you could to make sure I'd help you without ever *really* being responsible for anything yourself. Just like always."

Frannie looked stung, and I got a jolt of guilt, but it just blended with the anger. "I only wish I had your problems," I went on. My voice was shaking. "I'd trade places with you in a minute, and the thing is, you'd never want to be me. Has that ever occurred to you?"

"Don't try to change the subject," she said. "That's not what this is about."

"Oh, right," I said. "It's about you. How could I forget? Okay, fine. Let me tell you something else, then. You don't even know Jeffrey."

"What are you talking about?" she said. I was all over the map and we both knew it. I couldn't help myself, like everything I had never said was going to come out all at once or not at all.

"You don't know him—you don't *really* know him," I told her. "And that's because you've never really tried, and *that's* because you've never had to, as long as I've been around."

"Or maybe you've never given me the chance," she shot back. "Maybe . . . no, not even maybe. You've been keeping him to yourself. Don't you see that? You tell me I don't know Jeffrey; well, guess what? You don't even know *yourself*. You can't even see what you're doing here."

"What I see is how much of this you take for granted. Just like you take everything for granted." And because I just wasn't going to have any crying right now, I fought it back by yelling even louder. "This was all about you! Why do you think I'm even doing this?!"

♀ Ten

"Right, Marcus," I snapped, "why *are* you doing this?"

We just stood there, staring at each other for a full minute, the words hanging in the air like a strange scent. Everything was silent. From its place on Marcus's desk in the corner of the room, I could hear his computer hum and whir. Marcus's chest rose and fell with his breathing.

"I'm—I'm doing this for you." Marcus's voice had a strange, strangled quality. "Of course."

"You don't actually believe that, do you?" My voice was quiet. I hardly knew what I was saying, what I was feeling. I was furious, sure. And sad. Marcus was my friend. But he'd been hitting on my boyfriend . . . pretending to be

192

me? My throat tightened. The whole situation had this ugly quality—like Marcus had been making fun of me, laughing at me behind my back. But there was another feeling washing over me too, taking over the others. Was it—pity? What for? I felt dizzy; I couldn't think straight.

Marcus's narrow nostrils flared in fury. "Maybe I actually *like* Jeffrey," he growled. His face was contorted in anger—for a moment, I didn't recognize him. "Because I actually *know* Jeffrey, because I actually *talk to* Jeffrey."

"Right, you talk to him—behind my back!" I spat. "Only you aren't really talking to him, are you, Marcus? Someone who doesn't exist is talking to him!" I let out a little barking laugh. "You're so desperate, you're trying to seduce my boyfriend, but you don't even have the guts to do it for real."

The minute the words were out of my mouth, I wanted to call them back. I felt them reach out and claw Marcus across the face—he looked like I'd slapped him.

"He's not your boyfriend, Frannie," Marcus said finally. His voice was low and dangerous. "You can't talk to each other. He's never once tried to kiss you." Marcus's hazel eyes narrowed as he hissed, "Face it—he doesn't want you. Even with me at your back, you managed to blow it. As usual."

In the next moment, his face blurred. All I knew was that I had to get out of there. I was practically blinded by tears, but I managed to find my way out of his room. I stumbled down the hall and out the front door and didn't even break stride when I heard Marcus calling my name. He was supposed to be my best friend. How could he have hurt me like that?

I don't even remember fumbling for my keys or turning the ignition. All I remember is finding myself peeling down the street, wiping the hot tears from my cheeks as they streamed down my face. I turned on the radio and pumped the volume all the way up as I merged onto the highway. I had no idea where I was going. All I wanted to do was drive.

An hour later, I finally had to admit that I wasn't really going anywhere—I was just avoiding going home. I just couldn't face it. For one thing, I was totally afraid that Marcus would call, and then I'd have to figure out what to say to him. And for another thing, I was even more terrified that he might *not* call. Then I'd have to decide whether or not I wanted to do the reaching out.

Screw that, I decided as I hit the turn signal and headed toward my house. I can't just drive forever. I've got to go home. But I'm *not* calling Marcus. He's the one who owes me an apology, not the other way around.

"Hi, sweetie," Mom called from the living room as I walked in the back door.

Taking a deep breath, I managed to shout, "Hi." But that was about all I could handle. I had to resist the urge to go into the living room, put my head on my mom's shoulder, and cry until her sleeve was soaked through. I just didn't see how I could explain the whole situation to her when I didn't even really understand it myself. So I snuck up the back stairs and skulked into my room.

What happened?

That was the question that had been screaming in my brain the entire drive. I shoved a pile of books to the floor and sat heavily on the edge of my bed. Okay, so Marcus had a point. It wasn't like Jeffrey and I exactly had flow . . . . and maybe I'd been asking too much by having Marcus be my conversational crutch for so long. But that didn't give him the right to just start pretending to be me. Especially when I'd asked him not to. I mean, who knew what he'd been telling Jeffrey all this time? Besides, I'd only asked for Marcus's help because it was just so much easier for *him* to talk to Jeffrey.

God, why *is* that? I wondered. I guessed it was because he wasn't nervous, for one thing. I was always just so paranoid that I'd mess up and look stupid or say the wrong thing. It was easy for Marcus to be himself around Jeffrey. Okay, I didn't think Marcus had any idea about Eritrea, either, but for whatever reason, that wouldn't have made him feel like a moron. . . . He could just talk to Jeffrey about something else.

But that wasn't really the million-dollar question. No— the big question was, how could Marcus do this to me?

Looking down, I realized that my hand was hovering over the phone. Tears welled up in my eyes. Usually, whenever I had a problem, Marcus was the first person I called. But I'm not calling him on this one, I thought bitterly. He *is* the problem.

Okay, and Jeffrey was out, obviously, because that would require way too much explanation of stuff I wasn't sure I wanted explained to him . . . *ever*.

So I punched in Belina's number and pressed talk. "Come on," I murmured into the receiver as the phone rang four times.

"Hey, it's Belina. I'm not here, but my voice mail is. Talk to it."

I hung up before the beep. I couldn't leave a message. I needed to talk to a real person. I decided to try Jenn.

"Hello?" Jenn's voice sounded breathy.

"Hey," I said, "it's me."

"Oh, hey!"

The mere fact that she sounded so happy to hear from me made me feel a little better.

"I was just thinking about you," Jenn said.

"Yeah?"

"Yeah—I'm watching this movie about King Arthur, and everyone is dressed in armor, and it reminded me of you at the carnival. I know the movie is supposed to be romantic, but I just can't stop laughing!" Then, as if to prove her point, Jenn burst into hysterical giggles. "Ooh, they're attacking the castle!" I could hear the clash of sword on armor in the background.

I took a deep breath, wondering why in the world I'd ever thought it was a good idea to call Jenn. "Okay," I told her, "I guess I'll just let you watch your movie."

"No—wait a minute." The movie noise went silent. I guess Jenn had clicked it off. "Is everything okay?"

Her tone was really gentle. I couldn't help it; my eyes got hot and teary again. "No," I admitted.

"I didn't think so."

I gave a weak little sniffle-laugh. "What gave it away?"

"You sound really sad," Jenn said simply.

For some reason, that broke my heart.

"Tell me," she urged.

So I did. I told her the whole story about how Marcus had been helping me get to know Jeffrey—and how Marcus had started talking to Jeffrey behind my back, and how those two seemed to get along better than Jeffrey and I ever had. I told the whole thing really badly, because thoughts were whirling around in my brain the whole time like evil flying monkeys, so Jenn had to interrupt me a few times and ask me to clarify what had happened. I explained everything as well as I could, but I realized that I really had about as many questions as she did. At the end, we were both quiet for a long time.

It was Jenn who broke the silence. "Wow."

Sighing, I leaned back against my bed pillows. "Yeah," I agreed. "Wow."

"Why would Marcus do that?" she asked.

"I don't know." I picked up Molasses, a stuffed animal in the shape of a cat that I'd had since I was four, and hugged him to my chest. None of the answers I'd come up with seemed to fit: Marcus was jealous of me, he was afraid that he was losing me to Jeffrey and he had to put a stop to it, he was desperate enough to throw away our friendship for some weird vicarious action, he didn't care about me. . . .

"Do you think he's in love with Jeffrey?"

My body went cold at the suggestion. No, I thought. No, of course not. Marcus couldn't be in love with someone and not tell me about it. But then again, that was the only answer that really fit. And now that Jenn had said it, I discovered just how obvious it was. Marcus loved Jeffrey. That was why he could talk to him for hours. That was why he lit up whenever I mentioned Jeffrey's name. That was why he couldn't stop himself from talking to Jeffrey, even when he'd promised not to. . . .

"Yes," I whispered. A hot tear snaked down the side of my face and dripped onto my neck. Suddenly, an image of how much Marcus must have been hurting every time I talked about Jeffrey stabbed through my mind. I felt my breathing grow shallow. For the first time, Marcus's words made sense. Actually, he was right—this really *wasn't* all about me. He'd done what he'd done because he had all of these secret feelings . . . feelings he couldn't tell anyone about—not even me.

No wonder Marcus and I had been fighting so much lately. I mean, for the past few weeks, it had seemed like everything I did annoyed him. It had been worrying me a lot, hovering around the corners of my consciousness. Marcus was important to me. He was my brain twin. When we didn't get along, everything seemed . . . off. And now he thought things were sketchy between us? Just how sketchy were we?

Suddenly, it dawned on me. Marcus wasn't afraid that he was losing me to Jeffrey. I was losing Marcus to Jeffrey. He thought we were growing apart . . . and we were. I flopped sideways on my bed, knocking my head against a history book. Another tear flowed up my temple, into my scalp.

"And how do you think Jeffrey feels?" Jenn asked.

I stared at the receiver. I'd almost forgotten I'd been talking to someone. "Jeffrey doesn't know about all of this," I explained.

"Well . . . I know," Jenn admitted. "But—I mean . . ." Her voice trailed off.

"What do you mean?" I prompted, squeezing Molasses's neck.

"You know . . . it was stupid. Forget it."

"No. Tell me."

Jenn cleared her throat. "I meant—you said that you and Jeffrey don't exactly have flow. And that Jeffrey and Marcus have all these conversations . . ." Her voice trailed off again, as though she couldn't quite finish the thought.

What is she trying to say? screamed an evil flying monkey in my brain.

You have to struggle to talk to Jeffrey! screeched another monkey.

Another monkey shrieked, Marcus can talk to Jeffrey for hours!

Wait a minute.

Have you ever seen an old fluorescent light come on? It takes a really long time, and then it flickers, flickers, flickers, until finally it's on, casting its sickly glow.

Here is my fluorescent-lightbulb moment:

Jeffrey and I have no flow.

Marcus and Jeffrey have flow.

Jeffrey has been pursuing me. . . .

Then again, he's never even tried to kiss me. . . .

Marcus is clearly falling for Jeffrey. . . .

And Jeffrey is falling for whoever it is he's been talking to online. . . .

Ho.

Ly.

Crap.

Could Jeffrey be . . .

Gay?

"Oh my God," I whispered.

"Oh, good," Jenn said with a relieved sigh. "You got it."

"This is crazy," I told her, sitting bolt upright on my bed.

"Yeah," she admitted. "Maybe. I don't know; I'm just throwing it out there. I mean, how well do you really know Jeffrey?"

"Well enough to know that he isn't gay!" I cried.

"Mmmm . . ." Jenn sounded like she didn't want to say anything more.

"Even though he's never kissed me," I admitted.

"I didn't want to point that out." I could hear the wince in her voice.

"Okay, wait," I babbled. "I mean, he's well groomed."

"His shirts are always ironed," Jenn agreed. "Look at Keith—he's a slob."

"Jeffrey's sensitive," I went on.

"He reads poetry," she added.

"He's friends with European women," I ticked off on my fingers. "He's polite and arrives on time. He has never, ever mentioned sports in any context. . . ."

"Yeah," Jenn said slowly.

We were both silent.

"I'm so sorry," Jenn added finally.

Oh. My. God. How could I have been so blind? I think it's bizarre when people don't realize that *Marcus* is gay . . . and here I was, worse than they are! Was it really possible that I was so clued out that I had no idea that my best friend and my boyfriend were really in love?

Impossible.

Right?

Then again—don't people have that problem all the time?

"But wait a minute. . . ." My mind was reeling. "Wait—STF. That's pretty un-queer."

"True," Jenn admitted.

"And he's best friends with Glenn," I added.

"That guy's as straight as they come," Jenn agreed.

"And he always seemed to want to spend time with me alone." I bit my lip, trying to remember whether the one-on-one dates had been his idea or mine.

"Not that he ever acted on that," Jenn said helpfully.

"How am I ever going to figure this out?" I wailed. I yanked on my hair in frustration.

"Hmmm . . ." Jenn thought for a moment. "Maybe you could test him. . . ."

"Test him?" This weird mental image of Jeffrey taking a lie detector test flashed into my brain. "With what—a polygraph?"

"Well, you said yourself that you never really gave Jeffrey a chance to go for it with you," Jenn pointed out. "Maybe you should."

"You mean, like, seduce him?" I stared at Molasses—his one-eyed, torn-eared, smiling face. Is she crazy? he seemed to be asking.

Jenn giggled. "Or whatever."

"I think . . ." I said slowly. "I think I've got to go."

"Okay," Jenn said. "I'll be here all night, if you need me."

I had to swallow to clear my throat. "Thanks," I managed to choke out.

"Love you," Jenn said. Then she clicked off.

Slowly, I put the phone back into place on my nightstand. Then I leaned back, staring up at my white ceiling. The blankness felt good for some reason—uncomplicated. I tried to let it wash over me.

"Knock, knock," Laura said as she opened the door and walked into my room. "Are you okay?"

I looked up at her. My sister's hair was pulled back into a tidy blond ponytail. I, on the other hand, was a disheveled mess and was lying on my bed hugging an ancient stuffed animal. "Do I look okay?"

Laura stepped into my room. She was holding a red shopping bag. "Do you want to talk about it?" she asked.

"No," I snapped.

"Okay. Jeez," she huffed.

I heaved a sigh. "It's not because . . ." I somehow couldn't bring myself to tell her that it wasn't because I didn't want to talk about it with *her*. Because I really *didn't* want to talk about it with her. Little Miss Perfect Love, I thought bitterly. What's she going to say when I tell her that I think my boyfriend might be queer?

"It's just complicated," I finished weakly. "And I'm kind of all talked out right now." This part, at least, was true.

Laura's blue eyes softened. "Okay," she said awkwardly. "Well—I'm here if you need me. You can knock on my door anytime."

I pressed my lips together, surprised at how touched I was by the offer. "Thanks."

Laura smiled and then held up a bag. "Could you do me a favor?" she asked. "Mom needs to exchange this for the next size down before the end of the week. Neither one of us is going anywhere near the mall for the next few days, and I know you're always dropping by to see Marcus. . . ."

"No problem," I said quickly, not wanting to explain that I wasn't going to be visiting Marcus anytime soon.

"Thanks." Laura flashed her super-white smile and dropped the bag by my door. That was when I read what was written on the side of it. INTIMATE PLEASURES. My stomach lurched. "Oh no," I said quickly. I had to return Mom's negligee or whatever it was in that bag? Icky McBarf Bag—no way.

Laura had been halfway out the door, but now she turned in her tracks. "Frannie," she snapped, "it's not a big deal."

"It's gross!" I complained. "I don't want to think about Mom and Dad's sex life!"

"Then don't look in the bag," Laura said in that annoyingly reasonable way she has. "Just ask the saleslady to do an even exchange."

"It's still gross," I grumbled.

"Look, it's important that we all support Mom and Dad on their journey to re-energize their marriage—" Laura began.

Okay, that was clearly a quote from *The Romance*

Handbook. I didn't feel like arguing with a self-help book, so I decided that it was easiest to just give in. "Fine," I snapped. "Leave it there by the door. But I'm never discussing this again."

With a heavy sigh and an eyeball roll, Laura walked out the door.

Hopping off the bed, I kicked the bag halfway behind my dresser. Then I walked into my bathroom and stared at myself in my vanity mirror. I looked horrible. All of that crying had left my eyes and nose red, and my mascara had dripped dark tracks across my cheeks. I went to the bathroom sink and splashed my face, then repaired my makeup as well as I could.

I walked back into my room and looked at the phone. I really wanted to call Marcus, but I fought the urge. I wasn't ready to talk to him yet. I had to figure out what I wanted to say.

I sat down at my desk, drumming my fingers on the surface for a moment. Almost without realizing it, my eyes drifted toward the bag near my door.

Thump-thump.

It was almost like I could hear it beating, like the heart in that Edgar Allen Poe story we'd read last year. I hauled myself out of the chair, picked up the bag, and threw it into my closet. But it was no good. I still knew it was there.

I have to get out of here, I decided finally.

All of this noise—Jeffrey, Marcus, Mom and Dad and

the negligee—it was just too much. I knew it was getting late, but I just really needed to be alone.

Alone with the evil flying monkeys in my brain.

I walked into Smoothie King and immediately stumbled backward. There was a guy in the corner, reading a novel and sipping a pink drink from a clear plastic cup. For a moment, I couldn't place how I knew him. He had dark eyes and long legs. . . . Something about him was ringing a bell, but he wasn't from school. He was wearing a green polo shirt and dark jeans. . . .

Then my eyes shifted down to his shoes. He was wearing black cowboy boots.

Suddenly, it all came back to me.

Sundance.

Oh, *crap*.

Just what I needed—a confrontation with a guy who'd seen me whooping it up to "Cotton-Eyed Joe." My nerves can't take it, I decided. I've got to get out of here. I reached for the door handle—

Too late.

"Frannie!" Sundance called. He had put down his book and was waving at me with a huge megawatt grin.

"Hi!" I said, running my hand through my hair instead of yanking open the door. Crap! Crapcrapcrapcrapcrapcrap!

Sundance gestured to the chair beside his, and I managed

a wavery smile. Oh, crap, I thought as I made my way over to join him. What is his name? I was blanking . . . but it was kind of too late to ask him now without looking like an insensitive jerk. Oh well. What did I really need to know his name for, anyway? I was getting out of there as soon as possible. "Hey, good to see you," I said, thinking quickly as I slid into the chair. "I just want to warn you that I'm in a rush, though. I've got to meet my boyfriend down the street in ten minutes."

"Marcus?" Sundance asked.

"No." My face felt hot and I had to focus on breathing to keep the tears from coming. "Not him." My voice sounded strained, even to me.

Sundance was silent for a moment. His face was sympathetic, and for a moment he looked like he might ask me what was wrong.

Please don't, I thought.

I don't know if he got the mental message or what, but Sundance seemed to change his mind. "Well, then," he said, stretching out his long, lean legs as a smile crept up half of his face. "Ten minutes, hm? That still leaves nine minutes to talk to me."

Trapped. I giggled nervously. Stupid Frannie—why didn't you say five minutes?

Sundance picked up his smoothie. "These are mighty good," he said. "Want one?"

"Oh, no thanks." Actually, I was sitting right in front of the cooler, so I reached in and pulled out a Jones Cola. Don't think about how Marcus always teases you for drinking these, I commanded myself, and my brain was instantly flooded with images of Marcus teasing me for drinking Jones Cola. The cap bit into the skin of my palm as I twisted off the top.

Sundance took another sip of his smoothie and shook his head. "Right refreshing," he said. "I've been tryin' 'em all this week—kiwi strawberry, raspberry, mixed berry. . . . I even tried one with the extra protein powder in it. That didn't taste too good, though."

His expression was so serious that it cracked me up. "That stuff's like chalk dust." I had a weird out-of-body moment. Am I really talking about protein powder while my life is falling apart?

"Hm," Sundance drawled, nodding thoughtfully. "Reminded me of the prairie dust I slap out of my jeans sometimes."

I cocked an eyebrow. Something about the über-cowboyness of that statement made me wonder if he was just trying to get me to laugh. Then again, I thought, maybe he's serious. After all, he likes line dancing. I decided to play it safe. "When do you slap prairie dust out of your jeans?"

Sundance grinned. "Didn't I tell you I was from Oklahoma?"

"Yeah—but you said Tulsa, not the windswept plains."

"Busted." Sundance laughed, and his drawl went down about two notches. "Most people out here seem to think that Tulsa *is* the windswept plains."

I let out a giggle-snort. I usually hate it when I do that, but Sundance just smiled a little wider, so I let it go. "So, you've been coming here all week?" I asked, looking around the place. It seemed kind of weird—Smoothie King isn't exactly known for its ambience. I mean, it's clean, but it's kind of like any chain. Bright lights, Formica tables—it didn't really seem like Sundance's kind of place.

He shrugged, then smiled shyly. "Well, I heard you liked the place, so . . ."

For a minute, I wasn't sure I'd heard him right. Was he saying that he had been coming here looking for *me*? That was so sweet.

Then again, maybe that wasn't what he meant. Maybe he just really liked smoothies and wanted to find a good place in the area. I didn't want to read too much into any-thing. Besides, I so did *not* need some random hick crushin' on me right now. I had enough guy problems. "So," I said awkwardly, "what are you reading?"

He showed it to me. *Einstein's Dreams*. I'd read it last year—it was really good. Beautiful, in fact. Not exactly what I'd expected a cowboy to be reading. "How are you liking it?" I asked.

Sundance studied the cover, like he was really thinking

over my question. "I like it a lot," he said slowly. "It's kind of melancholy, though."

"Ooh . . . melancholy," I teased. "Nice fifty-cent word."

"You seem like a woman who appreciates a big word," Sundance said. He took another sip of smoothie.

I laughed. "I do?"

"Sure." Sundance leaned across the table. His shirt smelled clean, like Tide. "Do you know what else I bet you appreciate?" he asked in a low voice.

"What?" I asked dubiously. Ooh, I hope this conversation isn't about to take a turn for the weird. . . .

"A cheesy carnival." His dark eyes twinkled as he leaned back in his chair.

I relaxed against my chair. "I *love* a cheesy carnival," I admitted. "What gave it away?"

Sundance shrugged, but he couldn't stop smiling. "I'm not sure—maybe it was the way you entered that open-mike yodeling contest."

Oh, *yikes*. I'd actually managed to block that part of the Line 'Em Up experience out of my brain until that very moment. I felt myself flush a little. "I guess you can tell a lot about someone by the way they yodel."

"I guess you can." Sundance fiddled with his straw wrapper, and the muscles in his forearm danced and rippled. "So," he said finally, "how about it?"

"How about what?"

"Going with me to a cheesy carnival? There's a real old-school one here for the week down at the old ball fields in Chestertown."

Chestertown—that was only one town over. "I don't know. . . ."

"They have cotton candy," Sundance said temptingly. "And a shooting gallery."

"I'll bet you're good at that," I joked. "Being such a cowboy and all."

"I cannot tell a lie," he said with over-the-top sincerity. "Oklahoma state law—you've got to learn to shoot."

"Is that why you left Oklahoma?"

"Yeah—it's way too dangerous. Bullets flying every which way."

I laughed. "No, seriously. What brought you to Illinois?"

"College of the Midwest gave me a free ride," he said. "They've got a great animal husbandry program." He told me all about what he was studying. It was a pretty amazing course load—I had no idea how much you had to know in order to be a rancher. You practically had to be a veterinarian, it seemed like. I finished my soda and started another one.

Sundance cocked an eyebrow. "You sure you got time for that?"

"Why not?"

"Don't you have to meet somebody?"

"Oh, crap!" I'd completely forgotten about the little lie

I'd told him when I came in . . . and now I was half an hour late for my fake date. Suddenly, an intense sense of panic flooded my body—as though I really were late for something. What am I doing here? I thought as I yanked a five-dollar bill out of my purse and slapped it on the table. "For the sodas. I'm so sorry—I've gotta go—"

"What about the carnival?" Sundance asked.

I hesitated, unsure. I mean, I sort of had a boyfriend. Even though, as Marcus had pointed out, maybe he wasn't even all that into me. And he *had* been kind of accidentally cheating on me with my best friend. Not to mention the fact that he might be gay!

Still, I didn't want to sound like a slut. I'm not like *some* people, I thought meanly as an image of Marcus flashed in my brain, who just cheated on people without even thinking about it. "I don't know. . . ."

Sundance nodded. "The boyfriend you're meeting?" he guessed.

I sighed. "Yeah."

He blinked and looked down at the table, then back up at me. "Some guys have all the luck," he said.

I didn't know how to respond to that, so I just said, "I guess." I felt like I wanted to say something more—but I wasn't sure what. Finally, I had to give up. "Well, see you."

"Yeah." The corner of Sundance's mouth tucked into a smile, and he nodded. "I hope so."

♀ Eleven

"Marcus?" Patricia was back at my door again. "What just happened in there?"

That's exactly what I was trying to figure out. Ever since Frannie had stormed out of my room, I'd been sitting at my desk with my head in my hands, going over the whole thing. I'd said way too much to Frannie, at least, too much out of anger. It was true that she hadn't tried to see my side of this, but it was even truer that I had let the whole Jeffrey thing turn into one big lie fest. Now that it had blown up, I couldn't explain it, even to myself.

I heard the door open behind me. "Marcus, honey? Can I come in?"

"I don't really feel like talking right now," I told her.

"Just tell me if you're okay," she said.

"I'm fine. At least, I will be." I didn't even know if that was true, but it seemed like the fastest way out of the conversation.

Patricia came in anyway. She walked over and hugged me from behind. Purple gauzy fabric billowed around me and brushed my arms. At least she was fully clothed this time, in one of her goddess dresses. That's what Frannie called them—they were Patricia's version of sweats.

"Sugar, I know you want to be alone right now, but I can't just walk away from that hangdog look on your face. Now, why don't you tell me what's going on?"

I stared straight ahead, grinding a pencil tip into a pad of sticky notes. I was afraid I'd say the wrong thing or cry or throw up if I even opened my mouth.

"You know," she said, "Arthur and I had a tiff the other day, and I was so mad. But honey, it was nothing. With a little time, it was all fine." She gave my shoulders a squeeze. "And I hated to admit it, but he was right. My ass did look big in those jeans."

"He said that?" I asked, grateful for the change of topic.

"Well, not in so many words. But honey, the point is, it only seemed real big at the time. The fight, I mean, not my ass."

I knew she was trying to cheer me up, but she couldn't touch this one. "This is a little different," I told her.

"Of course it's different, hon," she said, sitting on the bed. "Every relationship is different, but—"

"No," I said. "You don't understand." As soon as I said it, that little warning siren in my head went off. Where was I going with this?

"Well," Patricia said. "Do you want to help me understand?"

Talk about an opening. If this were *Coming Out: The Musical*, that would have been the perfect song cue. But it wasn't a musical. It was just me sitting there, wondering if it was finally time to tell Patricia the truth.

Frannie isn't my girlfriend.

She has a boyfriend.

I wish he was my boyfriend.

It was so straightforward in the abstract. Getting it to come out of my mouth was, as usual, a completely different prospect. Once upon a time, I would have shriveled up and died if Patricia asked me outright, *Are you gay?* Now all I wanted was for her to ask the question. I guess I was ready to say "yes." I just wasn't ready to do the long version.

I looked at her, smiling back at me. I thought about it one more time.

And I caved.

"It's just that I've known Frannie longer than you've known Arthur," I flubbed. "It seems really . . . complicated right now. I don't think I'm ready to talk about it, if that's okay."

Patricia stood up to go. "No problem, hon."

I think she was surprised when I got up and hugged

her. I'm not so big on initiating physical contact, which is one of the few traits I get from my dad. Patricia tensed just a tiny bit but then squeezed me tight. Her goddess dress had long hanging sleeves, and for a few seconds, I was inside a gauzy purple cocoon. It was a nice place to be.

"You're going to be fine," she whispered in my ear. "You're going to be just fine."

"I know," I told her, which was another lie.

When she left me alone in my room, I realized I had to get out. It was too claustrophobic in there, with all my thoughts closing in. I needed a change of scenery, even if it was just a walk around the block. Dad told me to be home by eleven and that was it. I'm sure he'd overheard the fight I had with Frannie, and I'm sure he was glad to let Patricia go in for the follow-up. He did his part by not giving me a hard time about going out at nine-thirty on a Wednesday.

Somehow, I ended up on a bus and then at the mall. Maybe it was some kind of instinct. The mall was perfect right now, I realized. It was familiar. It was undemanding. And as far as I knew, there wasn't anyone here who I had recently lied to, fought with, or pretended to be.

I showed up at Scoops just after closing. The metal grate was halfway down and I ducked inside. Margaret was at the cash register counting the drawer. She still had her uniform on, but I could see she had already touched up her makeup for wherever it was she was going from here.

"Got a date?" I asked her.

"Where'd you come from?" she said.

"Hell."

She laughed tentatively, like she wasn't sure it was the correct response.

"Yo, Beauregard!" Cal was wiping down the stainless steel, his polyester tunic already unzipped. One of his Phish T-shirts showed through underneath. "What's going on, man?"

I went over and sat at the counter. "Nothing."

"You out on your own? Where's Frannie?"

My first impulse was to say, *Why Frannie? Why wouldn't I be out with some other friends?* But Cal pretty much knew I didn't have any other friends of my own.

"Whoa." He stopped what he was doing. The rag in his hand dripped dirty water on the floor. "You guys have a fight?"

Apparently, I had traded in my regular skull for the see-through kind. "How do you do that?" I asked him.

"The way you shrugged, man. If you don't know where Frannie is, something's wrong. You always know where she is."

"People like you are the reason people like me get paranoid," I said.

"Nah, man," he said. "Too much weed is the reason people get paranoid."

"So that means you—"

"Get just the right amount. Recommended daily

allowance." He went back to wiping the counters. "You going home from here? You want a ride?"

I knew Cal didn't smoke at work, but still. "No thanks," I said. "That's all right."

"Buses stop at ten." He pointed at the Scoops clock. "Looks like you've got a choice between me and your Adidas. So where do you live, anyway?"

The parking garage was nearly deserted, but Cal's car would have been easy to spot all the same. It looked like it had some kind of animal-print paint job, between the rust, the patches of primer, and the original brown color, or maybe it was red. I wondered who was older, me or the car.

"Is this thing safe?" I asked.

"Define 'safe,'" he said.

Since the alternative was walking home, I decided not to think about it. Cal opened the driver's side door for me.

"Oh. No thanks," I said. "I'll let you do the driving."

"I know, man. Passenger door doesn't work."

I crawled over the army blanket he had covering the front seat and found that the inside was both odor- and clutter-free. I'd expected it to smell like some combination of corn chips and/or socks and/or cigarettes and/or bong water. And I was surprised not to see a single butt, fast-food container, or Ziploc bag on the floor. Actually, I was just glad to see floor on the floor. Gaping holes with a view of the concrete below wouldn't have surprised me either.

"Not what you thought, right?" Cal said, sliding in. "Everyone always thinks I'm going to be this huge pig, when actually, I'm a pretty tidy guy. Oh, and don't bother with that." I was groping around with my right hand. "Seat belt got sucked into the vortex a long time ago. I don't think it's coming back."

We angled out of the lot and onto the dark streets. It felt good to move. I rolled down my window and let the wind come in over me. Calvin rolled his down too and lit a Camel unfiltered.

At first, the silence was uncomfortable. We always had plenty to banter about at work, but here, somehow, I wasn't sure what to say. Cal seemed fine with it. He drove and smoked and looked like he was exactly where he wanted to be. I was jealous of that.

When he finished his cigarette, he said, "You okay, M. B.? You've got sad all over you."

Why did everyone in the world want to talk about this except for me?

"I'm okay," I said. We were driving along Lake Michigan now, and I watched the water go by. There's something I love about a lake you can't see across. It's a lake, but it's something more, too, something bigger than its name. They should have another word for what that is.

"So tell me the story," he said.

"About what?" I said, even though I knew.

"Whatever happened with Frannie."

"I don't know," I said.

"You don't know if you want to talk about it, or you don't know what happened?"

"Both, I guess."

"All right." He lit another Camel.

"Frannie trusted me, and I . . ." What did I do? "I kind of went behind her back on something."

"Got it," he said. "So is she permanent mad?"

"That's what I don't know." I really liked that Cal wasn't asking me for more details than I wanted to give.

"Hm," he said, and then after a long pause, "Was it an accident, what happened?"

That question hurt, but it was fair. I couldn't even say sort of. "No. I knew what I was doing."

"Do you know why you did it?"

I looked over at him now. "Where are you coming up with all this?"

"Don't know," he said casually. "I just hang back and see what comes out of my mouth. The way I see it, there's me, and then there's my mind. Like I'm the tenant and my mind is the superintendent. I pay the rent, but the super does most of the work. He fixes things up and takes care of stuff for me, and the more I stay out of the way, the better everything goes. You know?"

"What is that? A metaphor? Simile?"

"Whatever."

I was still trying to sort out what he had just said when he came back with more.

"It's interesting."

"What is?"

"I asked if you knew why you did whatever it was, and you changed the subject, and then you didn't go back."

"You lost me again," I said.

"You either don't want to know why you went behind Frannie's back, or you do know, and you don't want to face up to it." He poked his cigarette in my direction. "And *that's* when you call the superintendent."

"Yeah, I still don't get that analogy," I said, or whatever it was.

"But that's not really the point, is it, Beauregard?"

"Are we almost there yet?" I asked, and he laughed. We both knew I was joking and avoiding at the same time. Still, Cal waited for me. "Okay," I said finally. "Remind me of the question."

He said it slowly. "Do you know why you did what you did?"

The first thing that popped into my head was the same thing I thought of when he'd asked the question the first time. In my mind, I saw Jeffrey's face. He was smiling. My stomach clenched.

"Yeah," I said. "I think I do."

• • •

The next couple of days were all about silence. Frannie not talking to me. Me trying to figure out what to say to Frannie and giving her space to cool off in the meantime. Me staying away from the chat room and from Jeffrey. Dad and Patricia not asking the questions they obviously wanted to ask. Me not telling Patricia what I wanted more and more to tell her. All silence, and nothing golden about it.

The only real conversation I had at school was with Ethan Schumacher. He popped up over the top of my study carrel in the library one day, where I was hiding out rather than risk the awkwardness of the cafeteria at lunchtime.

"So, you're coming to the next GSA meeting, right?" he said. "And I'll tell you right now, you have to say yes."

I stopped myself on the way to "I don't think so" and thought for a second. It was becoming clear to me that no matter what happened with Frannie, I needed to branch out. The Gay-Straight Alliance was as good a place to start as any, and for that matter, I was really glad that Roaring Brook had a GSA. I'd always taken it for granted and left it on its own. In the course of about two seconds, this whole new appreciation for Ethan Schumacher blossomed inside me.

"I'll be there," I said.

"Excellent. Bring Frannie if she wants to come."

Ouch. "I don't know if she can make it."

"Well, bring anyone," he said. "The more the merrier.

And for that matter, the more guys, the more merrier."

"I'll see what I can do," I said, and then suddenly, "Hey, Ethan? Do you want to go see a movie or something this weekend?"

He blinked and adjusted his glasses.

I wondered if he thought I meant a date, which I didn't.

"Uh . . ." he said. "I'm kind of overextended these days. But I'll see you at the meeting. Okay? Cool. Later." And he beat it out of the library even faster than his usual rabbity pace.

I had to laugh. It was either that or start crying and never stop. The person who was so far on my back burner that I didn't even know he was there wasn't interested in hanging out with me. Whatever the social version of body odor is, I obviously had it. I was going to have to start paying people to get close to me.

By the end of that week, I couldn't stand the idea of sitting home alone anymore, especially on a Saturday night, when I should have been videofesting with Frannie. So I called myself up and asked if maybe *I* wanted to go to a movie with me.

Thank God I said yes.

The local theater in Roaring Brook was playing *Crap*, and *Crap II*, and *Return of the Son of Crap*. For anything decent, you had to go into Chicago, but one of Dad's rules was no riding the El downtown at night by myself. It would have been easy enough to sneak away, but I was still hungover from the latest round of lies. I decided to opt for the dumb-movie/no-lying route.

I was standing at the counter waiting to buy some Twizzlers when I heard my name.

"Hey, it's Marcus of the South!"

I recognized Glenn's voice right away, not to mention that annoying Southern fixation of his. When I turned around, I found him standing there with Astrid, whose neon fuchsia clogs were enough to distract me for a second. Frannie definitely would have had something to say about those.

"What are you seeing?" Glenn asked.

I tore my eyes away from Astrid's shoes and looked at my ticket stub. "Um . . . *Head for Hell.*"

"Us too," Astrid said.

Glenn nodded. "Yeah, the preview looks terrible and the reviews are like, worst movie of the year, so we figured we had to see it." I noticed the way he used "we" and wondered if it meant something about him and Astrid. "Is Frannie here?" he asked.

"No," I said. "She's . . . not here." I was little surprised Glenn didn't know about our fight by now. Maybe he had been too busy with his own love life to obsess over his best friend's.

"Come. Sit with us," Astrid said.

"No thanks," I said. "I'm going to sit in the balcony."

"Okay, well—" Astrid moved toward the entrance to the theater.

"No, come on," Glenn insisted. "Do you really want to sit alone?"

"It's fine." Message to Glenn: Some people actually like to be alone.

"Why don't I meet you both up there?" Astrid said, like I hadn't even spoken, and she ducked off to the ladies' room.

"Listen, I don't want to bogart your date," I told Glenn. "I'll sit downstairs."

That didn't work either. Glenn blew a mouthful of air. "Dude, it's not a date. Don't worry about it."

I wondered if "it's not a date" was code for "it's *totally* a date." I hoped so, for Frannie's sake. If Astrid was otherwise occupied, Frannie would have nothing to worry about when it came to Jeffrey. I knew what a good friend would do in this situation. A good friend would confirm whether or not Astrid was truly out of the picture.

As some kind of penance, I followed Glenn up to the balcony.

"Third row center okay?" he asked.

"Yeah, perfect." We sat down with an empty seat in the middle for Astrid, although it made me self-conscious that someone would think I was one of those straight boys who always sit two seats apart in the theater So No One Will Think They're Homos. Obviously, that was more Glenn's gig.

"Twizzler?" I offered him. Maybe we could eat instead of talk.

No such luck. When he leaned over to take it, he said, "Can I ask you an honest question?"

No.

"I guess so."

"Do you think I'm, like, the most obnoxious person you've ever known?"

"Wow," I said. "That *is* an honest question."

He looked at me and smiled, but not in a hurt way. "I'll take that as a yes."

It seemed clear to me that this was my own doing, too. Whatever I had said about Glenn, as Frannie, to Jeffrey had obviously gotten back.

"No," I said automatically. "I didn't mean—"

Glenn stopped me with a ducked-chin-and-raised-eyebrow look that was something along the lines of, *Don't even try.*

"Well," I started again, "not the *most* obnoxious. There was a kid in third grade one time who threw up on me on purpose."

Glenn laughed and then I actually did too.

"So I get second place," he said.

Astrid came into the aisle and sat down. "What are you laughing at?"

"Vomit," Glenn said, and I laughed harder in spite of

myself. I didn't want to super-size his extra-large ego, but the look on Astrid's face was pretty funny.

"I'm not getting you," she said to Glenn. She put her big pink feet up on the seat, and my mind snapped right back to Frannie like a boomerang.

"So, is Frannie laying low or what?" Glenn asked me.

I looked over at him in that way you look at someone when they pluck a thought out of your brain. It seemed to be happening to me a lot these days.

"What is it?" Glenn asked.

"Nothing, I was just . . . thinking about her."

"Jeff said she's been kind of scarce lately."

I was starving for information here. Did that mean Frannie and Jeffrey weren't out tonight? Was she avoiding him? Why was she scarce? But the last thing in the world I wanted was for Glenn to know any more of my business than he already did.

"Yeah," I said in that way that sounds casual and detached but is actually very close to depressed. "I guess she's got a lot to do these days."

I could just imagine her to-do list:

1. Get some of Marcus's hair.
2. Make voodoo doll.
3. Stick pins in voodoo doll's head.
4. Skip funeral and go out with my new boyfriend.
5. Forget Marcus ever existed.

🚺 Twelve *Blink. Blink. Blink.*

The cursor on my screen just blipped on and off, daring me to write something. But it was so hard! Jeffrey and I were online, but the conversation wasn't going so well. Here's what we had so far:

<<FRANNO: Hi.>>

<<JEFFO: Sticking with this screen name?>>

<<FRANNO: For now, I guess.>>

The truth was, I'd racked my brain trying to come up with a clever new name, but the only thing I'd thought of was "total_jerkwad," which was what I felt like, but it seemed a little harsh for a chat. So I'd just gone with what Marcus had been using—which I instantly regretted, by the way, because it reminded me of how

I'd left things with him, which made me feel even worse.

So, back to *blinkblinkblink*.

Okay, I told myself. What would Marcus say?

Something clever.

Okay, think clever.

<<FRANNO: What are you doing?>>

I know, I know. The wit is blinding.

<<JEFFO: Talking to you.>>

Oh, jeez. Now what?

<<FRANNO: Me too.>>

<<JEFFO: LOL.>>

Yeah, right. Laugh out loud. More like groan quietly.

That cursor was really starting to get to me. Did it really have to blink so much? I mean, okay! I know you're ready for me! You don't need to constantly remind me that I'm not writing something.

The truth was, I didn't feel like talking to Jeffrey. Actually, I'd been avoiding him for the past couple of days. I couldn't face him . . . or Marcus. I guess I still just had so many questions that I wasn't sure I wanted answered. I mean, ever since my conversation with Jenn, I couldn't help thinking: Straight or gay? Straight or gay? Straight or gay? every time I saw Jeffrey.

<<JEFFO: Everything okay?>>

<<FRANNO: Yeah.>>

<<JEFFO: You've seemed a little down this week.>>

So he'd noticed. Did it mean he was sensitive—ergo, queer? Or really into me—ergo, straight? Typical Jeffrey—could be either.

<<FRANNO: Just been feeling a little sick. Think I'll just stay home and have soup.>>

<<JEFFO: Yeah—watch TV and drink fluids. Get sympathy.>>

<<FRANNO: Where's my sympathy?>>

<<JEFFO: Poor Frannie.>>

<<FRANNO: Awww . . .>>

Hey, I realized suddenly, this conversation is going better than it ever has before. So what does that mean? asked another voice in my mind. That doesn't mean anything. Maybe you and Jeffrey have flow. Maybe Jeffrey and Marcus have *more* flow. You have no idea, do you?

Grr. Hate you, evil little voice in my brain! I thought. Oof, if only Marcus were here right now! He was good at finding out information. But if he were actually here, then I'd have to talk to him . . . and that would lead to all kinds of problems.

Wait a minute. If I can't have Marcus with me, maybe I can channel him. I mean, what's a brain twin for? Okay, if Marcus wanted to find out if someone was gay, what would he do? Aside from ask, I mean . . .

Brainstorm!

<<FRANNO: Let's play a game.>>

<<JEFFO: Favorites?>>

<<FRANNO: You guessed it.>>

Heh, heh. It's also called "gay or straight?" And Jeffrey Osborne, step right up, because you're our first contestant!

<<FRANNO: Who's your favorite football team?>>

<<JEFFO: Uh—I kind of hate football.>>

Okay—that's definitely a couple of points on the queerometer, I thought. All straight guys like football. I mean, that's a real straight-guy thing, right?

<<JEFFO: Can we make it basketball?>>

My heart thudded hopefully in my chest. Basketball isn't very queer.

Wait—unless you're just watching it because you like guys in shorts . . .

<<JEFFO: Actually, I like hockey best. Can I change it to hockey?>>

Hockey? Okay, so now Jeffrey was *definitely* edging up the straightometer. Gay boys do not like watching men with no teeth bash each other on the head with sticks while wearing three tons of padding. At least, none of the gay guys *I* knew did. . . .

<<FRANNO: Okay, hockey.>>

<<JEFFO: New Jersey Devils.>>

Okay, so I had to try a different tack. <<Favorite supermodel?>> I typed.

<<JEFFO: Can't I ask you one?>>

<<FRANNO: Maybe later. I want to learn about you.>>

<<JEFFO: Okay. But I don't think I can name any supermodels.>>

Can't name a supermodel, eh? Well, come to think of it, that didn't really mean anything. I mean, I'd been thinking that a straight guy would know the names of supermodels because they were hot. But on the other hand, any gay guy who was into fashion would have been able to name his favorite supermodel too. I bet Marcus could have named twenty models with his brain tied behind his back. Dumb question, Frannie, you'll have to do better. Give him an arty one.

<<FRANNO: Favorite director?>>

<<JEFFO: Ridley Scott.>>

Oh, perfect, I thought with a groan. The guy who did both *Gladiator* and *Thelma & Louise*. I glared at the computer screen. Jeffrey, I thought at it, are you trying to make me insane?

Just then, my cell phone started to sing its cheery little song. I picked it up.

"Hello?"

"You are getting nowhere," Jenn's voice informed me.

"*What?*"

"Don't you want to find out if he's gay?" she asked. "Because this little game is *so* not working."

"Wait—have you been watching me online?" I peered at the screen. Jeffrey and I weren't in a private chat room.

We were just in the normal bulletin board, but we had it to ourselves. After all, it was Friday night, and most normal people were out doing normal-people things.

"Girl, what was that question about supermodels? Who has a favorite supermodel?"

Wait a minute—that wasn't Jenn's voice.

"Belina? Hold on—Jenn—do you have me on the three-way?"

"I just thought you wanted some help!" Jenn wailed.

"You let *Marcus* help you," Belina huffed.

"And look where that got me," I snapped. "And Jenn, I can't believe you told Belina the whole thing. Thanks a lot!"

"Okay, I am choosing not to take offense at that," Belina cracked. "Look, Jenn has a point—all chat and no action makes Frannie a very confused girl."

I sighed. Belina was right, and I knew it. My game was lame. "So what should I do?"

"Get him over there!" Belina cried. "Give him the big eyes and ask him to smear suntan lotion on your back."

I rolled my eyes. "Ha, ha."

"No, really," Jenn agreed. "You've got to put the moves on him, Frannie. That's the only way."

"There isn't a straight boy in this world who can resist a butt like yours," Belina added.

Why do we always end up talking about my butt? I

wondered. But the fact is, I knew that my best friends had a point—I'd never really given Jeffrey the chance to kiss me . . . so who knew if he secretly wanted to or not? So maybe it was time to put myself out there. . . . "Okay, you two," I said finally. "Thanks for the 'help.' Now please stop spying on me."

"We aren't spying," Jenn insisted. "We're helping!"

"Hanging up now," I singsonged.

"Good luck!" Belina called just as I clicked off.

<<JEFFO: Still there?>> scrolled up the screen.

Do or die, I thought grimly as my fingers flew across the keyboard.

<<FRANNO: Yeah. Hey—are you busy tonight?>>

<<JEFFO: Nope.>>

<<FRANNO: Why don't you come over for a little while?>>

Said the spider to the fly.

Okay, I thought as I scanned the living room, this place looks great. The soft music was playing, the lights were dim . . . I'd even lit a few candles. The family was gone, and I was ready.

"Hello, Jeffrey," I said, practicing my sultry voice as I fluffed a couch pillow. "I'm so glad you could make it—"

Just then, my cellie chirped its cheery ring.

"So what are you wearing?" It was Jenn's voice.

"Is this a pervert?" I asked.

Jenn giggled. "Is he coming over?"

"On the way," I announced proudly.

"So what are you wearing?" Jenn repeated.

"Frannie," Belina piped up, "if you are wearing that black-and-red T-shirt and those orange camouflage pants you were wearing in school, girl, you'd better get your butt upstairs to change."

I looked down at my outfit—which was exactly as Belina had described. "What's wrong with this outfit?"

"You have to wear something sexy," Jenn urged.

"Jenn, I don't do sexy," I informed her. "I do everything but sexy."

"Just wear your underwear," Jenn suggested. "Put a trench coat on over it, then give him a little peek."

I snorted. "That is the dumbest thing you've ever said to me," I informed her.

"Then just wear the underwear," Belina suggested.

"Hanging up again," I singsonged cheerfully. "Talk to you tomorrow!"

"Just remember to use physical contact!" Belina called before I could hang up.

Flipping closed my phone, I hurried into the kitchen, where my secret weapon lay waiting. I'd read online that ginseng increases "desire for the human touch," so I'd dug around in my mom's medicine cabinet and finally come up with a couple of her drugstore herbal tablets. Apparently, it's also supposed to be good for your memory or whatever. Anyway, I broke the tablets and dumped them into the hot chocolate (okay, pay attention, people—chocolate is another aphrodisiac) that I was warming on the stove. Looks good, I thought as I gave the sweet, dark liquid a stir in the pan. And smells just like normal hot chocolate. I turned the stove down to warm and hurried upstairs.

I dashed into my room and closed the door, then hustled over to my closet and started flipping through outfits. Something sexy, something sexy, I thought as my wardrobe flicked past. Peasant blouse, striped pants, ugly green sweater, sparkly thing I've never worn, comfy jeans, bathrobe—no, no, no, no, no, no!

"Ugh—what happened to all of my sexy clothes?" I murmured to myself. As if I'd ever had any. I mean, I had a couple of clingy tops. But I was already wearing the clingiest T-shirt I owned, and Belina had said it wasn't going to cut it. I needed something that screamed, "Jump me!"

At that moment, my eye fell on the red bag at the bottom of my closet.

Intimate Pleasures, it whispered at me.

"Oh no," I told the bag. "No way. You're grossing me out just with your very existence."

But you don't even know what's hidden inside my hot pink tissue paper, the bag murmured. *It's something a little*

too big for your mom, which means it might fit you. . . .
Besides, what choice do you have?

"Damn you, Intimate Pleasures," I growled as I reached into the bag. I couldn't believe I was actually so desperate that I was willing to borrow my mom's negligee. There's something sick about this, I thought as—wincing—I pulled the article of clothing that was supposed to rejuvenate my parents' sex life out of the bag.

I held up the whatever-it-was and opened my eyes wide enough to get a quick peek.

Actually, I thought as I inspected it, it's not so bad. It was supposed to be a slip, I guess. It was black stretch satin and had red flowers embroidered at the bustline. It wasn't even that revealing or anything.

I might just be able to pull this off as a dress, I thought as I held the thing against my body. A very, very sexy dress.

I pulled off my clothes and yanked on the Intimate Pleasure, then looked in the mirror. I looked . . . good. The slip thing was shoving my boobs up so that they were on prominent display somewhere near the vicinity of my neck, and the fabric glowed softly in a very "touch me" way.

"Oh, hello, Jeffrey," I cooed huskily. "Why, yes, my boobs have always been this rotund." I laughed out loud and spun around. If this doesn't work, then I'll *know*

Jeffrey's gay, I thought. Dang, even *I* want to jump me right now!

At that moment, the doorbell rang.

I froze.

"Ohmigosh," I murmured. "Ohmigosh! What am I doing?" I can't go downstairs in a negligee! I realized. Am I crazy?

The doorbell rang again, twice this time.

"Just a minute!" I shouted. What to do? What to do? Where's a trench coat when you need one? Finally, I grabbed my hot pink bathrobe off the hanger and scurried downstairs.

Once I reached the door, I fluffed out my hair and then remembered that I was supposed to be sick, so I shouldn't look too good, so I patted it back down a little.

Ding-a-ling-a-ling!

"All right," I snapped, then let out a tiny cough as I yanked open the door.

Jeffrey was standing there, holding a box of tissues and a stack of DVDs. He smiled that super-cute smile. "Hey," he said as he stepped into the entranceway. "Thought you might need some cheering up." He handed me the videos.

I flipped through them, my brain scanning for clues.

Young Frankenstein? Straight.

Casablanca? Not so straight.

Some Like It Hot? Totally confused.

"Thanks," I said, leading him into the living room. I put the videos down on the coffee table and perched next to him on the couch.

I smiled at him.

He smiled back.

Soft music played in the background.

And the silence between us yawned on.

Hmmm . . . I was starting to realize that I didn't really know what I was doing when it came to this seduction stuff. I mean, Jeffrey wasn't leaning toward me lustily or anything, despite all of the ambience I'd manufactured in the living room.

Well, okay, I realized, maybe I'm not looking too sexy in this huge pink bathrobe with the flowers on it. I remembered Jenn's suggestion—open up the trench coat and give him a little taste of what's underneath. Maybe I could do that with the robe, right? I shifted a little, subtly loosening the belt on my robe. The front fell open a teensy bit, but not enough to show any cleavage. I leaned forward, pretending to read the back of one of the movies, and loosened it a little more. Still not too wide open, but it was something.

"I love *Some Like It Hot*," I said, scanning the back of the movie. I was kind of trying to make it sound like maybe *I* liked it hot too, but Jeffrey didn't seem to pick up on it.

"It's one of my favorites," he said. "Totally cracks me up."

Suddenly, Belina's advice rang through my mind—
"Don't forget the physical contact!" With a jolt, I put my
hand on Jeffrey's knee. His eyebrows flew up, and he
stared at my hand. His mouth opened, but no sound
came out.

Hmmm, I thought. Too much? Or too much *girl*?
Either way, the response wasn't really what I'd wanted. So
I played it off like I was just giving him a pat, then I
cleared my throat and said, "Uh—I have a treat for you.
Close your eyes, I'll be right back."

"Okay," Jeffrey said. He looked kind of confused, but he
played along, closing his eyes as I scurried into the
kitchen.

"Still closed?" I called as I poured ginseng-spiked hot
chocolate into two mugs.

"Still closed," Jeffrey confirmed.

"Good." Quickly, I loosened my robe so that it was now
fully open, exposing my entire chestal region.

Deal with these, I thought as I picked up the mugs and
headed back into the living room.

"Keep them closed," I sang as I floated toward the
couch.

"Smells like chocolate," Jeffrey said as I sat down
beside him.

"Maybe it is," I cooed as I put down one mug and held

the other under his nose. "Maybe it's a special treat." I blew on the hot chocolate to make sure it wasn't too hot. "Now open your mouth and take a sip . . ."

Eyes still closed, Jeffrey obeyed. "Mmmm," he said as he swallowed the chocolate.

"Now open," I told him.

He did.

I looked deeply into his blue eyes.

A moment blinked by, then another as Jeffrey looked me up and down . . . and stopped at my Intimately Pleasurable bustline. A smile played at his lips for a moment, then wavered. His eyes fluttered closed, then opened. He cleared his throat.

This is it, I thought. He's going to make a move. . . .

I leaned forward slightly. . . .

"Frannie?" he whispered.

"Yes?" I whispered back. My lips were millimeters from his. I could almost taste the chocolate on his breath.

Jeffrey swallowed hard. "I think I'm going to be sick."

Before I even knew what was happening, Jeffrey had darted away. I heard a retching noise, then the sound of running water and the garbage disposal.

What the hell?

Oh my God, I realized, standing up from the couch. Jeffrey just barfed in my kitchen sink!

I raced into the kitchen. "Are you okay?" I asked

Jeffrey, who was splashing water on his face. He was a putrid shade of green.

"I'm fine," he croaked. "I don't know what happened. It's like some kind of allergy. . . ."

Yeah, right, I thought darkly. I handed him a dish towel and he dabbed his face with it.

Jeffrey looked up at me, apology stamped across his face. "Frannie . . ." he started.

"It's okay," I told him quietly.

He nodded. "I think I'd better go," he said finally.

"Yeah," I agreed. "Okay."

Jeffrey folded the towel carefully and laid it over the side of the sink. The he headed for the back door. "'Bye," he said, but he didn't turn around.

"'Bye," I whispered, but it was lost in the noise as the door slammed closed behind him.

So there it was. I had my answer. Jeffrey was definitely gay.

I mean, okay—I guess he *could* be allergic to chocolate, I thought. But then wouldn't he have said something when he smelled it?

No, I decided. More like he's allergic to girls in negligees trying to seduce him.

My chest tightened, and I sighed. I was sad about Jeffrey—sad that he wasn't really The One after all. But in a way, I was also relieved. I mean, we'd never really had much chemistry. So at least it wasn't because it was my fault. It wasn't because I was a romance reject or because I'd blown it, as Marcus had said. It just wasn't anybody's fault. The truth was, Jeffrey and I were almost totally mismatched, and now that I knew he was gay, it all made perfect sense. Jeffrey might be The One . . . but he wasn't The One for me.

The worst part of this whole thing, I realized, is that Jeffrey will probably want to talk about this night and explain what happened. Then again, maybe not. I mean, it's not like we were boyfriend and girlfriend and needed to break up. I'd just misread him from the beginning.

My mind spun back to the night this whole mess had started. *M or F?* Jeffrey had asked. Male or female?

Marcus or Frannie?

Well, I guess now I knew the answer to that one.

Jeffrey wasn't interested in me. But he couldn't help the fact that he really liked Online Frannie. Aka, Marcus.

Wow. So . . . this night had been really humiliating. I mean, illuminating. But I guess it was worth it.

Oh God, I thought as the memory of myself walking out of the kitchen with my mom's negligee exposed swirled in my brain. I couldn't even keep myself from groaning out loud. This had been one of the top three most embarrassing nights of my life—I didn't want to ever think about it again.

But at least it's over, I realized. At least it can't get any worse.

It was at that moment that I heard keys jingling in the front door.

"I'm telling you, Caroline, I don't know how you thought we'd get into that restaurant without a reservation," my dad was barking as he and my mom spilled through the door. They could see down the hall, all the way to the back of the kitchen.

My parents stopped in their tracks and stood there, gaping at me. For a minute, nobody said anything.

Please let me die now, I begged silently.

"Frannie? What are you doing in your mother's nightie?" my dad demanded.

My mom's blue eyes were round with shock, locked on my cleavage.

I sighed. Hey, I thought, at least *somebody* is impressed with my boobs.

There he is, I thought as I spotted Marcus in the lunch line the following Monday. He was getting mashed potatoes, peas, and Frosted Flakes—a very Marcus meal.

You will come and sit with me, I thought at him. You will walk over to our usual table and take the seat next to mine. I command you!

He didn't even glance in my direction.

I sighed. I can't take much more of this, I thought. I'd already had to endure a full weekend without him. Not that it had been horrible—Jenn and Belina and I had gone shopping and checked out a movie on Saturday, then I'd spent Sunday catching up on my class work—which I'd been ignoring ever since Jeffrey hit the scene. I know, I know. You're horrified that I didn't call Marcus the minute I was sure about Jeffrey. But I just didn't feel like I could deliver the news over the phone. Besides, I still needed a signal from him that he was ready to make up. After all, he *did* owe me an apology for going behind my back to talk to Jeffrey. But after waiting by the phone for almost five days, it was becoming obvious that I was going to have to be the one to make the first move. . . .

The only question was . . . how?

I'm embarrassed to admit that the first thing that popped into my mind was an image of myself standing outside his window with a boom box blaring "In Your Eyes," à la *Say Anything*. In my defense, Marcus is a movie freak, and that might actually have worked. But it seemed a little over the top. . . .

Okay, all I have to do is come up with a good opening line, I told myself. Something witty and clever so that Marcus will remember how funny I am and how much he misses me. Something like—

"Hey, what's up?" Marcus plopped his tray on my table

and slid it across from mine. Then he slid into the chair, just like we were best friends again, or maybe like nothing had ever happened in the first place.

I blinked at him. "Hey," I said finally. I held onto the bottom of my chair to keep myself from swaying back and forth. I couldn't believe how relieved I was. Just having Marcus say one word to me had made my muscles relax.

"I like your cowboy boots," Marcus said.

"Yeah?" I kicked out one of the purple boots, admiring it. I'd woken up in one of those I-hate-all-my-clothes moods this morning, so when I dug these up after ransacking my closet for something different to wear, I decided, Why not?

"They go freakishly well with that gypsy skirt." Marcus took a sip of his strawberry milk.

I smiled. I may be behind on my Jeffrese, but I speak fluent Marcus, and I knew just what he was telling me then. "I love you too," I whispered to him.

Marcus looked down at his tray. Setting down his milk carefully, he looked up at me. "Listen, Frannie, I know that you hate it when I say this . . . but I'm sorry." He swallowed hard, almost seeming to choke on his words. Without thinking, I reached out and took his hand. "I'm sorry that I hurt you," Marcus went on. "And I want you to know that I'll do whatever it takes . . . or *not* do whatever it takes . . . to make things work between you and Jeffrey. You both deserve it, and I never should have gotten in the way." His eyes were bright.

I gave his hand a squeeze and struggled to breathe through my tight chest. The truth was, Jeffrey and Marcus were the two who deserved to be together. They were the two who made sense. And it wasn't fair that Marcus was suffering, beating himself up for something that really wasn't even his fault.

At that moment, I caught a movement out of the corner of my eye. Glenn was headed toward our table, tray in hand.

Crap. Go away! Go away! Go away! I thought at him, but my brain waves were having no effect. He caught my eye and grinned.

I had no choice but to grin back, cursing myself silently. Horrible, horrible timing. But what I had to say to Marcus just couldn't wait. Glenn was still ten feet away.

"Look, this should really be a longer conversation," I told Marcus in a super-speed whisper, "but I really have to tell you this right now. I think Jeffrey's gay and you should go for it."

Marcus's hazel eyes were as round as a pair of shooting marbles.

"Hey," Glenn said as he walked up to our table. "Am I interrupting anything?"

"Not at all," I said, gesturing to the seat next to mine. "In fact, you're just in time. I was about to tell Marcus here everything I've recently learned about animal husbandry."

👤 Thirteen

The camera zooms in on my face while the cafeteria falls away behind me. The background swirls, and Frannie's voice comes in, all echoey like she's inside my head and my head is a cave.

I think Jeffrey's gay and you should go for it. . . .

I think Jeffrey's gay and you should go for it. . . .

I think Jeffrey's gay and you should go for it. . . .

It was possible that I had misunderstood her. Possible, but . . . what else could it have been besides "Jeffrey's gay"? Chef breeze day? *Je frieze que?*

I badly wanted to ask her a million questions, the first one being, *Whaaaaa???* followed by, *Are you sure?* and, *How can you be sure?* and, *Now what?* In that alternate universe where I can snap my fingers and stop time, it would have been no problem. Here in the cafeteria, Glenn had already hijacked the conversation and showed no signs of letting us go.

"Did Marcus tell you about our little date on Saturday night?" he asked Frannie. She looked across at me with confused eyes. I'm sure my own expression was as glazed as a doughnut.

"Oh," I said. "I ran into Glenn and, um . . ."

"Astrid," Glenn said.

"Astrid. At the cafeteria—"

"The movie theater," Glenn put in.

"Yeah, I mean the movie theater."

A little drool on my chin might have completed the picture. At least Frannie knew what was going on. If Glenn wondered, I didn't care.

"What did you guys see?" Frannie asked.

"*Head for Hell,*" Glenn answered. "The best terrible movie ever made."

"What's it about?" she asked Glenn. I'm sure she didn't care. She was giving me a little space so I could think. Thank you, Ms. Falconer. And thank you, friendship gods, for bringing her back to me.

"Well, there's this psychiatrist, right?" Glenn started in. "And he only has one eye, but it's blind . . ."

His voice morphed into a vague *blah blah blah* in the background as my thoughts went back to Jeffrey.

So Jeffrey was gay? Why did Frannie think so? And what if he was? God, what would that mean for Frannie, to know that the guy she'd been hoping for was . . . the guy *I'd* been hoping for? Yikes. Major hurt. But, the thing was, she didn't actually seem upset. In fact, it wasn't like the words she'd squeezed out in the point-five seconds before Glenn arrived had been, *"I think Jeffrey's gay and I'm going to become a nun after all."* She was all about me and Jeffrey, as if she'd breezed right through the getting-over-him phase and straight to the part where she's fixing him up with her best friend. Maybe that meant that deep down, she already knew he wasn't right for her anyway. Or was that just me, trying to make this all be what I wanted it to be?

And meanwhile, even if Jeffrey *was* gay, that didn't automatically mean he was into me. There was no sense getting too excited yet. Although . . . whoever Jeffrey thought he'd been chatting with all that time, it had been me on the other end. A version of me, anyway, but the chemistry was undeniable. That didn't make him gay, though. Of course, it didn't make him straight, either. Then there was also bi, bi-curious, hetero-curious, metrosexual . . . . assuming Jeffrey even *had* a label. Maybe even he didn't know what he was.

What I needed was more information from Frannie, and

I wasn't going to get it here in the cafeteria. Glenn was still going strong, somewhere in the middle of his movie review.

". . . so then the nurse pulls out this syringe that was for, like, spinal taps on horses or something, and she sticks it right into the guy's eye. Marcus, wasn't that nurse the worst actress you've ever seen? She couldn't play a statue if her life depended on it."

I nodded. "That's true. Hey, Frannie, can I talk to you in private for a second?"

Frannie reached for her purse. "Absolutely."

Before we could even stand up, Glenn waved at someone behind me. Frannie's eyes went wide. This part is in slow motion. Close-up on Glenn's face, his voice extra deep in that slow-mo kind of way.

"Yo . . .

"Jeff . . .

"Over . . .

"Here!"

Then everything speeds up again and Jeffrey's sitting down next to me, across from Glenn and Frannie.

My heart and my brain started competing to see which could race faster.

"Hey, guys," Jeffrey said. "What's up?" No kiss for Frannie, I noticed. I could feel her foot pressing down on mine under the table. "Nice vegetarian lunch there," he said, pointing at my tray.

Omigod, he is gay, he does like me, I will go for it, and it's going to be everything I ever wanted. . . .

Frannie rubbed my foot with hers.

And we're back. "Oh, uh . . . yeah," I said. "I'm not an actual vegetarian."

"But he does play one on TV," Glenn cut in with this fake-announcer voice. I was glad no one laughed.

I suppose Frannie and I could have stepped away for a conference, but now it seemed like a wrong move. And it wasn't like I could just turn to Jeffrey and ask him if he liked boys or girls. The only thing to do was . . . keep lunching.

"Glenn was just telling me about this movie," Frannie said. "So the nurse sticks a hypodermic in the guy's eye, and . . . ?" It was like she took Glenn off pause. He started right back up.

That left me quasi-alone with Jeffrey. I wondered if I had ever been this good playing for Frannie as she was for me right now. Not that I could think of a thing to say to him. All that advice I'd ever given Frannie—relax, just be yourself, yak yak yak—came back to me as the useless pile of recycled crap that I now saw it to be. Face-to-face is harder. It just is.

I took a big bite of Frosted Flakes mush and pretended that it needed lots of chewing. I was going to have to say something . . . anything . . . by the time I swallowed. Experience had shown that Jeffrey was not going to initiate the conversation even if he was interested; maybe especially if he was interested.

"What did you do this weekend?" I finally said. Not bad.

"My cousin was in town and we hung out. . . ." Was he avoiding my eyes? If so, was that a good sign or a bad sign? "Went downtown, went to the Peace and Justice Museum. You know, the usual touristy stuff."

"Yeah, sure," I said. "Did he have a good time?"

"Hillary? Yeah, she did."

Oops. Did Jeffrey already say it was a she? Was he annoyed with me now? Was I going to die a single and lonely old virgin?

All this time, Frannie was convincingly absorbed in what Glenn was saying. I sent off a silent bit of appreciation her way, glad to have her here and not here at the same time.

"What about you?" Jeffrey asked. I looked over and caught his eyes. Our shoulders were almost touching, and he sure didn't seem to mind.

"Not much," I said. "I worked a couple of shifts. Saw a really bad movie." Tried hard not to stalk you on the computer. Wondered what kind of kisser you might be.

"Hm." He nodded.

I nodded.

Frannie burst out laughing and put her hand over her

mouth, trying not to spit chocolate pudding onto the table. "So true," she said to Glenn through her fingers. "Did you see *Juicy Gossip*? The Botox did more acting than she did." I knew right away they were talking about Kitty Elizabeth Benson, who headed up mine and Frannie's most-overrated-actresses-of-all-time list.

Glenn cocked his head and widened his eyes in a dead-on Kitty Elizabeth Benson impersonation. "What do you mean, Frannie?"

Now she did spit out her pudding. "Sorry!" she practically screamed.

"Mmmm, nutritious," Glenn-Kitty said, pretending to scoop it up and eat it. Frannie waved her hands in front of her face and lifted her knees like she was going to wet her pants.

"Can't take him anywhere," Jeffrey said to me.

"I know what you mean," I said. "My best friend spits it out. Yours eats it up. Nice couple, right?" Then I stopped short.

"What is it?" Frannie asked me between gasps. I'm sure I was doing the deer-in-the-headlights thing.

"Nothing," I said. "I just remembered something I have to do." In truth, I was stuck on the "nice couple" comment from a second ago. Was I crazy, or were Frannie and Glenn good together? Not that I *wanted* them to be a couple or thought they should be, but . . .

Jeffrey was a good person, and he liked Glenn. Frannie seemed to at least find Glenn entertaining, and for that matter, had more to say to him than she ever had to with Jeffrey. The fact that I'd been outvoted about Glenn wasn't lost on me, either. And Glenn was . . . what? Funny. I'd give him that. He liked movies. That was a plus. He seemed like a loyal enough friend, even if he did always want to be the center of attention. I supposed I could relate to that. And . . .

My stomach lurched with another, whole new realization. I took a bite of my cereal mush just to stall for time while Frannie, Glenn, and Jeffrey went on talking.

Movie hound . . . loyal friend . . . uses humor . . . wants attention . . .

Glenn was *me*.

He was the straight version of me, whether or not I wanted to admit it.

Which made him totally perfect for Frannie.

The whole thing was starting to take shape in my head, and the only glitch I could see was that it was too perfect to believe. Frannie and Glenn. Me and Jeffrey. I didn't want to get attached to the idea, but I liked where it was going. And if Frannie was wrong about Jeffrey being gay, well, then I'd just have to kill her. No, maim her. Then she'd never be able to get away from me again.

"Hey, why don't we all do something after school?"

Jeffrey asked. I could see he was jumping on this opportunity. It was something he had suggested in one of our chats, and I (Frannie) had shot it down. Now for the first time, this little foursome seemed like a good idea to me.

"Sure," I said, but then remembered. "Wait. I promised Ethan Schumacher I'd go to the GSA meeting today."

"You did?" Frannie asked me.

"Well, yeah," I said. "He's been working it really hard, trying to get more people there." I felt a little sheepish since my original motivation had been more about shopping for new friends, even if Frannie didn't know that.

"What time's the meeting?" Jeffrey asked.

"Right after school," I said. "Three-thirty."

He looked around at us. "Well, it's the Gay-Straight Alliance, right? We can all go and then do something after. Get something to eat or whatever. How's that?"

Frannie and I exchanged a super-concentrated bit of eye contact—tiny on the outside, huge on the inside. This was perfect.

"That's perfect," she said.

"Can I meet you guys later?" Glenn asked. "Like five o'clock? I have to be home with my sister today until my mom gets off work."

Sure, you do, Glenn, I thought. He probably wouldn't have been caught dead at a GSA meeting.

"Sounds like a plan to me," Jeffrey said. "Frannie? Marcus?"

Frannie's face looked like a mirror of my own little smile. There was plenty of time to get the full lowdown from her before the meeting, and we both knew it.

"Sounds like a plan," we both said at the same time.

Room 108 was crowded at three-thirty. Apparently, Ethan had recruited more than just me to this meeting. Brendan Thomas had cracked open the closet door and shown up, I was glad to see. And there were about two dozen other people, many of them obviously queer, some obviously straight, and a few hard-to-tells, including the blue-eyed hottie sitting with Frannie and me on a wide windowsill at the back of the room. Jeffrey seemed perfectly comfortable to be there, no crossed arms, no tension on his face. I wrote it all down in my mental notebook.

By now, Frannie had told me the full story of her little seduction scheme and how that had gone. The more we talked about everything, the more I agreed with her that this had potential—if not for her, then for me. There was still the whole question of how—and if—she needed to break things off with Jeffrey, since maybe he'd been faking it all along, and/or maybe we'd been imagining that things were more "on" between them than they actually were. Either way, Frannie was now officially hands-off where Jeffrey was concerned, and I was hands-on, if I wanted to be, with her blessing. Still, I was going to need some kind of push or sign or something before I'd be ready to do anything about it.

"Okay, everyone, let's come to order." That was Ms. Bayonne, the well-meaning but clueless faculty liaison to the GSA, who tended to use phrases like *tolerance for homosexuals* and *life partner*. "It looks like Ethan's done a marvelous job turning out some new faces," she said. Ethan got a polite round of applause. "I thought we'd start with a little ice breaker to get things going. Let's go around the room and say one thing you think we can do to make RBHS a more tolerant place for everyone. Bridget, would you like to go first?"

Bridget thought for a second and said, "We should write our own nondiscrimination policy for the school."

Ms. Bayonne wrote the idea on a flip chart. "Good. Let's keep going around."

The girl holding Bridget's hand said, "We should have unisex bathrooms."

"I don't know about that," Ms. Bayonne said nervously, clicking the cap back onto her felt marker.

"I do," said Nicole, who was the closest thing to an out trans kid I knew at our school. "People shouldn't assume that everyone's either just gay or lesbian." Several people nodded supportively.

"Ethan?" Ms. Bayonne asked, anxiously moving things along.

"I think everyone who feels like they can be out at school should be. There's nothing more powerful than that." He got another little round of applause for that one. I whistled, too.

As it came around to us, I couldn't wait to hear what Jeffrey had to say. I didn't even think about my own answer ahead of time, so I just said, "I agree with Ethan. People should be out when they can." Then, in a mini-moment of inspiration, I added, "We should have some kind of buddy system for people who aren't ready to be out but want to talk to someone about it. I'd be willing to work on that." *Are you listening, Jeffrey?*

Frannie went next. "I think we should stop talking about 'tolerance' and start looking at real diversity," she said. "Correct me if I'm wrong, but tolerance is for things that you wish weren't there."

I love my brain twin. I couldn't have said it better.

Ms. Bayonne gave a tight smile. This clearly wasn't going the way she had planned. "Next?" she said hopefully.

Jeffrey looked a little uncomfortable with all the eyes on him. "Well," he said, nodding in Nicole's direction, "I like what you said. People shouldn't make so many assumptions about other people. You can't tell anything just by looking at someone." It seemed like he was going to say more, but then he just ducked his chin, as though he were putting a period on the sentence.

I looked down at my hands in case my face was showing more than I wanted it to. Jeffrey didn't know it, but he
had just given me the little push I was looking for. I knew
right then what I was going to . . .

. . . or at least, wanted to . . .

. . . but was scared to death to . . .

. . . but maybe just absolutely had to . . .

. . . do.

♀ Fourteen

"Hey, Mom," I said gently as I walked into the kitchen.

Mom looked up from a cup of coffee and smiled at me. She was wearing a black tank and black silk drawstring pants—pretty sophisticated for her. She looked really pretty—in a casual way. "Hi, sweetheart," she said, sliding a plate of oatmeal raisin cookies across the table in my direction.

"Are you going out?" I asked tentatively. She and I had never actually discussed the whole Intimate Pleasures moment—thank God. I was hoping that I might be able to spend the rest of my life pretending that it hadn't happened. Although I was pretty sure that Mom's silence wasn't going to last. Mom's a brooder. She'll process something for a long time, and then, once she has the right words—*bam!*—she'll bring it up. Permanent, total denial is more *my* style.

"Staying in," Mom corrected.

"Really?" I asked as I slid into the chair across from hers. "It's Saturday—don't you have a date with Dad?"

Mom chuckled softly. "Oh, sweetie, I think that's over."

I pressed my lips together as guilt stabbed through me. "You're giving up on *The Romance Handbook*?" I asked guiltily.

"Absolutely." Mom sighed.

I didn't say anything for a moment—I just sat there, feeling like the worst daughter ever. What was it that Laura had said? "It's important that we all support Mom and Dad on their journey to reenergize their marriage." Okay, so it sounded like something that a TV talk show host would spout. But it was still true. And what had I done? Borrowed Mom's slip and tried to seduce my gay boyfriend in it.

I'd never even returned it for the smaller size—I'd just put it back in the bag and kicked it way to the rear of my closet.

Way to go, Frannie, I thought. You're really supportive.

An image of Marcus flashed in my mind. Maybe if I'd been more supportive of *him*, he wouldn't have ever had to lie about chatting with Jeffrey—and then things wouldn't be as complicated as they were now. . . .

The fact was, despite incontrovertible evidence that Jeffrey was queer, Marcus still hadn't made his move. I wasn't sure what was holding him back. He knew that they got along great. So what was the risk? I wasn't sure. But whenever I tried to bring it up, Marcus shut me down. Not yet, he'd say. Soon.

So, okay. I didn't want to press him. But I couldn't help feeling that this whole mess was kind of my fault. If only I hadn't gone for Jeffrey in the first place. If only Marcus had felt he could tell me about his feelings. If only I hadn't been so focused on what *I* wanted . . .

So maybe permanent, total denial isn't really fair to Mom, I thought. Maybe it's time to start being a little more supportive. . . .

"Mom," I said in a soft voice, "I'm really sorry about your slip. . . ."

"What?" Mom's brow crinkled for a moment. "Oh, that." She laughed uncomfortably and sat back in her chair.

My breath left my chest in a rush, like air from a balloon you've just let go of. "I can get you a new one. . . ."

"Forget it," Mom said, waving her head dismissively. Actually, she looked like she didn't want to discuss this topic any more than I did. Still, there was something I needed to say. And I just couldn't wait until she had finished brooding. I mean, who knew how long that could take?

I cleared my throat. "I'm sorry," I told her.

Mom's pale eyebrows drew together. "What for?"

"For ruining your date with Dad," I said slowly. "For ruining *The Romance Handbook*. For everything."

Mom blew on her coffee. "Honey, you didn't ruin *The Romance Handbook*. . . ." She shook her head. "Look, seeing you in that nightie made me realize just how ridiculous the whole thing was."

"Um . . ." I wasn't really sure how to take that.

"It's just . . ." Mom toyed with a few crumbs on the table. "I realized that your father and I just aren't really romantic types. We're not spontaneous. Your dad likes to have a plan, and so do I." She shrugged. "We're never going to be Laura and Steve—drinking champagne on a sunset picnic. That's great—for them. But it's just not who we are."

"I guess . . ." I said slowly, "I guess that just because something seems ideal doesn't mean that it can work for everyone."

"Your dad isn't Mister Romance," Mom admitted, smiling. "But his style has worked for twenty-three years. I don't know why I thought I needed to change things now. The truth is . . . I just like being with him. We're perfectly happy sitting on the couch together. We don't need chocolate-covered strawberries or fancy lingerie."

I laughed, and suddenly, an image of Jeffrey popped into

my mind. Jeffrey—reading that poem in assembly, the first time I really noticed him. He'd seemed so perfect then . . . and so perfect for me. But he wasn't—that was just an illusion. I looked into my mom's sweet blue eyes. I guess I wasn't the only person who'd fallen into that "ideal love" trap. It was oddly comforting, in a way, to know that I wasn't alone. And to know that my mom wasn't as perfect as I'd always thought.

"Where are you off to?" Mom sipped her coffee.

"*King Kong*. Marcus is meeting me at Lincoln Park," I said, taking a bite of cookie. Wow. It really *was* good. I silently forgave Marcus for always oohing and aahing over Mom's treats.

Speaking of . . .

I looked down at my watch. "I really have to jet." I brushed a few cookie crumbs off my lap as I stood to go.

"You look great," Mom said, eyeing my outfit. "I really like that belt buckle."

"Yeah?" I looked down at the fat turquoise-and-silver buckle. "I stole it from Laura." I guess she'd bought it on our family's trip to New Mexico three years ago. I'd been in her room earlier looking to borrow a hair clip, and when I saw it in her drawer, I knew I had to have it. It reminded me of line dancing with Sundance. Besides, Laura never wore it, anyway.

Mom's eyes twinkled mischievously. "You look good. Not as good as in the nightie, but—"

"Mom!" I screeched. With a grin, I flipped my long hair behind my shoulders. Leaning over quickly, I gave her a peck on the cheek.

"Have fun, sweetie," Mom said.

"And you have fun staying in with Dad," I told her.

"Don't worry." A grin twitched at the corners of Mom's mouth. "I will."

Late, late, late. Marcus is always late, I thought as I paced back and forth in front of the Lincoln Park Cinema. Arty-looking people streamed past me, lining up for the three-thirty showing of *King Kong*. Why hadn't I volunteered to pick him up in Chirpy? But parking at the theater is always a nightmare and generally I end up in a lot, which costs somewhere in the neighborhood of twenty bucks for three hours—so Marcus and I had agreed to take the El instead and meet there. Brilliant. Now I had two tickets in my pocket, but no friend to see the movie with.

I checked my watch: 3:17. One minute later than the last time I checked. Come on, Marcus! I thought. I didn't want to miss the trailers. Normally, I wouldn't have cared, but at Lincoln Park, they play these hilarious old movie trailers whenever they show a classic film. It's the best part of the show.

"Frannie!" shouted a voice behind me.

"Nice of you to show up!" I turned, but it took a full

second for my brain to process that I was looking at Glenn, not Marcus.

He winced. "Sorry, I couldn't find parking—"

"Oh!" I said, although that really didn't make sense as a reply to what he'd just said. "I mean, I know—it's impossible to park around here. Uh . . . hi."

Glenn smiled. "Hi."

"Hi."

"You just said that."

"Right." I guess my brain wasn't really functioning. I was just confused—Glenn was acting like he was supposed to be here. And Marcus was still nowhere in sight. I felt like I was in some parallel universe, in which you make plans with one person and someone else shows up. "Um, don't take this the wrong way . . ." I started.

"But—what am I doing here?" Glenn asked, finishing my thought. His full lips curved into a smile. "Marcus invited me. Sorry—I thought he told you."

I rolled my eyes. "There's a lot he's been leaving out lately." Okay, so Marcus invited Glenn along on our hang. That was . . . weird. I guess. Although Marcus and Glenn had seemed to get along okay when the four of us—including Jeffrey—hung out earlier that week, after the GSA meeting. Maybe that was what Marcus was thinking. "Is Jeffrey coming too?"

"Not that I know of."

Curiouser and curiouser.

"So—where's Marcus?" Glenn asked, looking around. "It's three-twenty."

"Right. Let's find him. And yell at him." I pulled out my cellie, found his number, and pressed the send button.

"You rang?" Marcus sounded like he'd been expecting my call.

"Where are you?" I demanded.

"Actually, I've got a flat tire," Marcus said nonchalantly. "I don't think I'll be able to make it."

"Oh, a *flat*," I repeated, looking over at Glenn, who lifted his eyebrows in response. Very interesting, Marcus Beauregard, I thought. Considering that you don't have a car.

"Does he need us to pick him up?" Glenn whispered.

"Is Glenn there?" Marcus asked knowingly.

"Yes, he's here," I said into the receiver. "He wants to know if we should come and pick you up. He seems *very concerned* that you might be stuck on the highway, struggling with the spare tire." I made my voice as sarcastic as I could without giving away too much to Glenn.

"Why don't you two go ahead and see the movie?" Marcus suggested brightly. "Maybe you could catch some dinner afterward, too." Then he actually giggled.

I shook my head. So that was his little game. Marcus was trying to set me up with Glenn!

I looked over at Jeffrey's best friend, who was standing there in a crisp khaki button-down shirt and fresh jeans. He smiled uncertainly, flashing a set of white teeth. Dark hair, soulful dark eyes . . . Yeah, Glenn was cute. Shorter than Jeffrey but still tall and muscular. And we got along great. I could see where Marcus was getting this. But I just didn't have that vibe with Glenn. He was a friend— that was all. "Nice try," I said into the phone. "Why don't you just worry about fixing that *flat*?"

"Yeah . . ." Marcus's voice was playful.

"Yeah?"

"Yeah," Marcus repeated. "Well, I think it's time for a total overhaul, actually. And by the way, I'm meeting Jeffrey by Buckingham Fountain in ten minutes."

My heart leaped. "You *are*?" I screeched.

Glenn looked worried. "Is everything okay?" he whispered.

I waved him away, nodding. Yes, everything was okay! My best friend was about to go for it! Finally!

"I am," Marcus said.

"Well—good luck with that . . . flat. I hope it goes really well. I can't wait to hear all about it!" Marcus laughed and Glenn gave me a weird look as I flipped closed the phone. "Everything's fine," I said to Glenn. "But it's just you and me for the movie."

"Oh. Okay. Shall we?" He held out his arm, and I laced mine through his.

"I have the tickets already."

"Then I'll get the popcorn."

"That'll probably cost about ten thousand dollars more than the tickets did." I breathed in the clean scent of Glenn's shirt. I'd never been this close to him before. He smelled really nice. Suddenly, I felt unbelievably silly, out on this made-up "date" with Glenn. Marcus, you nut, I thought as we stepped into the cool, dark lobby.

"I'm sure the money will even out over the long course of our friendship," Glenn said.

I giggled.

"You're very smiley," Glenn remarked, looking at me suspiciously.

Suddenly, I just couldn't keep it to myself anymore. The joke was too good not to share. "Okay, I have to tell you something hilarious."

Glenn lifted his eyebrows, a smile creeping up half of his face.

I let out a little laugh-snort, then regained my composure. "Marcus is trying to set us up."

For a moment, Glenn just looked at me blankly. Then, all of a sudden, he busted out into this huge belly laugh, like I'd just told him the best joke in the world. He laughed like he couldn't stop. The sound echoed through the cinema lobby.

"Hey!" I griped, punching him on the shoulder. "Thanks a lot! I'm not that bad!"

Glenn shook his head, confused, a smile still playing at the corners of his mouth. Suddenly, I had this weird feeling that maybe I wasn't getting the joke after all. . . . "Frannie," he said slowly, "doesn't Marcus know I'm gay?"

I felt like the floor had just dropped out from under me. It was a physical sensation, like plunging down the far side of a roller coaster. It was just lucky that I was still holding on to Glenn's arm, because I had to grip his sleeve for support. "*What?*"

Glenn's dark eyes were serious. He looked kind of upset. "Didn't you know?"

"No," I whispered. "I'm sorry, I don't mean—" I didn't want Glenn to think that I thought it was weird that he was queer. Of course, I didn't care about that at all, although I was starting to wonder if my gaydar was seriously out of whack. I mean—what's the deal? I wondered. Is *everybody* gay? But something else was happening in my mind; I was struggling to make a connection. Glenn was gay. What did that mean? Could it mean . . . "Glenn— I hope you don't think I sound totally crazy," I said slowly, fitting the jigsaw pieces together in my mind, "but . . . are you and Jeffrey . . . together?"

He gaped at me like I had a fish growing out of my forehead. "Uh—*no*," he said, lifting one eyebrow. "Jeffrey isn't gay. He's really into *you*, remember?"

"He *is*?" I don't know why this shocked me so much,

but it did. Suddenly I had to wonder. . . . Maybe all of those times we hadn't been connecting, maybe it was just because we weren't on the same wavelength. . . .

"He's totally crazy about you," Glenn said. "He thinks you're sweet and funny and smart. . . ." He said a few more things, but I wasn't listening. My mind was working in overdrive.

Wait—

Jeffrey is into me.

Glenn is queer.

Jeffrey *isn't* queer. . . .

"Ohmigod!" I shouted. "We have to get out of here right now!" Dragging Glenn by the arm, I hauled him out of the cinema.

"Where are we going?" Glenn asked.

We're going to save Marcus from making the most humiliating mistake of his life! I thought desperately. But I didn't have time to explain. "To your car. I just realized that we have to go get Marcus." I yanked out my cell as we ran and pressed redial.

"I thought Marcus was okay," Glenn said. But he was running with me, thank God.

"I just realized that the spare has a leak," I told him. "He can't drive on it." Answer the phone, Marcus, I thought wildly. It rang and rang. No good. Clicking off, I tried again. Still no good.

Glenn's Honda let out a mechanical chirp as he used the remote to unlock the door.

I pressed redial again as I climbed into the car. I wasn't about to give up that easily. I was going to rescue my friend, no matter what.

"Where are we headed?" Glenn asked as he slid in behind the wheel and turned the key in the ignition.

To stop the madness, I thought crazily as I clicked off and punched redial yet again. "To Buckingham Fountain. As fast as humanly possible."

⟨⟩ Fifteen

"Who was that?" Jeffrey asked me as I turned off Dad's cell phone and stuck it in my pocket.

"I didn't recognize the number," I lied, hopefully for the last time. I couldn't pick up Frannie's call, not right now. I was about to do one of the most important things I had ever done in my life, and the whole point was to do this on my own.

The setting was perfect. I'd chosen it carefully. Buckingham Fountain was public but not too crowded, beautiful but not too sappy, and miles away from Roaring Brook. There was almost no chance of running into anyone we knew. Plus, if Jeffrey laughed in my face, I could just drown myself right there.

"So anyway," I said, "thanks for coming."

"Sure," he said. "I thought Frannie and Glenn would be here by now."

I wondered if I seemed as nervous as I felt. "Yeah," I said. "I guess I should start by telling you they're not actually coming."

He pushed his hair back from his eyes. The way he squinted at me asked his question for him.

"I know," I said. "This is all very James Bond, right? It's just that I wanted to talk to you alone."

"Why didn't you just do it over the phone?" he asked.

"Right. That's a reasonable question. Well . . ."

For all my planning, I realized, I hadn't put any thought into how to begin this conversation. But I couldn't stop now. Not after the twelve hours of rehearsal since he said he'd meet me, plus however many weeks it had been since this whole thing started, *plus* a lifetime of wondering if I'd ever even have this kind of chance. No. Whether or not I felt ready, I was ready.

"Here it is," I said. My voice was high. It didn't even sound like me. "I'm kind of afraid to bring this up, and at the same time, I feel like I have to."

"Is this about Frannie and me?"

"Can we sit down?" I practically fell onto the nearest bench. Jeffrey sat about a foot and a half away, somewhere between "touch me" and "don't touch me."

I looked at the ground and took in the cracks on the

sidewalk. A bike whizzed by. The fountain splooshed. The century churned on.

"It's funny," I finally said. "Frannie's the only one who knows I'm here. Just her and you."

"Why is that funny?" he asked.

"It's not," I said, throwing up my arms. "I don't know what I'm doing. I'm just putting this off, like maybe the person who has the guts to say it will show up if I wait around long enough."

"Well," he said quietly, "I can't say it for you."

Somehow, that changed everything. Jeffrey knew; or at least, it sounded that way. There was something in the way he spoke, like the secret I'd thought I was keeping wasn't a secret at all. All of a sudden, I was out of hiding places, and more than that, I was out of reasons for hiding. It almost didn't matter what happened after this anymore. I just needed to do what I had come here to do—if I could only find the words.

Then Jeffrey leaned the tiniest bit toward me and started to speak. "Marcus, I—"

And I realized that words weren't going to do it—not his, not mine. And no more thinking about this, either. In its own weird way, *not thinking* had gotten me to this point, and not thinking was going to get me through it. I let my mind go blank, I leaned in, I closed my eyes, and I put my lips to his.

"Noooooo!"

He might as well have had a thousand volts of electricity running through him. I literally jumped up and away from Jeffrey before I realized he wasn't the screamer. The voice I'd heard was Frannie's, and I saw her now, running toward us with Glenn right behind.

"Ohhh God. Ohhh . . . hi," she said looking from me to Jeffrey to me, then stopping to lean on her knees and catch her breath.

"Uh, what's going on, Frannie?" I asked her, trying to straitjacket my panic until I knew more.

"What's going on, period?" Jeffrey said.

"Ohhh God. Ohhh God," was all Frannie seemed able to say. Glenn hovered behind her, actually looking uncomfortable, which was something I'd never seen on him before.

I turned to Jeffrey. "I'm sorry. I don't know what's going on, but I'm pretty sure I just made a really big mistake."

Frannie raised a finger like she was ready to make her statement but was still out of breath. "What I told you before?" she gasped at me. "I was . . . misinformed."

"What the hell are you guys talking about?" Jeffrey's voice went sharp. I couldn't stand the way he was looking at me now, and I couldn't wait for Frannie anymore.

"We thought you were gay!" It just came out of me; not what I would have chosen, but I guess it was the one thought at the top of the pile.

"You did?" Jeffrey asked, looking at Frannie.

"Marcus!" Frannie yelled at me, and then turned again to Jeffrey. "Well . . . kind of, for a while there."

"Why?" Jeffrey didn't seem mad, exactly, but it was hard to tell.

Frannie shifted on her feet. "It was a lot of things, I guess, but . . ." She made a face like someone was squeezing her too hard. "Well, you kind of threw up the first time I tried to really kiss you."

"You did?" Glenn asked.

Jeffrey turned slightly pink. "Yeah. I don't know what that was about, Frannie, but it wasn't about you. I haven't thrown up like that since I tried one of my mom's ginseng tablets, but whatever. I still don't see how that makes me gay."

"Huh." I could see on Frannie's face that there was no way she was going to offer up the fact that she had, in fact, fed him ginseng-slash-poison-laced hot chocolate. "Well," she said, "even before that, you never really tried to kiss me or . . . *anything* me."

Jeffrey held up his hands in an I-give-up kind of shrug. "That's 'cause Glenn said that you said guys never tried to be friends first. You said the guy-girl friends-first thing was a lost art."

Now it was Frannie who looked confused. "No, I didn't."

"Um," I interrupted. "I might have said that along the way."

Jeffrey turned to me, freshly perplexed. *"What?"*

"Oh God." Frannie hung her head.

"Okay," I said, "Let me start where I should have started. Here's the thing. You know all those online conversations? All the instant messaging and the different screen names?"

"Yeah?" he said slowly.

"That was me," I said, rounding the point of no return. "Actually, it was both of us at first, me and Frannie. I was just helping her out because she really liked you, but then, I don't know, it kind of got away from me and I started doing it on my own. There was something about those conversations. They were great. *You* were great."

Jeffrey turned a little more pink and he looked over at Glenn, like for help.

I kept going. "I was supposed to be Frannie all that time, and I can only imagine how screwed up this sounds, but something about it just felt so right, and I never would have taken it this far, but—"

I stopped. A new thought hit me like a smack in the head. "Hang on a second," I said, and turned to Glenn. "You told Jeffrey what I said about guys and girls being friends, but . . . how did you know about it before he did?"

Glenn smiled, a little cocky and a little sheepish looking. "Well," he said, "that's the thing."

"What's the thing?" I said. "I thought my thing was the
thing."

He took a deep breath. "I guess Frannie wasn't the only
one with a little online helper."

"And he's gay!" Frannie blurted. We all turned to look
at her and she shrank back. "Sorry. I couldn't hold it in
anymore. This is so huge. Go on."

I have no idea how the movie will capture whatever
was happening in my mind at that moment, but it will
have to be something good. Some kind of special effects
that haven't been invented yet.

Glenn thought for a second. "I guess that's it," he said.
"Jeff would get into one of those conversations, and then
he'd call me and I'd help him out. Or sometimes I'd be
over at his house. Then after a while, I just started going
online for him and telling him about it later. It was supposed to be a temporary thing."

"I think I owe you a huge apology," Jeffrey said to Frannie.
"Glenn was just so much better at that stuff than I was, and—"

Frannie cut him off. "Believe me, I understand. Don't
worry about it."

I was still piecing everything together in my head.
"So . . . Jeffrey knew what you were doing the whole
time?" I asked Glenn.

He nodded. "I guess that means Frannie didn't?"

"Not until last week," I said.

"Wow," he said. "And I thought Jeff and I were being screwed up."

It felt good to laugh.

"But it was great, wasn't it?" Glenn asked me, suddenly serious. "The chemistry? The whatever that was?" I felt uncomfortable looking into his eyes. He was right about the chemistry, but I didn't know how to respond.

"That's our cue," I heard Frannie say. "We'll see you guys later." It took me a second to realize that "you guys" meant me and Glenn.

"You don't have to go," I said, turning to her. She looked right into me, the way only she can do, and I knew she was going to leave, and she knew I knew, and we both knew that it was fine. No conversation required.

"I'll call you later," she said. She kissed me and then Glenn on the cheek, then turned and left with Jeffrey. We watched them walk away, following the huge curve of the fountain until they disappeared on the other side.

"She's the best," Glenn said, breaking our silence.

"Yeah," I answered. "She really is. Literally."

He sat down on the bench and looked up at me. "So?"

"So," I said, sitting down next to him. "This kind of changes things."

"Does it?"

I stopped to think for a second. "Well, actually, I don't know. I mean, until about a minute ago, you were straight."

"Riiiiight," he said with a smile. "And the second-most obnoxious person you've ever known."

"Right," I said, keeping his eye contact.

"Which means I probably don't have anything to lose if I do this."

He leaned over and put a hand on my shoulder, and before I could have any opinion about it either way, he kissed me right there. And no one screamed when he did it. Not even me.

This would be a good place in the movie for some corny fireworks. It could be a totally stylized thing, all colors and music and explosions in a night sky, even though it was the middle of the day. Sitting there with Glenn, the only fireworks I saw were the ones inside my head, but they were much more real than any movie and much more my own. I didn't question it; I just let them happen.

When we pulled apart, I felt like I was looking at a whole new person. "Why am I just learning this about you?"

"You never asked," he said, and before I could speak, he added, "And I don't exactly advertise it, especially at school. You're a lot braver about that stuff than I am."

The first thing I thought of was Patricia. "I don't know about brave," I said.

We sat there through another silence that would have been uncomfortable if I hadn't had so many thoughts distracting me. I just couldn't figure out which of them to say out loud.

Glenn tilted his head to catch my eyes. "What are you thinking?" he asked.

"Good things," I said.

"Like what?" He was fishing for compliments—typical.

"Well," I said, "you've probably dropped all the way down to like, fourth- or fifth-most obnoxious person I've ever known."

He threw back his head and laughed out loud. "Hey, I'm making progress with the Southern kid."

"And that's another thing," I said, poking him on the shoulder.

"What is?" His brown eyes bored into mine.

"You know what?" I said. "Never mind. I'll save it for later."

♀ Sixteen

"So . . ." Jeffrey said as we walked past the fountain. Cool mist blew across my face as the water shot into the air in a perfect stream, brilliant in the warm spring sunlight. "That was . . . interesting."

I laughed, feeling lighter than I had in weeks. I felt like I did the night I peeled off that horrible plastic shoot-the-freak costume—it was so good to be back in my own clothes, my own skin. After hours of lurching around in a costume, I'd forgotten what it could feel like to just be . . . comfortable.

We walked along in silence for a while. But it wasn't an awkward silence. For the first time, I didn't feel like I had to rack my brain for things to say to Jeffrey. I really didn't need to impress him anymore.

"You know," I said after a few moments, "I just wanted to tell you that I'm sorry." I looked into his sincere blue eyes. "I never should have had Marcus talk to you for me. It's just—I don't even know how it happened. . . ."

"Look, I'm sorry too. I mean, I was having Glenn do the same thing." Jeffrey shook his head, shoving his hands deep into the pockets of his khakis. "God, I still can't believe I did that. It's so unethical."

I gave a little snort-laugh.

"What?"

"Nothing," I said, punching him on the arm lightly. "'Unethical.'"

"Did I just make myself sound like a serious wanker?" Jeffrey actually looked worried, which totally cracked me up. "Kind of," I admitted.

He laughed too as we plopped down onto an open bench near a soft pretzel cart. The wooden slats beneath me were warm. Interesting, I thought, studying his profile. I never would have guessed that Jeffrey would need backup—just like I did. I mean, I'm this slightly chubby girl with a big nose and a weird wardrobe who doesn't write well. But Jeffrey was tall and gorgeous—he was really smart, really sweet, and he seemed comfortable talking in front of people. . . . It was funny to think that he felt self-conscious sometimes.

I guess that kind of stuff doesn't always make sense.

"Well . . ." Jeffrey's voice trailed off as he studied the fountain. A little girl with pigtails and a pink dress was walking back and forth on the lip. If I were that little girl, I would have jumped in a long time ago. The clean water on a warm day was just too tempting.

"Maybe we should try again."

Jeffrey's sentence was so out of the blue that for a minute, I thought he was saying something about the fountain. But when I turned to face him, I saw that he was staring at me.

"Maybe we should start over." Jeffrey picked up my hand and turned it over, studying my palm. I wondered vaguely whether my future was written there and if he could see it. "I mean, we have a lot of fun together, don't we? You know—with shoot the freak, and the Polish food festival . . ."

"Right . . ." I said vaguely. I guess those things had been fun, in a bizarre kind of way. But, you know, not in a way that I necessarily wanted to repeat.

Jeffrey's blue eyes were hopeful. My heart ached. He really was such a sweetheart. "Jeffrey," I said, squeezing his hand, "I think you're really great. . . ." I paused, unsure what else to say. The truth was, I really liked Jeffrey. And I still really wanted someone . . . especially now that it looked like Marcus was going to be with Glenn. I mean, it would be so great if the four of us worked out—we could all get married in a double wedding and have homes on the same block.

There was only one thing wrong with the picture.

"You're really great," I repeated.

My words hung in the air.

"It sounds like you want to add a 'but' to that sentence," Jeffrey said after a few moments.

I looked down at our interlaced fingers. "But I just think we're better off as friends."

I felt Jeffrey's body deflate as he let out a long sigh. But eventually he nodded.

I peered up into his face. "Is that okay?"

"Well . . ." Jeffrey shrugged. "I guess it will have to be."

I gave his hand a squeeze. "So," I said finally. "What are you doing right now?"

"I don't have any plans."

I felt in the pocket of my low-rise jeans and fished out a pair of movie tickets. "Well . . . since we're friends . . . want to go see a movie with me?" I asked. "We missed the three-thirty, but there's another show in about an hour."

"Sure." Jeffrey stood up, then tugged on my hand, pulling me up with him. "What's the movie?"

I smiled down at the *King Kong* tickets in my hand. "Oh, you'll love it," I promised him. "It's all about animal rights."

"Quit hogging it," Marcus griped as he reached for the popcorn.

I smacked his hand. "Hey—I did the cooking. I do the eating." I stuffed a handful of kernels into my mouth.

Marcus rolled his eyes. "I'd hardly call shoving a bag of Orville Redenbacher's into the microwave 'cooking.'"

"That's because you understand nothing about the domestic arts," I told him. "If you're going to complain so much, why don't you just go hang out with your new *boyfriend*?" I teased.

My best friend gave me a bored look. "Saturday night is *our* night, remember?"

I grinned and held out the big bowl of popcorn. "Good answer."

Marcus took a handful of kernels, then pressed play on the remote as I settled back onto the comfy old couch in his family's rec room. I love the furniture at his place—all of it is old and sturdy and comfy, and Mr. Beauregard doesn't care if you put your feet on the table or anything.

An Indian voice blared from the TV as the opening credits for *Kal Ho Naa Ho* rolled. It was a Bollywood musical, and I'd seen it before—but it was such a tear-jerker that when Marcus had said he wanted to watch it, of course I'd said yes. Plus, it had this really great number called "It's the Time to Disco."

"Hey, kids!" Patricia chirped as she stuck her head into the room. "Whatcha watchin'?" She was wearing a pink straw cowboy hat and a pink blouse, long denim skirt, and cowboy boots.

Marcus eyed her skeptically and hit the mute button. "Where are you headed? Back to Line 'Em Up?"

"Not till tomorrow!" Patricia said brightly. "I'm just tryin' on all my outfits. How about this one, honey?" she asked me.

"Perfect," I told her.

"Arthur is picking me up at six. You two want to come with?" she asked, giving Marcus a heavily mascara-ed wink. "Another double date?"

Marcus looked at me, and I lifted my eyebrows at him. *How are you going to handle this, Marcus?* I thought at him. I knew he'd always played it off with her as though he and I were a kind of quasi couple. And I wasn't about to blow his cover. But the fact was, he had a date with Glenn the next day—they were going to catch the Sunday double feature at the Fairlane.

"Actually," Marcus said finally, "I've got a date with someone else tomorrow. This guy named Glenn."

A popcorn kernel got lodged in my throat and I choked. Seriously. Like the face-turning-blue kind of choke.

"You okay, honey?" Patricia asked. "Marcus, sweetie, pass Frannie that glass of water."

Marcus handed me the water that was sitting on the coffee table, and I took a long gulp. The kernel dislodged itself, and I stared at him, fish-eyed. He'd just come out with it! Just like that! What the hell? Had Patricia even noticed?

It was almost like, ever since Marcus had confronted Jeffrey, he just *said* stuff. Stuff that wasn't in code. It took a little getting used to.

Marcus grinned at me as I finished the water and wiped my lips with the back of my hand. "Thanks," I gasped. "I'm all better now."

"So," Patricia said to Marcus, "you finally have a boyfriend." She walked over and sat on the arm of the couch. "Is he hot?"

Marcus looked a little weirded out. "B-b-but don't you . . ." he sputtered. "I mean . . . you're not . . ."

"Totally," I answered for him. "He is totally and utterly hot."

Patricia grinned. "That's my boy!"

"Wait a minute," Marcus said, staring at his grandmother. "Aren't you surprised?"

"Surprised?" Patricia laughed. "I was just waiting for you to tell me!" She looked at me like, *Can you believe this guy?* and shook her head.

"I have to admit," she continued, "I'm just a little jealous."

"Jealous?" Marcus repeated. "What about Arthur?"

"Oh, Arthur," Patricia said dismissively, waving her hand, "He wants a boyfriend too. Meanwhile, we've got each other." She winked again, this time at me. "Just like you two."

Marcus stared at me like he thought he'd just been beamed onto a strange planet. So—Patricia had had our number all along! She'd never bought that we were a couple. We should've known better than to try to put one over on a sharp Southern lady like her. What were we thinking?

"So, Frannie," Patricia said, "sounds like you're free tomorrow. Do you want to come with?" She waggled her eyebrows at me. "A certain super-cute cowboy was asking about you last week. . . ."

My heart did a skippy little thud at the thought of Sundance—his dark eyes and lean limbs. Maybe I'd actually ask him his name this time. "Sure," I said.

"Great!" Patricia hopped off the arm of the couch. "Then it's a date. See ya tomorrow!" Whistling, she bounced out of the rec room.

I turned back to Marcus, who was staring at me skeptically. "What?" I demanded.

"A cowboy?"

"Well . . . I've got boots. And a big belt buckle," I told him. Besides, I mused, why not a cowboy? I thought about Glenn—about how Marcus had been so sure that he didn't like him when, really, he'd been falling in love with him all along. And I thought about Jeffrey—how he was the perfect guy for me . . . on paper. But when it comes to love, these things don't always make sense. "I guess you just never know. Do you?"

Smiling, Marcus sat back against the couch and put his arm around me. I rested my head against his shoulder. "I guess you never do," he said.

👨👩 Coda

<<I'M_NOT_JEFFREY: "The Matrix?" Marcus, are you crazy?>>

<<I'M_NOT_FRANNIE: Not the sequels. The first one. Best movie of the '90s, period.>>

<<I'M_NOT_JEFFREY: You know, Frannie warned me you had some weird opinions.>>

<<I'M_NOT_FRANNIE: With a little time, I could convince you.>>

<<I'M_NOT_JEFFREY: I'll give you the time.>>

<<I'M_NOT_FRANNIE: That is, if I even liked you.>>

<<I'M_NOT_JEFFREY: Oh yeah, I forgot, you can't stand me.>>

<<I'M_NOT_FRANNIE: Right.>>

<<I'M_NOT_JEFFREY: Should I come over there and make you take that back?>>

<<I'M_NOT_FRANNIE: Maybe you should.>>

<<TDIXON35: WHAT? But everyone loves Willie Nelson!>>

<<SMOOCHIE_FRAN: I'm just not a huge fan of the whole C/W oeuvre . . . unless I'm dancing to it.>>

<< TDIXON35: Tell you what. You come with me to the concert on Friday, and you can pick what we do on Sunday.>>

<<SMOOCHIE_FRAN: Fine. Then you can come with me to the Franz Marc exhibit at the Chicago Institute.>>

<<TDIXON35: Great. Been meaning to go.>>

<<SMOOCHIE_FRAN: Really? I didn't realize cowboys liked expressionism.>>

<<TDIXON35: Cowboys like lots of things. As I'll be happy to show you later.>>

<<JEFFO: Anyone up for a rally on Saturday?>>

<<LOLA227: I'm in.>>

<<JEFFO: Astrid, don't you want to know what it's for?>>

<<LOLA227: Jeffrey, I will tell you the truth. I really do not care.>>

<<JEFFO: Wow, I admire your commitment.>>

<<LOLA227: I knew you'd say that.>>

<<SMOOCHIE_FRAN: Mine's taller.>>

<<I'M_NOT_FRANNIE: Mine's a better singer.>>

<<SMOOCHIE_FRAN: Mine's a better line dancer.>>

<<I'M_NOT_FRANNIE: Mine's smart-ass-ier.>>

<<SMOOCHIE_FRAN: Mine can lasso yours.>>

<<I'M_NOT_FRANNIE: That would probably be the thrill of Glenn's life. Do you think Trent would teach me how to do that?>>

<<SMOOCHIE_FRAN: Actually, I'm not sure that he knows how to lasso things. I just made that up.>>

<<I'M_NOT_FRANNIE: Maybe you should find out.>>

<<SMOOCHIE_FRAN: What's the emoticon for blushing?>>

<<I'M_NOT_FRANNIE: I never found one.>>

<<SMOOCHIE_FRAN: What good are you, then?>>

<<I'M_NOT_FRANNIE: I'm good for watching movies with. And giving style advice. And playing favorites.>>

<<SMOOCHIE_FRAN: You're right. I guess I do love you after all.>>

<<I'M_NOT_FRANNIE: I love you too.>>

<<SMOOCHIE_FRAN: Wow. You just said it.>>

<<I'M_NOT_FRANNIE: Sometimes using code just isn't good enough.>>

<<SMOOCHIE_FRAN: Even when you're talking to your brain twin?>>

<<I'M_NOT_FRANNIE: Even then.>>

Acknowledgements

Lisa Papademetriou

A big, fat THANK YOU to all who helped and supported me throughout the strange and wonderful collaborative process that was the creation of this book. Extra-special shout-outs to Kristen Pettit, Liesa Abrams, and—of course—the fabulous Christopher Tebbetts.

Chris Tebbetts

Many people have asked me what it's like to write a book with someone else. The answer is that it's a huge pleasure, as long as that someone else is Lisa Papademetriou. Working with her was like finding a room in my brain I never knew was there. Meanwhile, we had two fairy god-mothers at Razorbill, in Kristen Pettit and Liesa Abrams, who make me want to put quotation marks around the "work" that this whole thing was. Thanks also to the Friday night gang at Outright Vermont and the Champlain Valley Union High School GSA for their time and opinions. And, lastly—and always—thank you to Jonathan Radigan and Laura Wasserman, for being my real-life M and F.